PRAISE FOR

THE KEEPER OF STORIES

"I absolutely loved it! So different, clever, funny, and charming."
—KATIE FFORDE,
Sunday Times (London) bestselling author

"A treasure of a book. Beautiful, emotional, and heartfelt with a cornucopia of characters you'll love spending time with."
—PHAEDRA PATRICK,
author of *The Library of Lost and Found*

"Funny, wise, moving, and full of lovely moments . . . The characters are endearing and unforgettable."
—HAZEL PRIOR,
author of the Richard & Judy Book Club Pick
Away with the Penguins

"Absolutely spellbinding . . . Warm-hearted, thoughtful, funny, and yet deeply poignant."
—CELIA ANDERSON,
author of *59 Memory Lane*

THE KEEPER OF STORIES

BOOKS BY SALLY PAGE

FICTION

The Keeper of Stories

NONFICTION

The Flower Shop:
A Year in the Life of an English Country Flower Shop

The Flower Shop Christmas:
Christmas in an English Country Flower Shop

Flower Shops and Friends:
A Year's Journey around English Flower Shops

Flower Shop Secrets:
A Book of Florist's Tips

THE KEEPER OF STORIES

SALLY PAGE

Published in 2023 by Blackstone Publishing
Cover design by Ellie Game
Cover photographs: Shutterstock.com

Printed in the United States of America
Originally published in hardcover by Blackstone Publishing in 2023

First paperback edition: 2023
ISBN 979-8-212-17059-8
Fiction / Women

Version 1

Blackstone Publishing
31 Mistletoe Rd.
Ashland, OR 97520

www.BlackstonePublishing.com

THE KEEPER OF STORIES

Prologue

Everyone has a story to tell.

But what if you don't have a story? What then?

If you are Janice, you become a collector of other people's stories.

She once watched the Academy Awards acceptance speech of a famous English actor—a National Treasure. In it, the National Treasure described her early life as a cleaner and how, as a young hopeful, she had stood in front of other people's bathroom mirrors holding the toilet cleaner as if it was an Oscar statue. Janice wonders what would have happened if the National Treasure hadn't made it as an actor. Would she still be a cleaner, like her? They are about the same age—late forties—and she thinks they even look a bit alike. Well, (she has to smile) perhaps not that similar, but with the same short build that hints of a stocky future. She wonders if the National Treasure would have ended up as a collector of other people's stories too.

She can't recall what started her collection. Maybe it was a life glimpsed as she rode the bus through the Cambridge countryside to work? Or something in a fragment of conversation overheard as she cleaned a sink? Before long (as she dusted a sitting room or defrosted a fridge) she noticed people were telling her their stories. Perhaps they always had done, but now it is different, now the stories are reaching out and she gathers them to her. She knows she is a receptive vessel. As she listens to the stories, the small nod she gives acknowledges what she knows to be true: that for many, she is a simple, homely bowl into which they can pour their confidences.

Often the stories are unexpected; at times they are funny and engaging. Sometimes they are steeped in regret and sometimes they are life-affirming. She thinks maybe people talk to her because she believes in their stories. She delights in the unexpected and swallows their exaggerations whole. At home at night, with a husband who swamps her with speeches rather than stories, she thinks about her favorites, savoring each of them in turn.

ONE

The Start of the Story

Monday has a very particular order: laughter to begin with; sadness toward the end of the day. Like mismatched bookends, these are the things that prop up her Monday. She has arranged it this way on purpose as the prospect of laughter helps get her out of bed and strengthens her for what comes later.

Janice has discovered that a good cleaner can pretty much dictate their days and hours—and importantly, for the balance of her Monday, the order in which they do their cleaning on a particular day. Everyone knows reliable cleaners are hard to come by and a surprising number of people in Cambridge seem to have discovered that Janice is an exceptional cleaner. She is unsure about the accolade "exceptional" (overheard when one of her employers had a friend in for coffee). She knows she is not an exceptional woman. But is she a good cleaner? Yes, she thinks she is that. She has certainly had enough practice. She just hopes this isn't going to be the sum story of her life: "she cleaned well." As she gets off the bus, she nods at the driver to distract herself from this increasingly recurring thought. He nods back, and she has the fleeting impression that he is going to say something, but then the bus doors sigh as if exhaling and shudder closed.

As the bus pulls away, she is left looking across the road to a long, leafy avenue of detached houses. Some of the windows of the houses gleam with light; others are shaded and dark. She imagines there are many stories hidden behind all those windows, but this morning she is only interested in one. It is the story of the man who lives in the rambling Edwardian house on the corner: Geordie Bowman. She doesn't think her other clients have ever met Geordie, and she knows they are unlikely to meet through her (that is not how Janice thinks her world should work). But, of course, they have heard of Geordie Bowman. Everyone has heard of Geordie Bowman.

Geordie has lived in the same house for over forty years. First, he took a room as a lodger—the rents in Cambridge being considerably cheaper than they were in London, where he was working. Then, eventually, when he married, he ended up buying the house from his landlady. He and his wife could not bear to throw the other tenants out, so his growing family lived alongside a mixture of painters, academics, and students, until, one by one, they moved out of their own accord. That was when the fight for the newly vacant room would start.

"John, now he was the canniest," Geordie often recalls, with pride, "he just moved his stuff in before they had finished packing."

John is Geordie's eldest and now lives in Yorkshire with a family of his own. The rest of Geordie's brood are scattered around the world but visit whenever they can. His beloved wife, Annie, has been dead for several years but nothing has changed in the house since she left it. Each week Janice waters her plants—some now as big as small bushes—and she flicks the dust from her collection of novels by American writers. Geordie encourages Janice to borrow these and occasionally she takes

Harper Lee or Mark Twain home with her, to join her selection of comfort reading.

Geordie has the door open before she can reach for her key.

"They say timing is everything," he booms at her. Geordie is built on magnificent lines, with a voice to match. "Get yourself in and we'll start with a coffee."

This is her cue to make strong coffee for them—with lots of hot milk, just the way Geordie likes it and exactly how Annie used to make it. She doesn't mind. Most of the time Geordie fends for himself (when he is not in London, overseas, or in the pub) and she feels Annie would approve of her spoiling him now and again.

Geordie's story is one of her favorites. It reminds her of the fortitude within people. There is definitely something in there too about using your talents, but she does not like to dwell on this. It is too close to the Bible stories of her childhood and leads her back to her own lack of talent. So, she pushes these thoughts away and concentrates on fortitude, as demonstrated by the boy who was to become Geordie Bowman.

Geordie (unsurprisingly) grew up in Newcastle. She thinks his name is actually John or possibly Jimmy, she is no longer sure; over time he simply became "Geordie." He lived in the streets by the docks, where his father worked. They had a dog that his father adored (more than his son) and a cocktail cabinet shaped like a gondola that was the family's pride and joy (until plasma screens were invented). When Geordie was fourteen, he was out on the streets of Newcastle early one evening. The family dog had bitten the neighbor and his father was out for blood—the neighbor's. As reason and logic had gone out of the window Geordie had legged it out of the back door. It was a cold night with snow on the ground and Geordie was only wearing a thin jacket. Still, he had no desire to be at home, so instead of turning right to go toward the docks, he turned left into an alleyway and snuck in through the side door of Newcastle City Hall.

In the concert hall, Geordie climbed up high into the gods where it was warm and he was unlikely to be spotted. And this is where he was, tucked behind a lighting unit (extra warmth) eating a bar of chocolate he had pinched from the kiosk, when the singing started. The first soaring note tore like a javelin into Geordie's chest, rooting him to the spot. He had never heard of opera, let alone listened to it, yet the music spoke directly to him. Later, in television interviews, Geordie would say that when he died and they opened him up they would find the score for *La Bohème* wrapped around his heart.

He returned home for a few days, a few weeks—he barely noticed how long. In that time, he came up with a plan. He had never heard of opera in the Northeast, so his assumption was that this was not the place to be. It must be London. Surely that was the home of opera? The home of anything posh. He needed to get to London. But without any money, the train or bus was out of the question. So the answer was that he would have to walk. And that is exactly what he did. He filled a rucksack with what food he could carry and a bottle stolen from the gondola and headed south. Along the way, he met a tramp who joined him for much of the walk. During this time, the tramp taught him things that he might find useful in the city and showed him how to keep his clothes clean on their journey. This involved taking clean clothes from one washing line and replacing the stolen clothes with the dirty ones they had been wearing. This was repeated at the next suitable washing line, and so on.

Once in London, Geordie made his way around the various concert halls (the tramp having given him a list of places to try) and eventually he secured a job as a props boy. The rest is history.

Janice's husband, Mike, has never met Geordie. This does not stop him talking about him in the pub like he is an old friend. Janice doesn't contradict him in public—not that Mike is grateful for this; in his mind he has chatted to Geordie many times. As he talks about the world-famous tenor ("Was the queen's favorite, you know") she holds on to the thought that this meeting is never, ever going to happen. Occasionally when he has "nipped to the john" and left her to pay the bill (again), she thinks about Geordie singing her one of her favorite arias as she cleans his oven. These days, Geordie's singing is louder than ever before, and this has started to worry her as she has also noticed that sometimes she has to shout to get his attention and he misses some of what she is saying.

Coffee over, Geordie cannot resist following Janice around the house. He loiters in the doorway as she cleans the wood burner and re-lays it with kindling and logs. It seems he needs coaxing. For such a big man, he can be surprisingly coy about putting himself forward.

"Have you been away?" Janice asks, hoping this might lead him to what he clearly wants to tell her.

She hits gold first time, and he beams at her. "Just a bit of a stretch in London. Ay, you get some right tossers there, pet."

"I imagine you do." She hopes this is enough encouragement.

It is.

"I was on the tube and there was this right knob. It was crowded but not that bad. You know, we were all making the best of it, like. This posh twat pushed on at the last minute before the door closed and starts really mouthing off . . ."

Here Geordie does a pretty good imitation of the posh tosser, making Janice grin. She had been right; she knew Geordie was the place to start her day, her week.

Geordie's posh twat is in midflow. "Oh, come on now. Just

move on up a bit. I'm sure there's plenty of room if only people make way a tad. There is plenty of room. Really! Come on now, move down the train."

Geordie pauses to make sure he has her attention. "That's when I heard a voice from down the carriage. Another lad, a Londoner, I'd say. Anyway, he calls out, 'Open up your gob a bit more, mate. I reckon we could get a couple in there.'"

Janice laughs out loud.

"That shut him up." Geordie is delighted by her response.

She is not fooled. She knows it was Geordie who called that out on the tube. He was the one who took the shine out of the tosser's eye. He is too modest to say it, but she knows. She can almost hear his voice booming down the carriage and the eruption of appreciative laughter all around him.

Pleased with her response, he leaves her to get on with her work. She reaches for her duster. Perhaps being with people like Geordie should be enough for her? Many of the people she cleans for do bring something special to her life and she hopes, in some small way, that she contributes to theirs. She pauses with her duster halfway up a bookshelf. The truth is that she is unconvinced, uneasy. These are other people's stories. If she does have a part to play in them, she knows she is a bit part, an extra. She thinks again of the National Treasure and tries to picture her in Geordie's music room, duster held aloft above his shelves of musical scores. Would this be enough for the National Treasure? Would she settle for this? She continues dusting, embarrassed she even asked.

Janice sees Geordie again when she's heading off for an early lunch and then on to her next cleaning job. It is gray outside and she can feel the bitter February air seeping through the crack in the door. Geordie helps her into her coat. "Thanks, I'm going to need that. It's getting cold out."

"You want to look after yourself if you're getting a cold," he suggests.

"No, I'm fine," she tries again, this time at full volume. "It's just it's a cold day."

He hands her her scarf. "Well, see you next week, and you look after that cold."

She gives up.

"I'm feeling better already," she tells him, with perfect truth.

As he closes the door behind her, she wonders if the story of life is a tragic comedy or a comic tragedy.

TWO

Family Stories

"Of course all libraries have ghosts. Everyone knows ghosts like to read."

The young man coming down the steps of the library is talking earnestly to his companion—a girl of about twenty-five. Janice wishes she had time to follow them, to hear more of their conversation and find out about the ghosts. He sounds so completely sure of himself, as if he were telling his friend that there are birds in the air and clouds in the sky. Janice is fascinated by the thought of the ghosts in the library and wonders if she will meet any today. She often pops into the library at lunchtime to change a book and surreptitiously eat a sandwich at a table tucked at the back between the shelves.

Today there are no ghosts, only the sisters, for the two librarians could be nothing other than sisters. They have the same particular shade of auburn hair—strawberry-blond woven with touches of copper. One sister wears her hair shoulder-length, curling under; the other has one long plait drawn slightly to the side. This reminds Janice of a little girl, even though this sister must be close to fifty. Janice thinks it suits her and likes the way she has woven multicolored threads into her plait. Janice knows little about them apart from that they are indeed sisters and there are four sisters in all. The younger of the sisters (with hair worn loose) had once said to her, "Mum had four of us. Dad never could get himself a boy." Her elder sister had added for emphasis, "Four, can you imagine that? The poor man. A houseful of women." The younger sister had gone on to explain that all the sisters were very close and all looked remarkably similar. "Of course," the elder had stressed, "we are all very different." Her sister had nodded. "Yes, we call ourselves Brainy, Beauty, Bossy, and Baby." They had both laughed. "A family joke," the eldest had said. "Yes, a family joke," the other had repeated, smiling at her sister.

Janice had thought of her own sister and tried to imagine the two of them working together, sorting through books in a library in Cambridge. She knows it is a fantasy—thousands of miles and unspoken memories separate them—but she draws the imagined thought out sometimes in the same way that she selects stories to revisit. The sisters have no idea she is a sister too, but they do know she loves books and they chat to her about her favorites. The sisters are not women who believe you should keep quiet in a library. "Well, of course people who love books are going to want to talk about them," the younger sister had once said.

Janice has tried to work out which sister is which but hasn't liked to ask for fear of getting it wrong. She privately thinks the younger must be Beauty and the elder sister Brainy, or possibly Bossy. She has seen her clear the library at closing time in less than two minutes.

Today they both greet her in unison. "Janice, your book is in."

Janice is currently rereading old favorites and has ordered a copy of Stella Gibbons's *Cold Comfort Farm.*

She takes the book with a word of thanks, and then thinks to ask, "Have you ever thought the library might have a ghost?" As she says it, she feels foolish and wonders how the young man could have talked about the subject with such assured certainty.

The elder sister leans a little further over the counter. "Well, it's funny you should ask that. You're the second person who has been in today talking about the library being haunted."

Ah, the young man. "And are you? Haunted, I mean?"

They appear to give the subject their serious consideration. The elder sister says, "Well, I don't know. I have sometimes thought the books have a life of their own. But I just think that is old Mr. Banks, who never puts anything back where he finds it." The younger sister considers her sibling for a moment. "But of course, everyone knows ghosts like to read. So maybe . . ."

Before Janice can ask another question—how do you know? Or maybe, how come everyone seems to be aware of this but me? Or is this just what you heard the young man say?—they are interrupted by a gaggle of young mothers with their toddlers who need the sisters' attention.

Janice takes her thoughts, her copy of *Cold Comfort Farm*, and her cheese sandwiches to the hidden table at the back. She sits for some time, her book unopened in front of her, considering the question: are people's stories defined by where they fit in a family? But if so, where does that leave her? She has no desire to follow this thought so instead imagines a ghost browsing the shelves after closing. She finds the prospect calming rather than worrying—any ghost that likes books can't be all bad. And this calm is a relief. The truth is, Janice is a worrier. And the list of things she worries about seems to be growing daily. She worries about the state of the oceans, plastic bags, climate change, refugees, political unrest, the far right, the far left, people who have to feed their children from food banks, diesel cars, could she recycle more? Should she eat less meat? She worries about the state of the NHS, zero-hours contracts, why in this day and age, many people she knows get no sick pay or holiday pay. She is deeply concerned about all the people who rent with little security, or live at home until they are nearly forty. And she worries about why anyone would want to troll another human being or shout at a person in the street just because of the color of their skin.

She used to read the newspaper and enjoy the crossword. Now she checks her tablet quickly each morning, just in case there has been an earthquake or some major royal has died. But she cannot read on. Each news story adds to her list of worries. And the worry seeps into the rest of her life too. Instead of challenging herself with new and exciting books from the library, she comfort reads old classics and familiar favorites: Austen, Hardy, Trollope, Thackeray, and Fitzgerald.

She opens up her copy of *Cold Comfort Farm*, ready to sink into the humorous familiarity of the story. Plus, here is a heroine she can really relate to: Flora Poste is a woman who likes things to be kept in order, and so is Janice.

Half an hour later, Janice is leaving the library, retracing the path of the young man who believes in ghosts. She is on her way to her next job—Dr. Huang—before, finally, the last job of the day. She is halfway down the steps when she sees a familiar figure on the opposite side of the street. The tall man has an unmistakable rolling gait. He sways from the ball of one foot to the other as he walks. It always surprises her that her husband, Mike, is such a bad dancer when he walks with such a lilting rhythm. But what is he doing here? She checks her watch. He should have been at work hours ago. As he disappears from view, Janice finds little relief in the fact that she does not have to add worrying about her husband to her list. He is at the top of her list already.

THREE

Stories within Storeys

It is nearly four p.m. when Janice reaches her final job on Monday: sadness. Laughter to start her day, sorrow to finish it. The red-brick semi-detached house is set back from the road, broad and squat, as if it had once settled down here on its haunches and decided not to budge. The modest front is deceptive; like all the other houses in the street, it has been extended at the back, with long, light kitchen/dining rooms stretching into each parallel garden. And in the lofts all along the street are home offices, playrooms, guest rooms, and, in this instance, Janice's favorite room which she thinks may be the center of a story. Fiona's story.

Opening the door, Janice immediately knows Fiona and her son, Adam, are out. An empty house has a singular sound all of its own. Not only does it feel like the inhabitants have gone but that the house has in some way closed itself off, stepped away somewhere else. The silence is so absolute she can hear it. She has noticed this with houses at other times. A house early on Christmas Day can be devoid of noise—but not quite. The house is clearly not asleep (unlike the inhabitants), but instead is breathing very softly and from the walls, she can almost hear the plea for, "Just five more minutes," before the onslaught begins. A house on the morning of a funeral has a particular sound—or maybe it's a feel, she's never been quite sure: tense, waiting, steady. Two years ago, she felt this here. It was the day Fiona buried her husband. The last time Adam said goodbye to his dad.

There is a note from Fiona on the hall table.

Taken Adam to the orthodontist
(more problems with the braces!)
Money on the kitchen table.

Janice exhales with a deep sense of relief and then immediately feels guilty. She likes Fiona and looks forward to a coffee break with her in her study, but the truth is, sometimes she hopes she won't be here. On consideration, she thinks there are probably three reasons for this. Firstly, she knows she can get the cleaning done quicker without her around. Secondly—and this is where she knows her guilt comes from—she wants to avoid the sadness she sees in the pleasant, middle-aged woman who sits opposite her, sipping the coffee she has just poured them from the bright red cafetière. The truth is that she worries about Fiona (another one to add to her list). But, of course, Fiona's life has nothing to do with her. She is just their cleaner, as her husband keeps reminding her.

By the time she has accomplished the bulk of the cleaning, she can acknowledge the third reason she is glad Fiona is out. It gives her more time to spend in her favorite room in the house—the long, low room in the loft. She will still be cleaning, of course,

(Janice has strict rules about this) but she will be thinking about Fiona's story too.

In the loft, on a broad table that once held a train set—the marks from the tracks still visible on the green felt—sits a doll's house. It is a large, Regency-style house with three storeys and—like Fiona's home—extra rooms in the attic. But on the ground floor, instead of dining rooms, kitchens, and pantries, is a commercial property. Living space above, business premises below. In gold-leaf paint, Fiona has created an elegant miniature sign for the business: Jebediah Jury: Undertaker. Janice has no idea where the name came from, but she must admit it has a certain ring to it.

She sits down and opens the front of the house. Most of the rooms are complete, perfect in their miniature form. Bedrooms, a drawing room, a nursery, and Janice's favorite, a beautifully fashioned country-style kitchen with pastry part-rolled on the table alongside a bowl of plums the size of pin heads. And there is a new addition since last week; Fiona has finished one of the bathrooms. She thinks the blue and cream paisley print wallpaper looks perfect with the mahogany suite and claw-foot bath. Janice reaches out and straightens the tiny navy bathmat that hangs over the miniature towel rail. There is another change she spots too. Downstairs in the back workroom, she sees that Fiona has made another coffin—walnut, with tiny brass handles. She does not think this is something any doll's house emporium sells. Why would they, when most people look for minuscule dressers, a piano, or even a dog basket? No, she knows Fiona will have made this herself. She sits frowning at it, not knowing quite what to think.

When Fiona's husband died, she had been working as an accountant in a law firm. Within two months of his death, she had given up her job and was retraining as an undertaker. Over coffee she explained to Janice that it was something she had always been interested in doing but had never said it out loud as she thought people would think it was rather odd.

Janice did not find it odd at all. She knew that when people marry there are magazines and online guides to help you. Everyone gives you advice; you can't stop them. But when someone dies, you can find yourself alone in a world of self-conscious silence. Janice sometimes helped out a friend who ran a catering business and over the years had found herself volunteering for the wakes and avoiding the weddings. At a funeral people were often lost, not just in their grief but, being English, immobilized by the fear of saying or doing the wrong thing. A gentle word from the "staff," rather than from a fellow mourner, was often welcomed. So, yes, she could quite see why Fiona would want to be a funeral director.

Fiona had worked part and then full-time for an undertaker's, completing the required training to become a funeral director, and Janice had no reason to believe she had ever regretted her decision. But another coffin? Were there not too many already stacked up in the back? Since then, Fiona had gone on a series of residential courses and moved away from undertaking and specialized as a civil celebrant, focusing on nonreligious funerals. Janice can understand this too—the need to bring order and offer security when you do not have religious rituals to follow. She knew people—atheists—who had received a religious funeral purely because the family had turned to established doctrines, unsure what else was available.

Janice draws a long thin tube from the pocket in her apron and from it pulls a metal wire on which are attached rows of tiny green feathers. Fiona is not the only one who can make things. She sets about dusting each room in turn, marveling at the detail that has gone into creating each setting. Is building this tiny world in miniature enabling Fiona to make sense of her world? She isn't at all sure it is.

Janice does think her new job has helped, and she knows Fiona has eased and guided others with great kindness through the shock and sorrow that comes with death. And it was because of Fiona's work that Janice had first heard her laugh after her husband's death.

They had been having coffee together in Fiona's study. Fiona had been curled up in the low leather armchair, feet tucked under her tweed skirt. She wore a pale green jumper, and all Janice had felt she needed was the addition of a dog collar, for her to be the picture of a country vicar. Perhaps that was why the bereaved found her so comforting? Fiona had pushed her glasses up into her short, ash-blond bob and put aside the piles of notes in her lap. She'd explained that these were her numerous attempts at a eulogy for a man who appeared to be universally disliked by all who had known him.

"You'd be amazed," she had said, looking up at Janice, "how many families leave the eulogy to me."

"Maybe they're afraid of speaking in public?" she had tentatively suggested. Janice knows she is not only a worrier, she is also a mouse.

"Doesn't seem to stop them yelling and fighting in public," Fiona had replied, smiling.

Janice had nodded. She had seen that at the wakes too. For a mouse she was surprisingly effective at breaking up fights.

"How about this?" Fiona had said and picked up her top page of notes. "He was a man of his generation."

"Hmm, not sure."

"He was a real character?" Fiona had suggested doubtfully.

Janice had considered for a moment. "How about . . ." She paused for a while staring out the window. "He was a man who will not be forgotten by those who knew him best."

Janice had turned back quickly at the sound of Fiona's laughter. It had been months since she had heard her laugh. She found she wanted to cry.

"Bloody perfect," Fiona had said, grinning.

She finishes dusting the exquisite doll's house and clips the door shut. She wants Fiona's story to be represented in this beautiful piece of furniture. An allegory for a new, unexpected direction that leads to healing and recovery. That is a story she would like in her collection. But she is less and less sure that Fiona's story has a happy ending. There is a darkness hidden in the story—a huge, unspoken issue that she thinks is being ignored. Something is lurking. This makes her uneasy, leading her to think of her own childhood, and if there is one place she has no wish to be, it is back there.

FOUR

Everyone Has a Song to Sing
(And a Reason to Dance)

Waiting at the bus stop, Janice finds herself wondering if it will be the driver from this morning. She can't rid herself of the feeling of something left unsaid in that fraction of a second just before the doors sighed and shuddered closed. She begins to imagine the driver sighing along with the doors. What was he going to say to her? When the bus arrives and she pulls herself on board, she nearly laughs. This bus driver could not be in greater contrast to this morning's driver. She wonders if someone up there (whatever that means) is mocking her. This evening's bus driver is a man in his early thirties, and he is simply enormous—she suspects more muscle than fat. He has a bald head, a tremendous beard, and tattoos running up the side of his neck. This man looks like a Hells Angel. This morning's driver looked like a geography teacher.

Only when she sits down does she realize how tired she is and for a while she debates easing her shoes off her swollen feet. The trouble is, it can be so tricky to get them back on again. Instead, she lets her weight sink into the seat and she relaxes her body so it sways in time with the movement of the bus. She empties her mind and prepares to idly tune in to the conversations around her. She does not consider this eavesdropping; she just lets the talk wash over her. Then, occasionally, her mind may reach out and catch at a thread of something. Sometimes these loose threads lead nowhere, but if she is lucky, she may follow one and get a tantalizing glimpse of a story. The journey from the center of Cambridge to the village where she lives only takes half an hour, so usually it is up to her to fill in the gaps in the stories from her imagination. She is more than happy to do this—and it occupies the time walking home from the bus stop. However, she is very strict about where she keeps these stories: they are filed somewhere between fiction and nonfiction in her mind.

She is not hopeful about tonight's journey. The bus is only half full and for the moment there is only the barest murmur of conversation. Not that she would ever claim to have developed a second sense of where a story will lie—that is the joy of being a story collector, you can find the unexpected just about anywhere. She recalls the frail, elderly lady in the launderette (Janice had been washing a client's duvet) who it turned out had been an air stewardess on the first commercial jet flight from London to New York. As the woman had carefully folded her satin-edged blankets (her husband could never abide a duvet), she'd told Janice of the moment they landed. "You see, PANAM had taken out adverts saying they were going to be the first to break the record, but my boss at BOAC had pulled me aside about a week earlier and made me sign a confidential document and told me they were going to beat them to it—and did I want to be in the crew. You can imagine what I said to that." She recalls the old woman pausing to straighten her nondescript, quilted anorak. For a split second, her hand had wavered midway to her head, as if to check her cap. Instead, she had curled her gray hair about her ear and continued. "Well, we were always very smart, us girls. More military than the uniform stewardesses wear today. But oh, on that day we pulled out all the stops. I still remember the shade of red lipstick I wore: Dashing Delight. I thought it was rather apt. Well, we did it. And when we landed and walked away from the plane, all the PANAM staff came out and booed us. But we didn't care. I walked across that runway as if I were six feet tall." The woman had smiled up at her and Janice had tried to imagine the younger face that would have held that same triumphant smile. She had helped the old lady carry her blankets to her car and that was the last she ever saw of her. But she still has her story. She pulls it out on the days when she can't summon a smile herself. The woman's smile had been so bright it would have lit a space far larger than a launderette in a back street of Cambridge. It would have illuminated something as large as, well, as large as an aircraft. And Janice thinks, it probably did. She catches sight of her reflection in the rain-streaked bus window. She can see the ghost of a smile on her face. Yes, a good story. And yet another reminder—not that Janice believes she needs it, but no harm in repeating it—that you should *never* underestimate the elderly.

She is suddenly caught by a line of conversation. She couldn't really fail to be—the man is talking so loudly. A young couple. Friends rather than lovers, she thinks.

Him: "You heard of banana Jack Daniel's?"

Her: "That sounds gross!"

Him: "It is. I can't get enough of the stuff."

And that's it. It looks like it ends there, and she has no desire to follow it.

From behind her she hears a couple of women talking. Lower tone, middle-class. Pleasant women, she imagines. Friends.

"I was walking through the theater car park and there he was."

"Who?"

"You know . . . that actor. He's everywhere."

"Hugh Bonneville?"

Good guess, Janice thinks, on so little information.

"No, not him. He was in *The Observer*. You must have seen it."

Why should she?

"Bill Nighy?"

"No, not him. He's black."

"Bill Nighy's not black! Oh, you mean the man in the car park. Idris Elba?"

That would have been Janice's first guess too.

"No, older, he was in that film with . . ." and here the woman mentions the National Treasure and for a split second, Janice thinks they know she is listening. She shuffles a little uncomfortably in her seat.

"Oh, I do like her . . ."

And they are off about the National Treasure. She doesn't blame them; she really is a very good actor. But this is not where Janice wants to go, so she returns to studying the raindrops on the window. And that's when she sees her.

First it is her reflection. Janice turns her head slowly so she can watch her from the corner of her eye. She had noticed her earlier as she is standing up when there are plenty of seats available. She is a young woman, probably in her late twenties, tall and willowy. She wears a striped woolen dress and long matching cardigan in shades of deep green and gold. Her black tights are a shade darker than the skin on her hands but the same color as her hair. She appears to be standing still, eyes half-closed. Motionless—but not quite. One leg is stretched out a little further than the other in front of her and Janice can see the muscles in it flexing slightly. Her head is moving too, just a fraction. Tiny movements back and forward. That is when she notices the headphones almost hidden in the corkscrew curls of her hair. Suddenly, as if in spasm, her arm sneaks out in a rippling wave. It is an elegant, joyous movement, and Janice wonders if the young woman is a dancer. Then the arm is tucked back by her side, but the other infinitesimal movements continue.

Janice wonders what the young woman is listening to. She would give much to hear the music that made an arm sneak out and dance on its own. She used to love dancing. She never had this woman's dancer's build but when she heard certain songs her body sang along with them. Her muscles would flex, her toes tap, and she knew, whatever she looked like to others, that she was completely in tune with the music. In those precious, glorious moments when her hips swayed in rhythm and her arms snuck free from her sides, she really didn't care what anyone else in the room, or even in the world, thought of her. When she dances she is a lioness.

As her bus stop approaches, she pulls herself reluctantly to her feet. She is loath to leave the young woman, but in this moment, in this life, she is far too much of a mouse to interrupt her private reverie and ask what she is listening to. Stepping onto the pavement she hears the bus doors sigh behind her and in that gap between the last gasp and the noise of them shuddering closed, she hears a voice. She turns expectantly.

"Night, love," the young bus driver throws out cheerfully after her.

As she walks away, she begins to think maybe the gods really are mocking her.

FIVE

A Husband's Story

There are some days when she approaches their (undeceptively) small semi that Janice thinks it will take two hands to get her through the door. One each side of the doorframe to pull her reluctant body over the threshold. If her husband is speaking at her before she has even got her foot over the step, it can take all her strength from both arms to propel herself forward. She wonders if one day she is going to need a stiff push in the middle of her back to get her across. She knows not to expect an extended arm, a helping hand from her husband. She does not allow herself to listen to the breath of a voice that sometimes whispers in her ear. *"Would you not just think of turning on your heel, Janice, and walking back down that path?"* For some reason, the whispering voice has an Irish accent. She thinks maybe this is to do with the kindness of Sister Bernadette—one of the few nuns she has ever met who seemed to actually fancy the idea of loving thy neighbor.

Tonight the house is quiet when she opens the door, and it is easier to get over the threshold. It is not the absolute still silence of an empty house but the hushed quiet of a house in which someone is sleeping. She finds her husband, Mike, sitting on the sofa, head thrown back. His feet are up on the coffee table, and he has a half-empty bowl of chips balanced on his stomach. She returns to the hall, kicks off her shoes, flexes her toes, and heads for the kitchen. She knows the first thing he will say when he wakes is, "What's for dinner?" He doesn't ask this in a nagging or demanding voice, but in a jolly tone that suggests they are all in it together. She is no longer fooled.

When he appears in the doorway, eyes bleary from sleep, he surprises her—really surprises her—by asking about her day. This distracts her from her worry about seeing him by the library earlier, when she knows he should have been at work. As she begins to describe her day she wonders why, tonight of all nights, has he asked about her work? Then, there it is. He starts before she has even finished her sentence, which makes her realize he wasn't really listening. She can't believe that after all this time she fell for it, that her heart had lifted when he had taken an interest in her.

"It's good you like your work."

Had she said that?

"Good, you're busy. Oh, what's for dinner?" he smiles at her.

"Shepherd's pie."

She had been thinking of making pancakes for pudding. They had come into her mind in that moment, that heartbeat, when he had asked about her day.

"No pudding tonight?" He is a large man with a sweet tooth and his mum always made fantastic puddings, as he often reminds her.

"There are yogurts in the fridge."

As a rebellion, she knows it's pathetic.

"You were saying it was good about my work?" she prompts. She wonders why she is helping him. Maybe just to get it over with.

"Yes, yep, the truth is, Jan . . ."

Here it comes, with the affectionate name she hates . . .

"I don't know how much longer I can stick this job."

And there it is: her husband's story.

In the thirty years she has known Mike, he has had twenty-eight different jobs. The one thing she can say about Mike—and maybe this is what has kept her coming back through that door—is that the man is not work-shy. The twenty-eight jobs he has had have been remarkably different. He has been a salesman, a health and safety trainee, a driver, a fitness instructor, a barman, a hospital porter, and now a porter at one of the largest colleges in Cambridge. He has worked in small businesses, large companies, and on the road on his own; at different stages in their marriage, they have had everything from BMWs to secondhand vans parked in their drive. One summer it was an ice-cream van. Mike has also driven tractors and forklift trucks, but thankfully never brought those home. In his different capacities, he has strolled, with his easy rolling gait, through shops, factories, warehouses, bakeries, colleges, and hospitals offering all around him the benefit of his advice. He even spent some time working as a financial advisor, the irony of which is not lost on Janice.

Mike is a pleasant man. He has a sense of humor and does not immediately push his ideas onto others. Janice thinks this is one of the reasons he is so successful at getting new jobs. Mike can be very likable, the reasons for his varied career can appear plausible, and she is certain many employers have taken him on feeling rather sorry for him. She certainly knows of one or two female bosses who saw him as a man who has never been understood. For all his growing paunch and flabby jowls, Mike is still a good-looking man.

The thing that all his employers come to realize in time

is that Mike knows so much more than they do. The first few weeks can go well. Sometimes this stretches into months. But soon they will find Mike correcting them. It will be a small suggestion to start with, but before long Mike has singled out someone who, in his opinion, is doing a shocking job and he feels this needs to be addressed. He becomes passionate about this and talks about the good of the company. He identifies the issues and has, on occasion, got that individual removed from their role. One down, just a few more to go.

Over time—and it can take some time—his employers start to ask themselves, how can this man have the time to pull the planks out of so many other eyes? He often turns up late and when he is needed to complete a task, perhaps deliver a consignment on time, he is inexplicably missing. (She sees him again in her mind's eye, walking past the library in the middle of the day when he should be in the Porter's Lodge.) Then the doubts start to creep in. Janice understands this transition period better than most. In the early days of their marriage, she lived each job with Mike, she felt for him as he tackled the problems, was annoyed with the colleagues who let him down, angry with the bosses who didn't appreciate him. It was only when he was fired from his fourth job that she had had a light-bulb moment of disturbing brightness: maybe it's not them, maybe it's Mike.

Over the years, Mike's timing has gotten better and he has learned to jump before he's pushed. Not that the timing has always suited her—pregnant with their son, Simon, or when they had just taken on a mortgage, and now, when she is . . . What is she? She has no idea. But she knows this is not the time to tell her what is wrong with the college authorities, especially when she has Sister Bernadette whispering in her ear.

Janice lets Mike launch into the latest diatribe about who is at fault and why he needs a new opportunity. She is no longer listening. She wonders, what exactly is her husband's story? Is he simply the man of a thousand jobs? Is he Walter Mitty? Certainly, his world bears little resemblance to anybody else's, as far as she can tell. Or is it more sinister than that? Is it the story of an illusionist? A hypnotist? Because as much as she tries to pull herself away from the world he has constructed for himself, she can't help feeling that he has got some part of her wedged in there with him too. He may not hold her hand, but she is pretty certain he's got the end of her coat caught firmly in one fat fist and he's not going to let it go. When she asks herself if she is frightened of this fist, she knows the answer. Mike is not a man to be physically feared. He is too large and slow for that. She knows it is the small sinewy men you need to be truly afraid of.

When dinner is over and Mike has gone to bed, leaving her to clean up ("You don't mind Jan, do you? I've got a lot of thinking to do.") she closes the kitchen door and stands for some time staring out of the window at the crescent of identical houses and the green beyond. She wonders where the young girl on the bus is now and what she might be dancing to. She would like to listen to some music in the kitchen as she tidies up but doesn't want to bring Mike, complaining, down the stairs. Then she remembers the headphones Simon bought his dad for Christmas. Their son is now twenty-eight and he works in the city, doing she knows not what. It has been many years since he has spent any proper time with them. One foundation of Mike's constructed kingdom was that his only son would go away to private school, and it needed to be one that other people would have heard of.

"You can't deny him the best, Jan."

"You wouldn't want him to suffer because we"—he meant *she*—"didn't do everything we could."

That had been the start of her cleaning career. She had little else to offer, and any thought of studying to improve her opportunities had been squashed early on.

"You have to put the lad first, Jan. And with this job not working out like I wanted . . . They really are the biggest bunch of incompetents. The things I'd like to tell the board about the way things are run . . ."

The irony now being that their well-educated son wants little to do with her or his dad. His dad, maybe, because he has seen through him. Her, she fears, because he blames her for letting him be sent away. Visits from Simon are rare, and a few Christmases ago he gave up sending presents and just sent them a check. It was a generous check, but she ripped it up into tiny pieces before stuffing it deep into the recycling. Perhaps he realized it had never been cashed because since then he has given them John Lewis vouchers. Easy to send and he need never know if they have been used. She still has hers from this Christmas tucked into her purse, but she remembers her husband used his on a pair of expensive headphones.

"Look at these, lads"—to the boys in the pub—"great bit of kit from our Simon. He only gets the best."

As Janice goes searching for Mike's headphones, she wonders if it is pity, or maybe atonement for colluding in sending Simon away, that keeps her living with a man she no longer loves or even likes.

Mr. Mukherjee (who played cricket for the under-twenty-one Indian team) stops to wait for his dog, Booma. He averts his eyes politely from the squatting form beside him and watches as his neighbor, Janice, shimmies across the backlit kitchen window. She spins on the spot and one arm snakes up in an arc above her head. There is something rather beautiful about her rhythmical movements, and for Mr. Mukherjee, not a little surprising. He thinks perhaps he should turn away, but the small dancing head and shoulders (that is all he can see) are mesmerizing, and he finds himself standing on the green, in the cold winter air, smiling.

SIX

Every Story Needs a Villain
(The Notable Exception)

A good cleaner can, in the main, pick and choose who they work for. Janice likes all the people she cleans for, with one notable exception.

The large modern house in front of her is built in a V-shape, which is made of interlocking concrete blocks. It sprawls arrogantly across a plot that once formed part of the grounds of one of the more modern colleges. The house reminds her of a large man—legs akimbo—taking up far more room than is necessary or polite. As she crunches up the Brazilian slate shingle drive, she feels a mix of dread and happy anticipation.

The door is opened by the owner of the house (she is not allowed a key here). The woman in front of her is a handsome, fifty-something-year-old. She is wearing one of her own creations—a dress coat in royal blue slashed all over with brass zips the color of urine. Out of these slashes, Janice can see silk fabric printed with neon horse heads. Each week she wears a different dress coat, and Janice has gathered that she sells a range of these at fairs held in her friends' houses. When she is not selling her dress coats, she likes to "give back" to charities. This seems to involve gathering staff from any number of charities in her house and donating her acquired wisdom. "You can't put a price on that. It would be worth, literally, thousands." Occasionally she donates a dress coat to charity. Janice likes to be there when she does this just to see the faces of the fundraisers she has gathered around her.

The woman has a name but to Janice, she will always be Mrs. YeahYeahYeah. This is what she says when on the phone, when talking to friends, and when discussing her wisdom with the staff from whichever charity is flavor of the month. She presumes the woman is actually trying to say, "Yes," or maybe even, "Yeah," but one is never enough for Mrs. YeahYeahYeah.

Mrs. YeahYeahYeah's husband also works from home. Janice thinks he was something very successful in the city and, having made his money, he spent part of it on building the architectural monstrosity they now call home. It is a house full of large spaces and gleaming empty surfaces—so in some ways, she shouldn't complain. There may be a lot of it, but it is very easy to clean. At the back of the house is a large cube that the husband uses as an office. If Janice ever tries to venture near this area to clean (as instructed by Mrs. YeahYeahYeah) her husband waves a paper/folder/finger at her, and without ever looking up, barks, "No, no! Not now." So Mrs. YeahYeahYeah is married to Mr. NoNoNotNow. She wonders if her husband is the reason they never had any children.

Mrs. YeahYeahYeah pays Janice well for the work she does. She does not shout at her or leave revolting saucepans/toilets/baths/ovens for her to tackle, but she has committed two cardinal sins for which Janice cannot forgive her. In the kitchen, one of the few things allowed to sit on the side is a state-of-the-art Italian coffee machine. It is a thing of real beauty. Janice can dismantle it and clean all the working parts, but she has never been invited to drink coffee from it. In the cupboard above the machine is a jar of Tesco's own brand of instant coffee just for Janice's use. As far as she can tell (and she has looked) this is the only thing Mrs. YeahYeahYeah has ever bought from Tesco.

The second sin is that she calls Janice, "Mrs. P." Janice cannot recall ever allowing this—but she also knows she would never have found the words to object. And now it is far too late. Janice may think what she likes of Mrs. YeahYeahYeah in her head, but she knows she is far too timid to say anything even approaching these things to her face.

Because of all this, Mrs. YeahYeahYeah does not have a story. On a point of principle, Janice will take no more interest in her than is strictly necessary and she certainly will not allow her into the precious library in her head. She does allow her one "incident," which falls far short of a story, but for her, sums up Mrs. YeahYeahYeah.

A group of fundraisers from a children's charity was at the house where Mrs. YeahYeahYeah had organized a team-building session. The exercise involved imagining they were all in a rowing boat cast adrift on the sea. On various bits of paper were descriptions of imaginary people who were in the boat with them. These varied from philanthropists, campaigners for children's rights, a number of different children, and some less savory characters, such as politicians and journalists. The aim of the session was to decide—since the boat was sinking—who, including the staff and Mrs. YeahYeahYeah, should stay and who should be thrown out.

No one seemed to want to start until a small, dark-haired girl from the children's charity tentatively suggested that to make the discussion easier shouldn't they at least rule the children out and just think about which adults might have to be sacrificed. Mrs. YeahYeahYeah immediately objected and leaped in with,

"Why? Do you think my life is worth less than a child's life?" And so it went on. By the end of the session, Mrs. YeahYeah-Yeah had thrown a number of people overboard including an imaginary child with cystic fibrosis. "Well, they probably weren't going to live long anyway."

Janice was pleased to hear the small, dark-haired girl throw herself in after the child. But Mrs. YeahYeahYeah was not amused. "You can't do that. You can't jump out of the boat. No one would really do that in real life." The girl was adamant and refused to get back in the boat. Janice was not sure whether this was because she would have jumped out of any boat that had Mrs. YeahYeahYeah in it or because she genuinely believed a person would sacrifice themselves for a child. She liked to think it was the latter and gave her extra chocolate cookies when she was called in to circulate with more coffee.

Today, Mrs. YeahYeahYeah is hanging around as Janice cleans, which is unusual—in fact, it's more than unusual; it's unnerving. It is making her very uneasy. Mrs. YeahYeahYeah is chatting generally about her week and about a play she went to see. She is talking to Janice like she might go to a play herself and even be a woman who could drink a cappuccino made from a coffee machine. This is far from normal and as she talks Janice becomes acutely self-conscious, aware of each circle she makes on the wooden floor with the specially designed, long-handled floor duster (with cashmere filaments). She thinks if, like Mike, Mrs. YeahYeahYeah actually asks her how her day is, she will pick up her coat and leave.

Instead, eventually, Mrs. YeahYeahYeah says, "Mrs. P, I have a proposition for you."

For one ridiculous moment, she wonders if Mrs. YeahYe-ahYeah and Mr. NoNoNotNow are swingers. She sweeps the floor in an exaggerated arc to turn her back on her employer and hide her laughter. Apart from that, she says nothing. There is nothing she can think of to say.

Even with her back to her, Janice can tell Mrs. YeahYeahYeah is unusually nervous (which, when Janice looks back, should have warned her).

"Mrs. P, I know it's always nice to have a bit more money, so I immediately thought about you."

Janice's mind is a complete blank. What on earth is she going to ask her to do? What could make her this anxious?

"It's not going to take much of your time, and we will make sure the pay is good. Arrange the hours to suit you—five or six hours a week should do it. The thing is, my mother-in-law really needs some help. She's in her nineties and, well, her house . . ."

Mrs. YeahYeahYeah flinches and can't seem to finish, but then, realizing her mistake, quickly recovers. "It's not really that bad. It is quite full of her things, but I am sure you've seen worse and once you get on top of it, of course, it would be much more manageable."

After a pause, she adds, "It's attached to one of the colleges and in many ways is very beautiful."

Janice keeps sweeping very slowly, trying to buy herself time. "I am pretty full at the moment, I'm afraid," is as much as she can manage.

"But not completely full." Mrs. YeahYeahYeah sees the opportunity and wedges the toe of her alligator pump into the gap.

"Well, I mean, I'm busy every day," Janice tries.

"You could make it any day you liked, and the money would be good."

This does give her pause. It looks like Mike is out of work again, and she can't imagine he's going to stop his trips to the pub.

Mrs. YeahYeahYeah hasn't finished. "The thing is, Mrs. P,

either she gets some help where she is, or we will have to consider a home for her. We don't want that, but, at ninety-two . . ."

Great. Now the prospect of being the cause of an old woman being thrown out of her own home into a nursing home smelling of wee and cabbages is to be added to her list of worries.

"Well, I suppose I could visit her. I'm not promising anything though."

Mrs. YeahYeahYeah is no longer listening. "That's fantastic, Mrs. P. I knew I could rely on you. I'll get you all the details." She rubs her fingertips over the edge of the counter a couple of times before adding, "You have to remember, she's a very old lady, and I'm sure you understand what they can be like. But I know nothing will faze you. You are always so calm and steady."

Janice barely takes this last part in, as suddenly, there, sitting at her feet, is the reason she keeps coming to clean for Mrs. YeahYeahYeah. The source of her happy anticipation. A small, untidy fox terrier is sitting there looking up at her. He has an expressive face and sometimes (well, if she's honest, quite a lot of the time) it is as if he is speaking directly to her. His expression simply says it all. And now she could almost believe he is taking his mistress to task for presuming to know what Janice is like. He glances in Mrs. YeahYeahYeah's direction and in that look Janice hears the unspoken words. *"And how the fuck would you know what Janice is like? You never even talk to her!"*

SEVEN

A Shaggy Dog Story

"This is Decius, he's a fox terrier."

This was one of the first things that Mrs. YeahYeahYeah had said to her. Quickly followed by, "I hope you like dogs we'd like you to walk him."

Not, "We hope you like dogs." Pause, "We'd like you to walk him." Or even, "Would you possibly mind walking him?" Like her yeahyeahyeahs, she ran it all in together in her eagerness to get the words out and the mutt off her hands.

All Janice had been able to say was, "Decius?"

"Yes, he's named after a Roman emperor."

And that's when she first noticed it. She looked at Decius. He looked at her and his expression said, as surely as if he had barked it out loud, *"Don't say a word. Not a fucking word."* She didn't blame him, but after all this time it still amazes her how much he swears. For a fox terrier.

She has known Decius now for four years and she is not afraid to admit (to herself at least) that she loves him. She loves the feel of his fuzzy, wiry face between her hands; she likes the way he walks like a ballerina about to go on pointe. She adores the way he bounces like there is a string somewhere around his middle and she knows she is happiest when walking Decius across the fields and meadows around Cambridge. She is thinking of starting a section within her library for animal stories, just so she can include Decius.

She did once try out "Decy" on him, as Decius seemed such a formal name. And it is she, not Mrs. YeahYeahYeah or Mr. NoNoNotNow, who has to stand in the fields shouting his name out loud. However, he gave her a look from under his shaggy brows that silently but eloquently said, *"Please. Just don't."* As he walked away, kicking up mud furiously with his back paws, she could almost believe he muttered, *"For fuck's sake."*

To start with, Janice walked Decius when she went over for the cleaning or to help with the refreshments for some charitable event—roughly twice a week. But it wasn't enough, for either of them. So Janice had volunteered to come more often as a dog walker, and Mrs. YeahYeahYeah had jumped at it. So on other days she fits in his walks around her cleaning jobs and at the weekend often drives over in the car. When Mrs. YeahYeahYeah first saw her pull into the drive she had exclaimed, "Oh you drive!" As if (as Janice told Decius later) she had found a performing monkey behind the wheel. They had been sitting on a bench in the woods sharing some cooked chicken bits. Decius is meant to be vegan (even though neither Mrs. YeahYeahYeah nor Mr. NoNoNotNow embraces this food choice for themselves) and she thinks one of the reasons he loves her (and this is a two-way thing) is that she brings him food he actually wants to eat. She recalls he had looked up at her enquiringly and she had felt the need to explain to Decius, why, if she can drive, she doesn't come over in the car on other days—especially when it is weather you wouldn't send, well, a dog out in. She admitted to him that it was complicated.

She and Mike own one car—an old VW estate. He has always claimed this for his journeys to work. It occurs to her now that maybe that might change since he is going to be unemployed but somehow, she doubts it.

"You don't want to take the car in, Jan, it'll be more trouble than it's worth. Parking's a nightmare in the city."

This is true, although it is also true that most of her employers have parking for visitors or drives. She has pointed this out in the past.

"Whatever you say, but I think you'll find I'm right." He had beamed good-naturedly at her. "I tell you what, I can give you a lift in and out when I'm going."

She had been foolish enough to think this might indeed work. He had parking through the college where he was working as a porter, and sharing a car could help her with her worry about her carbon footprint. But it never seemed he was going in when she was. And when she turned up at the college knowing his shift had nearly ended, hoping for a lift home, he was often inexplicably missing. It became too much to face the looks from the other staff who were clearly getting increasingly annoyed with her husband and his erratic timekeeping.

She thinks back to that day in the woods, Decius sitting on the bench beside her, his head in her lap. She had put her face close to his fur for comfort, because she'd realized that the car problem just led her to think about another problem: she has very few friends. Cambridge, it turns out, is quite a small city when you go through as many jobs as Mike has done. It amazes Janice that he doesn't turn away when he meets old colleagues and business acquaintances. She genuinely believes the man has no shame and in his mind, he has emerged somehow the victor from these associations. So she carries the shame for both of them, and she finds the weight of it pulls her whole body down so she can no longer look people in the eye—some of whom she would have liked to know better. She recalls the relief she felt on meeting a friend of Geordie Bowman's, who was there to deliver some silver wine coolers. She knew he knew Mike, but he had no idea she was married to him. When his name came up in passing, he had laughed out loud (which Janice thought was very forgiving when she recalled the run-around Mike had given him). He had snorted and exclaimed, "The man's delusional! Completely and utterly delusional." He had then gone back to arranging the coolers in the old bread oven that Geordie stored his wine in, and she had gone back to removing the rust from the oven door with her sander. However, it was with a lighter heart. It was good to know that other people got it and that it *could* be said out loud. It made her feel less alone.

For now, she is alone with Decius in the kitchen (which is never really alone) and her work is nearly done. After their "chat," Mrs. YeahYeahYeah had scribbled her mother-in-law's details down as fast as her Mont Blanc could manage and left to go shopping. Janice unclips Decius's lead from the hook in the boot room and unlocks the back door. She has decided she is going to take Decius for a walk across the fields over to where Fiona lives. She has been worrying about her. She is not due to clean for her until next Monday but she hopes she won't mind her calling in a few days early as she has a present for her.

The house is dark and there is no sign of life when she rings the doorbell. She debates trying to post her present through the letterbox, but it is very small and might easily get trampled underfoot. So, after knocking and ringing a further time, she uses her key to let herself in. She is sure Fiona will not mind and she thinks her gift will make her smile when she next looks into her doll's house. She wipes Decius's feet carefully with the cloth she keeps in her coat pocket and holds him on a tight lead close to her side as she heads up to the attic. It is one thing her popping in for two minutes to drop off a gift, another thing to let a stranger's dog explore Fiona's house.

When she opens the doll's house door, she sees that Fiona has been busy. A whole range of electrics has been added and in a few of the rooms, tiny standard and table lamps have been carefully positioned. She spots the switch unit on the table to the right of the doll's house and cannot resist turning it on. The spark and *crack* from somewhere in the house make her jump, and in dismay, she pulls the door open wider to see what has happened. It doesn't take her long to find the issue: two wires have crossed, and the ensuing spark has split them apart and broken the circuit. One wire she thinks she can twist together, the other wire she thinks may need soldering. She knows Fiona's son, Adam, keeps a soldering iron in his bedroom, which he uses to work on his mini robotic figures, but going into a twelve-year-old boy's bedroom and rummaging about is very definitely breaking her rules of cleaning.

She is so immersed in working out if she can mend the wires without a soldering iron, it is a while before she hears the voice from below. She looks down at the side of her chair and Decius is missing and the attic door is standing slightly ajar. She springs out of the chair, her face already burning at the thought of the forthcoming explanation. She finds Decius one floor down, sitting beside Adam who has knelt down to talk to him. Decius has his paws on the boy's thighs and is nuzzling his nose into Adam's hand.

"Adam, I'm so sorry. I had no idea anyone was in. I just wanted to drop something off for your mum."

Adam is completely unfazed by her sudden appearance (she presumes he is used to a stream of people coming and going through this house with little reference to him). It seems she falls into this category. He is much more interested in Decius.

"This your dog?"

She is tempted to say, "Yes." In fact, "Hell, yes!" comes to mind, but instead she tells the truth. "I'm just his dog walker."

At this, Decius turns to look at her, and she thinks he appears rather hurt. Before she can think what to add, Adam continues. "He's kind of weird-looking and he seems to walk on tip-toes. Is that normal?"

She sends a silent prayer to Decius to stop him swearing but it seems he likes Adam and climbs up higher on his lap. She knows what comes next: he will soon be lounging on Adam. This is exactly what happens, and the boy laughs, and, in that moment, Janice thinks her heart is going to break. She steadies herself by sitting beside them on the floor. "He's a fox terrier, and I believe that is a sign of good breeding."

"Blimey, looks a bit dorkish to me."

Janice daren't catch Decius's eye.

But Adam saves the moment by adding, "He's kinda cool though, isn't he." It's a statement not a question and Decius looks at her as if to say, *"Told you."* Then it occurs to her that Decius would never swear in front of a child, and for all his long limbs and large feet, Adam is still very much a boy. The neck emerging from his hoody is long and skinny, and though his hair is big and floppy, his face is small and still spot-free. In fact, he has a beautiful peaches-and-cream complexion. He has also given himself away by the use of "blimey" and "cool." Adam is still happy to use the mild exclamations that his mother (who looks like a vicar) would use.

"Did they get your braces sorted?" she asks.

"Oh, them," he says, flicking his tongue unconsciously over his teeth, but offering nothing else.

This reminds her of previous conversations with Adam, responses that lead nowhere until they move around each other in an awkward silence. Then she thinks of the laugh and tells herself to just try harder.

"Do you have a soldering iron?"

He looks up from Decius in surprise. "Yep?"

"Can I borrow it?"

"Yeah, I suppose."

He gets up reluctantly, holding on to Decius's warm body until the last moment when he has to tip him on the floor. "I'll get it." He half turns and then looks a little anxiously at her. "Will he stay there? He won't go away?"

Oh, such a boy. And again, her heart aches. This time for Adam and she thinks a little for Simon and for herself too. She keeps her tone cheerful. "I think he wants to come with you."

Adam flashes her a grin and Decius glances back as if to say, *"A smelly boy's bedroom? Are you kidding? Of course I'm going in."*

She leaves them together in Adam's room and goes up to mend the wiring in the doll's house. It doesn't take her long. Once she has returned everything to its rightful place, she reaches in her bag for the tiny present she has brought Fiona. It is a miniature, pretend birthday cake. Of course, she couldn't fit forty-five candles on it, but she thinks Fiona will get the idea when she opens up the house—as she hopes she will do tomorrow—and finds it on the kitchen table. Before she closes the doll's house door, she catches sight of the new miniature coffin propped up in Jebediah Jury's workroom. A familiar feeling of disquiet creeps over her. She knows (better than anyone) she is only the cleaner. This has nothing to do with her. She can't pretend to know how the family is really coping without John: Adam's father and Fiona's husband. But unease settles in her like mist in a hollow.

John had been a thoracic surgeon at Addenbrooke's hospital. He had loved camping and cycling trips with the family. He had built a train set up here for his son and helped build his mini robotic figures in his bedroom. She can't really know what it feels like to lose him, but she has a strong sense of an unanswered question hanging over them and she can feel it blighting this family, crushing this house. And the question she keeps coming back to is: why did that lovely man kill himself?

When she returns the soldering iron to Adam, she finds him on his bed with Decius lying on top of him.

"Thanks, Adam, we'd better be going."

Decius jumps down and returns to her side. She looks at Adam's face and as she makes the suggestion, she wonders what she's getting herself into. Deep water, that's for sure.

"Would you like to help me walk Decius sometime?"

"Could I?" he asks, and she thinks Decius looks at him with approval, for this is clearly an unequivocal, "Absobloodylutely!" from Adam. He then spoils it by adding, "Bit of a crap name." And she knows it is time to go. There is only so much a fox terrier can take.

EIGHT

Never Judge a Book by the Cover

The globule of spit hits the pavement less than an inch from her shoe. It is either a very good shot or Mrs. YeahYeah-Yeah's mother-in-law has missed. Janice stands looking at the small, elderly woman in the open doorway, trying to ignore Sister Bernadette who is whispering in her ear, *"Well, will you look at the state of the woman."* Followed by the inevitable, *"Will you not just turn around, Janice, and walk back down the path?"* She thinks Sister Bernadette has a point, or rather two points. Does she really need to be here? And what is this woman wearing? It seems to be some sort of kimono thrown over a pair of men's cords (rolled up many times at the ankles), and on her head she has a red hat with artificial cherries on. The cherries appear to be covered in what Janice suspects is mold.

When she speaks, the woman's voice is clipped, each word beautifully formed before it is spat like the phlegm, out of her mouth. Janice thinks she sounds like a 1950s BBC newsreader who is really, *really* pissed off.

"I do not need your cleaning services. This is *my* house, and I will not be dictated to as to my personal arrangements."

Janice can't help asking, "How did you know that's why I was here? That I'm a cleaner?"

"Well, look for yourself woman." With this, the old woman points at a packet of vacuum bags and Marigold rubber gloves that are poking out of the top of her handbag. "What else could you be?"

Janice can hear Sister Bernadette's disapproving sniff in her ear. Then suddenly she takes in the color of the kimono—a bright, lurid purple. She had noticed it before, of course, but not really *seen* it. She recalls the famous poem about old age—something about wearing purple, a red hat, and learning to spit. She reaches into her memory for another line, and asks, "May I ask, do you spend your pension on brandy and summer gloves?"

The old lady on the doorstep looks at her for some time before replying in a more moderate tone. "I am partial to brandy but I have no need for more gloves." She then stares at Janice for a few more seconds before proclaiming, "I will not have fools in my house. And my daughter-in-law is the biggest fool of them all." With that, she turns on her heel and shuffles back down the hallway. Janice presumes she is meant to follow so steps in and closes the door behind her.

It is a struggle to get past all the stuff littering the narrow space: magazines—piles of them—golf clubs, an Anglepoise lamp with a broken base, suitcases, a stuffed squirrel, two step-ladders, and what looks like a didgeridoo propped up by two snooker cues. Janice's practical side cannot help taking over—this woman just needs more storage space. She wonders if the college has a lock-up somewhere that could be rented. The old woman comes to the end of the hallway and Janice sees her reach for two sticks she has hidden there. As she relaxes her weight onto them, she gives a grunt of pain, and Janice realizes what an effort it has taken for her to perform her little pantomime unaided. Before she turns the corner into the body of the house, the woman pulls off her hat and kimono and drops them on the floor to join the other things littering the place. Janice has to stop herself from instinctively bending down to pick them up. Instead, she purposefully steps on them and feels the satisfying pop of an artificial cherry splitting under her foot. She is *not* going to work for this woman. If money is that tight, she could easily get another job through one of her regulars.

The house appears to be built into the wall of one of Cambridge's oldest colleges. The door Janice has come through is set into a red brick outer wall facing onto the street. As she turns into the main building at the end of the corridor, she sees that the house opens out to form one side of a quadrangle. The room she walks into is vast. It is open from the floor to the rafters and appears to have no upper storey, apart from a gallery that runs around the entire room. Spiral stairs lead up to this and at the far end, she can see the legs of what looks like an unmade bed. Below this, under the gallery, is a small kitchen. Well, she presumes it's a kitchen; piles of clutter obscure the surfaces, but since many of these are plates and saucepans, she assumes this is what it is. The internal walls of the room are warm terracotta, like the bricks of the outer wall. On the street side, there are three windows placed well above head height. On the main internal wall looking onto a grass quadrangle is a massive window made of latticed glass. There are coats of arms in stained glass arranged in a row at the top of this. The light in the room is glorious but it does nothing to hide the mess. Dust hangs in the air and everywhere Janice looks there are piles of books. This is in addition to the books in the many cases that line the room.

A groan of what sounds like pain draws her attention back to the owner of the books. Her shoulders are stooping low over the sticks that still hold her up—just. She stares at Janice from under white shaggy eyebrows but says nothing. Everything about this woman seems aggressive—a challenge. Janice wonders how she gets up the spiral staircase each night; she suspects it is achieved through sheer bloody-mindedness. Janice feels something softening within her and suggests quietly that they sit down. She does not go so far as to offer to make them both a coffee; she has no desire to go anywhere near that kitchen.

The old lady shuffles over to a leather armchair by a small electric fire and lowers herself into it. It folds around her, making her look smaller and frailer than she had on the doorstep in her purple and red. Her small feet poke out from the ends of her rolled-up trousers like a child's. Janice starts to head for the chair opposite but the woman barks, "No! No, not there," and she suddenly remembers whose mother this is. Taking one of the few free chairs that don't have books on it—a beautiful dining room chair that she suspects might be an original Chippendale—she pulls this toward the fire and sits down. She then realizes her mistake. All she wants to say is that, since a cleaner is not required, she will say good morning and leave. How long can that take?

She doesn't even get the first word out. The old lady sniffs suddenly and demands, "So, what's your story?"

No one has ever asked her this before. And it floors her—nightmares of being naked in front of a crowd and memories of Mike insisting she try karaoke with him and then leaving her alone on the stage, are nothing compared to this feeling. She tries to tell herself maybe this is a polite opener (although going on the performance so far, she doubts it). Her employers (unlike her husband) usually do ask about her day, and together they chat about films, music, the ubiquitous weather, and holidays—theirs not hers. But no one has ever inquired about her life. If indeed that is what this unpleasant old woman is doing.

"Are you deaf? I thought that was my prerogative."

This forces Janice into speech. "I'm a very good cleaner and I suspect that is all you need to know." Why did she say that? She is not going to work for the woman. And where did the mouse go? Both of them know this came out as a challenge. God, at this rate, unless she can make her escape, she will have this awful, old woman calling her "Mrs. P," too.

"Ah, but everyone has a story," the woman insists, ignoring the challenge, and making things a whole lot worse for Janice. It is as if she is digging her (very dirty) fingernails under a flap of loose skin, trying to get a hold so she can rip great strips of it off Janice's body.

All Janice can manage is an unconvincing laugh and, "I'm afraid you'd find me very dull. I wouldn't say I had a story."

She wishes she could say this more forcefully, but the mouse has reestablished itself. She wants to hammer home with true conviction that *she* is the story collector. That she gathers stories because she doesn't have a story. She wants to shout this loudly to drown the little voice within her that is trying to add, "Certainly not a story I would ever tell you."

They appear to have reached a standoff. The old woman is looking up at the ceiling. Janice is looking at the woman looking up at the ceiling. She is grateful the (probably original) Chippendale is supporting her shaking legs.

Janice is not sure she can actually stand up, but manages a, "I think I'd better go. It doesn't appear you want a cleaner."

It seems that the woman has reached a decision. Still staring at the ceiling, she says, "I didn't say that. I said I would not be dictated to as to my personal arrangements. I may be a very old woman, but I am not mentally deficient. I know I am struggling to manage and that unless something changes my son will put me in a home. There was a time when I had a certain standing in the college—my late husband was Master here for a number of years—but now it seems few remember him, and the authorities would like this building back for 'more productive purposes.'"

She now looks directly at Janice. "I believe my son is offering to help fund one of these. I understand he would like the 'new cohesive initiative' to be named after him."

Janice looks back at her and—not knowing what to say—reaches for her natural lifeline. "It sounds like you've had a very interesting life. I'm sure you have a story to tell." She then adds, as if on autopilot, "Shall I make us a coffee?"

The old woman leans forward and heaves herself to her feet. "No, you have a look at some of the books. They will tell you all you need to know about me. Start over there." She points to a pile on what looks like a dining room table. "I'll make the coffee."

With that, she shuffles off to the end of the room. Janice notices she does not attempt to put the kettle on but sits down on a stool near the sink. She wonders if Mr. NoNoNotNow's mother is giving her some time to herself. It strikes her that she could just get up and walk out. But then, she could still do that after looking at the books on the table. And ever since she entered the room, she has wanted to look a little closer at what appears to be a sumptuous library.

There are many tomes stacked on the table—and this, she can see, is just a fraction of what is in the room. There are books in French and, she thinks, Russian. Classic English novels—a whole set of beautiful leather-bound copies of *Barchester Chronicles* by Trollope. Weighty hardbacks on Caravaggio and Bernini. Books about Hadrian's Wall and a guidebook to the Roman Baths at Herculaneum. Toward the bottom of the pile, there are more books about art, this time featuring modern artists.

"So?"

Without her noticing, Mr. NoNoNotNow's mother has drawn closer and is sitting at one end of the table.

"You are well-traveled and obviously well-read." Janice looks up and nods at the rest of the room. "You have an interest in art and history and you and/or your husband can speak Russian and French."

"We both can . . . could."

Janice thinks it is time to leave; that pause, that change of tense is drawing her in. And she does not want to spend any more time than is necessary with this tricky woman.

Suddenly, Janice laughs out loud; she has caught sight of one of the modern art books.

"What is it?" the woman asks, but Janice guesses she already knows. She can't rid of herself of the feeling that she is being tested in some way.

Janice holds it up and reads out the title, a book by a contemporary artist, "*Your Saliva is my Diving Suit in the Ocean of Pain*."

There is a snort of laughter from down the end of the table. "Yes, I bought that to remind myself how fucking ridiculous people can be."

Before she can stop herself, Janice asks, "Have you ever met Decius?"

"Decius who?"

Now Janice feels ridiculous. What is she going to say? *I know a fox terrier who in my imagination swears like you. Your eyebrows are rather like his.*

"Oh, nothing, it's your son's dog, that's all."

The old woman puts both hands on the table and bows her head over them. Her wheezing startles Janice, and she wonders if this is an asthma attack and if there is any medication she should get. Then she realizes this is laughter, great hacking guffaws of it. Eventually, the old lady wipes her eyes and says, "So Tiberius called his dog Decius. His father would have loved that." She adds by way of explanation, "My husband had a great interest in Roman history."

Tiberius?! Janice just can't go there. She doesn't want the villains to have a story. She doesn't want to think of a little boy going to school with such an appalling name or consider why the boy grew up to name his dog after a Roman emperor. (A joke against his father? A gentle reminder of him?) She suddenly wonders if, in wanting to name the "new cohesive initiative" after himself, he is thinking of "Tiberius" or his family name—his father's name.

She gets to her feet. She really doesn't need this. "I will have to be going," she says, picking up her bag.

However, Tiberius's mother hasn't finished with her. "One last question. It is a desert-island question." She sees the look on Janice's face (probably the look of a mouse in a trap) and continues quickly. "If you could have one book, one novel on a desert island, what would it be?"

"*Vanity Fair.*" She hadn't meant to answer, but the words are out before she can stop them.

Tiberius's mum looks surprised. Then she nods slowly. "Good choice, lots of stories within stories. Well-written, great humor, delightful sense of the ridiculous, and *what* a cast of characters."

Janice is beginning to resent this dissection of her favorite book and edges closer to the door.

"So, tell me, are you a Becky Sharp or an Amelia?"

Janice says nothing as she fears it might come out as, "Who the hell do you think I am?" She yearns to be more like Becky Sharp but knows she's foolish, deluded Amelia.

By now Janice is in the doorway to the corridor, but it seems that she can't escape the old woman. She shuffles over to her.

"I have such a wonderful story for you. Yes, I would say it is the perfect story, just for you. It is all about a girl, a woman, just like Becky Sharp. In fact, we will call her Becky for the purposes of our tale. It is a story about two princes and a pauper. Well, one was a real prince who grew up to be a king and one was never really a prince at all. So you can see it is going to be a story of intrigue and mystery."

Janice is now stepping over the purple kimono and navigating her way around the suitcases and stuffed squirrel.

The woman behind her is relentless. "Now Becky, our heroine, grew up in Paris, a truly beautiful city. Her mother was a milliner, and her father was a lawyer's clerk. It was a loving family. She had two elder brothers, big brave boys who protected her and who grew up to be soldiers."

By now Janice is outside the door, and out of sheer habit she turns around to take her leave of Tiberius's mother.

"Of course, this is Becky we're talking about. And all that story, all the talk of family and brothers and bravery, well, naturally, it was all lies."

And with that, she shuts the door in Janice's face.

NINE

In Search of a Heroine

It is Thursday and Janice is standing outside a block of well-maintained, Art Deco–style flats. She tries to concentrate on the story of the woman who lives on the first floor, but Becky's story keeps intruding on her thoughts. What had she lied about? And why did the old woman think it was a story for her?

As Janice removes her shoes with a practiced one-two of toe on heel and steps onto the softness of pure wool with double underlay, she is struck by the contrast between this entrance hall and Mrs. YeahYeahYeah's mother-in-law's. Everything is white; everything is spotless. She can hear Carrie-Louise calling from the small kitchen to the right of the front door. "Darling . . . is that you? Now, Janice . . . you really have to be very kind to me today."

Carrie-Louise's speech is slow, each word stretched out to its fullest extent. Her "really" ripples midstretch, trembling like her hands that no longer stay still, even when lying in her lap. She emerges from the kitchen, her movements composed and sure—strangely at odds with her voice and hands. When Janice thinks of Carrie-Louise, the phrase, "neat as a pin," always comes to mind. She is not a woman who would ever wear a hat with moldy cherries on. Her clothes are smoothed over a form slightly thickened by age but still bearing the evidence of earlier, ethereal lines. Silver-framed photographs that Janice dusts each week bear witness to this younger, breathtaking beauty. Janice has no idea how old Carrie-Louise is but assumes she must be late eighties. Not far off the age of . . . but she has no desire to think of her.

Carrie-Louise is off again—rippling laughter and her slow, aristocratic speech. "Darling, you will have . . . to forgive me . . . if I am rather ponderous today. A bit of an old tortoise. Last night . . . I got *so* drunk . . . really, I should have been with the down and outs . . . under the arches." She nods and raises an eyebrow at Janice. "And today we have Mavis coming."

Mavis is Carrie-Louise's oldest friend. They met on their first day at boarding school and decades later came to settle in neighboring suburbs in Cambridge—more than enough time to become experts in each other's foibles. And even though they move much more slowly than they did when they flew across the lacrosse field, they are still quick to spot an emerging weakness in the other. Currently, Mavis likes to flaunt her greater mobility in Carrie-Louise's face: "Madeira in May, just a few days walking among the gardens, it will be a complete tonic. What a shame that's all too much for you now. We used to have such fun, the four of us, didn't we, when your Ernest was still with us? We always think of you two when we are there among the flowers." Mavis does not go so far as to boast about her robust husband, George. If she did, Janice thinks Carrie-Louise might laugh out loud. In fact, Janice is surprised Carrie-Louise does not throw George into the mix of verbal returns. Or, maybe, some things are out of bounds. And perhaps reminding your friend that she has been married to the most boring man in the world for well over fifty years is one of them.

For this visit, Carrie-Louise reaches for an old favorite. She turns to her recipe book. Mavis is an inadequate cook and they both know it. "Darling . . . shall we make . . . some lovely . . . madeleines?" Gurgles of laughter this time. Mavis has never been able to master these delicate French cakes.

"Oh, I think so." Head half in the hall cupboard, Janice can't help smiling as she reaches for the vacuum. "Let me get the drawing room straight for you first, then I can get them started and keep an eye on them as I clean the kitchen." It is an unspoken pact that Mavis must not know that these days Janice does the more intricate baking. Janice knows Carrie-Louise need not worry. Mavis views her as a woman who would buy her cakes from Mr. Kipling. This thought makes her add, "And would you like two varieties of madeleines?"

Carrie-Louise's laughter is gleeful. "Oh, yes, shall we . . . ?" She peers around the edge of the drawing-room door, where Janice is now plugging in the vacuum. "That . . . should sock it to her."

Carrie-Louise returns to the kitchen and Janice can hear her opening and closing cupboards, merrily chatting to herself, until the vacuum drowns out all other noise. Later, as she plumps each of the blue-and-white tapestry cushions on the sofa, she catches the sound of singing and wonders whether the breadth and depth of Carrie-Louise can really be contained in just one story. As she arranges the last cushion in the perfect place, she leaves this thought with them on the sofa. Order matters. (At times she thinks it is all that keeps the rising panic at bay). Rules matter. She tweaks the edge of one of the cushions. Her rule is one person, one story. And better to have one story than none at all.

Carrie-Louise's story is one of the oldest in Janice's collection. She discovered it very early on in their relationship, way before she became a serious collector (she was bleaching the grouting and Carrie-Louise was sitting on the side of the bath). It is a good story, and she draws it out when she wants reassurance that, for some people, love can last a lifetime.

As a much younger woman walking through London's theater district, Carrie-Louise had come across a man being attacked by a gang with baseball bats. Apart from the horrifying tableau in front of her, the street was completely deserted. Carrie-Louise had reached into her bag and grabbed the first thing she could find—her Harvey Nichols store card as it turned out. Bearing this flimsy bit of plastic aloft she ran toward them roaring, "Police!" The men fled from her but not before she was caught on the side of the head by a flailing bat. The impact knocked her out and she crumpled where she stood. When she came to, she was looking up into the face of a young doctor, who had joined the people spilling out of the theater, and who were now forming a crowd around the two prone figures.

Janice recalled the deep satisfaction in Carrie-Louise's voice as she had drummed her heels delightedly against the side of the bath and said, "Darling, I thought I had died and gone to heaven. He really was the most delicious young man and there he was holding my hand and telling me it would be all right and he wouldn't leave me." Carrie-Louise's laugh had filled the small bathroom. "Well, he was right about that. I thought, *I'm not letting you go*, so I just held on tight. And I was still holding his hand fifty years later." She had sighed and, in a voice totally devoid of laughter, added, "I held his hand right until the end, you know.

"Still," she had continued, and Janice had heard the smile returning to her voice, "it showed Bloody Daddy. He had been absolutely ghastly about it all. Ernest was just a lowly houseman at that time. Not what Bloody Daddy had in mind for me at all. But I just kept on holding on tight to his hand and in the end, no one could say it wasn't a success. Even Bloody Daddy had to admit Ernest was really very special when it came to looking after me."

Janice knew this was an oblique reference to the many hospital visits over the years. ("Far too boring to talk about, darling.") Now she gathers it is the long-term damage from the original injury that the neurologists believe is causing the irreversible deterioration of her speech and motor movement.

When she revisits Carrie-Louise's story in her mind, she sometimes changes a few of the smaller details (often adding a second doctor who looks after the man that was attacked). But there is one thing she never alters. It is the phrase, "I held his hand right until the end, you know." Janice cannot remember the last time someone held her hand.

The oven timer breaks in on her thoughts. As she tests the rise of her madeleines, it occurs to her that maybe Carrie-Louise's story is not about one event but about the courage demonstrated during the whole of her life. A special kind of courage that made her run toward the danger and that has held her firm as she faced the physical consequences of her action. Shouldn't she take some inspiration from Carrie-Louise? Dusting and polishing her possessions over the years, Janice hoped some of the older woman's courage had rubbed off onto her.

Frowning, she arranges the *two* varieties of madeleines in perfect symmetry on the best tray. Beautiful cakes in perfect order. Then she wraps a clean white apron about her and forces a smile. A smile that, as she ties the apron strings about her, relaxes more naturally onto her lips. All she has is the here and now, and in the face of Carrie-Louise's courage, she feels the least she can do is to keep playing the game. And part of the game when Mavis appears is that Janice acts the part of loyal retainer—a "domestic" from some 1950s drama. She thinks she plays the part rather well. Although Carrie-Louise draws the line at her bobbing a curtsey, which she had once done to make her laugh. It had worked too well, and Mavis had been sprayed in crumbs, which of course only made Carrie-Louise laugh even harder. As she straightens her apron and smooths her hair, Janice reflects that whatever the future may hold, she has no doubt that Carrie-Louise will always be able to say that she has been the heroine of her own story. Oh, that she could say the same about herself.

As she pushes open the door to the drawing room and hears Mavis's dull, flat voice describing her recent trip to the Channel Islands, she lifts her chin and comes to a decision.

TEN

Every Man Should Leave a Story Better Than He Found It

Janice is sorry she is wearing large lime-green headphones when she gets on the bus. It is foolish of her, she knows, but when she sees that the geography teacher is driving, she wishes her hair wasn't plastered to her head, clamped down by green earpieces that she suspects make her look like a frog. He nods pleasantly at her but does not say anything. Why would he? She clearly can't hear him. But he gives no indication either that she might be a woman he would like to talk to, and the idea that he might sigh at that moment when the bus doors sigh is frankly ludicrous. Her palms turn sweaty with embarrassment, and all she can do is repeat silently to herself, "No one knows. It's okay, no one actually knows. He has no idea." What makes it worse is that he looks nicer than she remembers. He *does* look like a geography teacher—one possibly on the verge of retirement—a man who has photographs in his office of him and his smiling students halfway up Snowdon or Ben Nevis. She moves further down the bus. There is no point in watching him anymore; it is only making her feel mortified and vulnerable—and that is the last thing she needs this morning.

She turns her music up and tries to concentrate on that. The headphones are a new purchase (part of her John Lewis voucher from Simon), and she knows she is going to need them for what lies ahead. They are not anywhere near as expensive as the headphones Mike bought—she suspects they were on sale because they are so very green—but they do the job perfectly well. She hopes they will help her follow through on the promise she made to herself in Carrie-Louise's flat. Her playlist is carefully chosen from Spotify. A dance mix commencing with Sam Cooke (nice, gentle start, great melody) and Stealers Wheel (toe-tapping, irresistible), moving on to George Ezra (bouncy, feel-good), then a swift shuffle through Walk the Moon, T. Rex, Paolo Nutini, and others. By the time she gets to The Commitments and "Mustang Sally," she hopes nothing will be able to stop her and she will be ready to face Tiberius's mother. For she has something she wants to say to her. Well, four things, actually.

She had tried to discuss it with Mike, but he had other things on his mind. He is full of what he might do next. She can't really understand what this might actually involve; he talks of "finalizing negotiations," "getting his ducks lined up," and "keeping her in the loop." None of it fills her with confidence, but she tries hard to stay positive and encouraging, and not let her cynicism show. The only thing that did seem to register about her situation was the name of Tiberius's father. It seems he had been an important man—not just at the college, but nationally—and had received many honors during his life.

"You know he was head of MI6 or something like that?"

She hadn't known, but thinking back to the Russian books, it didn't surprise her. This had naturally brought her back to thinking about his wife. Had she been a spy too? Frankly, she wouldn't put anything past that woman.

Over the past few days, she has thought about her a lot: the purple kimono, her trickiness, the mess, the beautiful room filled with books, and, she hates to admit it, the intriguing story about Becky. She has also thought about her rapier-like stare and that question, "What is your story?" This worries Janice a lot more than her incredible rudeness. But at the end of the day, she's a ninety-two-year-old woman. How scary can she really be? She always has the option to get up and leave. It's not like the woman could run after her. But Janice is uneasy, undecided. Should she take the job? Mrs. YeahYeahYeah had left a message telling her she *is* acceptable to her mother-in-law. She didn't call her back and, thankfully, Mrs. YeahYeahYeah has been out when she has called in for cleaning or dog walking.

In the fields with Decius, she has tried outlining all the pros and cons of taking the work, but for once she hasn't been able to read his expression. At times it looks like he is thinking, *"Give it a go; it's only a job. Why worry when there are far more important things in life—like me?"* At other times it's a definite, *"Fuck her, the old trout."* Perhaps he can't make his mind up either.

Eventually, she reminded herself of the promise she had made herself at Carrie-Louise's—to try to find the courage to take more control and maybe, just maybe, then she could be the heroine of her own life. With this in mind, she came to a decision. She will take the job if, and only if, the old trout gives the right answers to her four questions.

She arrives at the front door with David Bowie blasting through her headphones. She really believes she can do this. The woman who opens the door is remarkably different from the mad figure in the purple kimono and red hat of a few days ago. The old cords are still there, rolled up around her ankles and she seems to be wearing a man's V-neck sweater, but her short white hair is brushed, and her nails are spotless. Oh, she's tricky all right—so all that was part of the act too. Before she loses her nerve, Janice starts, "Thank you for offering me the job, but before I take it, I would like to ask you four questions."

Tiberius's mother regards her with her head tilted slightly to the side. "Go on then."

"Will you tell me Becky's story?"

"Yes."

So far, so good.

"Is Becky's story true?" This is an important question as Janice only collects true stories. She has thought long and hard about this. She believes the stories need to be based on real life because they convince her that the unexpected can happen, that there is extraordinary strength and goodness within normal, everyday people and, because of this, there is always hope.

"Yes, it is a true story. But like any story told and retold, there will be exaggerations here and there."

Janice accepts this. After all, she is a woman who is happy to swallow exaggerations whole. She understands the art and rules of storytelling. She nods.

The old woman continues. "In the retelling, a few extra details may have got thrown into the mix—to add color, shall we say. I subscribe to the novelist and suffragette, Mary Augusta Ward's point of view that 'Every man should leave a story better than he found it,' but I believe the essential facts of the story to be correct, yes." She shifts her body on her sticks as she talks, and Janice can tell she is getting uncomfortable. She would like to say, "Sit down, we can do this inside," but she knows if she pauses now, she will never finish.

"Question number three?"

"Will you let me help you organize your books?"

"Yes."

Now for the tricky one. At first, she had considered asking for an extortionate amount of money for the cleaning job as number four, but this left her feeling uncomfortable. She thought she would always, ever after, be on the moral back foot and she wants her two feet planted firmly on the ground. She does not want to be off balance with this woman around.

So instead, she says, "I will take the job if you call me Janice. And I shall call you Mrs. B."

"That's not a question," she fires at Janice. Her face is deadpan, but Janice thinks that the twitch to the left of her mouth could possibly be a suppressed smile.

"I know it's not really a question. But do you mind?"

"Would it matter if I did?"

Emboldened by Paulo, David, John, Paul, Ringo, and George, Janice says, "No, it wouldn't."

"Then call me Mrs. B." And with that, she performs a slight bow and closes the door once more in Janice's face.

Question four, or, as it turned out, statement four, was important to Janice for three reasons. Firstly, it is for the years of having Mrs. YeahYeahYeah call her "Mrs. P." She knows it is going to infuriate Mrs. YeahYeahYeah when her mother-in-law mentions that Janice calls her Mrs. B. And she is absolutely certain that Mrs. B will tell her—it is just what a troublemaker would do. The second reason is because Mike is already telling everyone in the pub of her latest client, Lady B, wife of the ex-head of MI6, soon to be his close personal friend. Janice's demotion of her through a nickname will irritate the hell out of her husband. The final reason for the "Mrs. B" is simple payback for the comment, "What else could you be but a cleaner?" For once, Janice wants the cleaner to have the last laugh.

She walks away from the door on shaky legs. She doesn't know how she did it. But she has to admit it feels good. She clamps her headphones to her ears and turns up the volume.

The bus driver (who was never a geography teacher but has climbed Snowdon and Ben Nevis) watches from the opposite side of the road as the woman in green headphones (with nice eyes and an excellent bottom) gives a tiny skip and side step on the pavement before walking on. He would give much to hear what she is listening to. He turns his attention back to the road, closes the bus doors, and, with them, lets out a gentle sigh.

ELEVEN

Choosing Your Own Story

Decius is upstairs in Adam's bedroom and Janice is downstairs having coffee with Fiona.

"Thank you for the birthday cake. It made me think of *The Elves and the Shoemaker* when I saw it. Did you ever read that story as a child?"

She hadn't. There had been very different sorts of stories back then.

"I'm glad you liked it. I hope you didn't mind me letting myself in to put it in the doll's house?"

"Oh, not at all," Fiona reassures her, "and it meant that Adam got to meet . . . what did you say his name was? Decius?" She raises anxious eyes upward as if she would like to see through the ceiling and check on Adam in his room. "Is that Greek or something?"

"No, he's named after a Roman emperor." She doesn't add, *by a man called Tiberius.* Instead, she wants to check something with Fiona. "I mentioned that Adam could walk Decius with me sometimes. Would that be all right with you?"

"Of course." Fiona leans forward to pour more coffee, but

when the cups are full, she does not sit back, but stays staring at the smooth, dark surfaces. Janice wishes she were dusting the Venetian blinds or polishing the desk; she knows Fiona would find it easier to confide in her if her attention appeared to be somewhere else. This was often how story collecting worked—not a rule as such, more of a guideline for best practice. As this is clearly not an option now, she sits quietly, not moving.

"He's finding it very hard without John. I try my best, but he won't really talk about it. I did get him to agree to some counseling but he refused to go back after the first session. Said the counselor was, 'some dumbnut who believed all the shit he told him.'" Fiona looks up and tries to smile. "I think John . . . sorry, Adam—" She stops dead. "Jesus, sorry, I keep doing that, calling him John. I don't suppose that's helping much." She shrugs, still trying to smile.

This is breaking Janice's heart.

"Anyway, he said he had told the counselor what he wanted to hear and that he was a dummy for believing him. He said his dad would have thought he was a twat." She shakes her head. She is no longer smiling. "But when you had been over with Decius, he was full of it. Told me what were signs of good breeding in a fox terrier. Wanted me to call you to get him over."

Janice is mortified; it is over a week since she introduced Decius to Adam. "Always call me. I can easily pop over and collect Decius. I'm really the only dog walker he has. Adam can come with me as often as he likes." She wonders if it would help if Adam was earning some money for this; she could give him part of what Mrs. YeahYeahYeah pays her for taking Decius out. Then she decides this is not about money. It is about love. And that can't be bought.

Fiona is back to studying the full coffee cups. Janice dares not pick hers up, although she would dearly like to.

"The thing is, I don't want him to be defined by this. I don't want him, forever, to be the boy whose father killed himself."

And there it is, out on the table, with the duck-egg-blue coffee cups (from a local potter) and the plate of all-butter hazelnut cookies from Waitrose.

"I keep telling him that," Fiona repeats. "That this mustn't be what defines him."

"What does Adam say?"

"He says it doesn't work like that. He says you can't choose your own story."

What can Janice say? That she fears Adam may be right?

"And you?" Janice asks gently.

"Oh, me." Fiona sighs. "You know, I think I started this work as a way of punishing myself. Making myself do something so painful—as if that could make up for letting John and Adam down."

Janice shakes her head as if to contradict her, but Fiona ignores this and continues. "The thing is, it's strange, but I find working with the bereaved really helps. And I have done some funerals for other people who have killed themselves. My mum can't understand how I can bear to do that, but it makes it something that is part of life. It makes me feel it doesn't consign John to the shadows. I can talk about him, and people know that I understand their pain."

Janice can see that Fiona is miles away. She resigns herself to drinking cold coffee. It couldn't matter less.

Fiona continues. "I think maybe it is easier for me because I saw much more of what John was going through. Knew about the depression, the medication, the days of doubt and hopelessness. We hid that from Adam as much as we could. For me, whilst it was a hideous shock what he did, in some ways I had been expecting it for years." She looks up at Janice. "Don't get me wrong, thinking about it is not the same as actually going through it. It can't really prepare you for how you are going to feel, but afterward, you have some context. I don't think Adam has that. To him, John was the best dad in the world, and he chose to leave him. How on earth is he supposed to get his head around that?"

Janice has no answers, although somewhere inside herself she wonders if Adam really was that ignorant of what his dad was going through. As she herself knows, children notice a lot more than adults think they do.

As she cannot explain this to herself, let alone Fiona, she thinks of two things that she can do. "If it's okay, I'll bring Decius over tomorrow after school for a long walk." Then, ever practical, she adds, "and after that would you like me to defrost your freezer? I saw it was getting so you couldn't close the door."

On the way home on the bus that night (no sign of the geography teacher; maybe he only works mornings?) she thinks about Fiona. She can understand how having some purpose through her work would be helping her. She remembers the story of a young woman (a friend of Geordie's son, John) who, after a number of miscarriages, had eventually given up trying to have children. She and her husband, a zoologist, had moved to Botswana and she is now a woman who makes elephants angry. This is quite an art because she may want to make them slightly annoyed, a little bit pissed off, proper cross or, as Decius might put it, fucking furious. Obviously, all without getting trampled. Her husband is studying how elephants communicate using their ears and apparently anger is one of the easiest emotions to monitor. When she last heard about her from Geordie, he'd told her that she and her husband now have a nine-month-old baby.

Janice tries to be analytical and scientific about her story collecting—like the husband-and-wife team who study elephants' ears—but the truth is that she is a sucker for a happy ending. She just isn't sure she can see how Fiona is ever going to get one for Adam.

TWELVE

Every Story Has a Beginning

By her second visit to Mrs. B's, Janice has cleared her hallway of clutter. It had been a relatively easy task. She was right: the college did have storage space that Mrs. B could use. Chatting to the porters and university cleaners (a short, middle-aged woman being an easy and nonthreatening confidante), she gathers that the college hopes that this will be the first step in Mrs. B changing her arrangements and possibly, hopefully, fingers crossed—"because she really is a right pain in the arse"—moving on. She didn't disabuse them of this notion and kept her comments vague (apart from allowing herself a silent look of understanding at the use of "pain in the arse"). She certainly didn't suggest that many Roman generals (as she has been reading in Mrs. B's books) often created diversions, when in truth they were fortifying their positions ready for battle. Nonetheless, storage space has been found and Janice had persuaded Mrs. B to part with some crumpled £20 notes to pay a couple of students to move her belongings.

The kitchen is taking a bit longer, and Janice is still trying to scrape the last bits of solidified food from the counter when

Mrs. B starts to circle. She moves from chair to chair, each time getting a bit closer. To begin with, she limbers up with a rally of what Janice presumes is unusually polite chit-chat for her.

"Janice, do you have to come far?"

"No, we live in a village just outside of Cambridge. I get the bus in."

"Where is it that you're from originally?"

"I grew up in Northampton, mainly."

"Ah, famous for its shoes I believe."

Janice says nothing but raises an eyebrow at her.

This is all a warm-up for the main event. Janice has not asked Mrs. B about Becky's story, although she dearly wants to hear it. Nor has Mrs. B broached the subject, despite the fact that Janice is pretty certain she wants to tell it. It has become a game of chicken. Mrs. B is the first to break, which surprises Janice. But at ninety-two, maybe she feels she hasn't got time for any more of this shit.

"So, do you want to hear about Becky or not?"

Janice can't stop herself from beaming at her. "You know I do." She adds by way of a thank you, "Would you like me to make you a hot chocolate?" She has discovered Mrs. B has a fondness for 70 percent dark chocolate in all its forms. This is too much for Mrs. B and it seems that having given in she wants to redress the balance. "No, I do not. Do you think I want to end up with an arse like yours?" She glares at Janice, challenging her to object to her rudeness.

Janice returns to her scraping with a cheery, "Right you are, Mrs. B."

She thinks she hears a small snort from the wife of the life peer, but cannot tell if this is anger or laughter.

Janice takes pity on her and meets her halfway. "So what was Becky lying about?"

"Oh, pretty much all of it. She did grow up in Paris though—"

"When was this?" Janice interrupts.

"The 1890s. Are you going to listen to this story or not?" Mrs. B glares at her.

Janice stays quiet, and watches Mrs. B settle down more comfortably in her chair. "There was no happy family, at least not for Becky. I think she was a girl who felt like an outsider within her own family. Paris was a beautiful city at this time, just before the dawn of the new century, a city of parks and boulevards, filled with sunlight and fragrance. But of course, like most things in life, it depended on which side of the tracks you were born. And Becky was definitely born on the filthy, smelly, decrepit side of the tracks. Becky's mother was not a milliner and did not preside over an elegant shop selling exquisite confections, and her father was not a valued member of a prestigious law firm. Her mother was a chare woman." Mrs. B cannot resist adding, "Rather like yourself."

Janice had been thinking of putting the milk on the hob to make Mrs. B the hot chocolate despite her protest but changes her mind.

"Her father," Mrs. B continues, after a pause, "drove a common Hackney cab. There were no gallant elder brothers who would grow up to be soldiers. I believe, later, Becky could move many to tears when she described the death of *both* of her brothers in the First World War. There was a younger sister of whom she was inordinately jealous—I suspect she fitted in, you see—and a blond-haired baby brother who was as chubby as he was cheerful.

"Do you have brothers and sisters, Janice?" she suddenly asks.

"I have a sister," Janice finds herself saying before she can stop herself. She continues, more slowly, more carefully, "She lives in Canada now. She is five years younger than me and works as a pediatric nurse; her husband is a doctor."

"And do you see much of her?"

"Not really. They come to England every couple of years and, of course, I make a point of meeting up with her then, usually in London." She doesn't add that her sister has little time for Mike, and so it is better this way. "I went over to stay with her for three weeks a couple of years ago and that was . . ." She can't quite finish the sentence and she senses the change in Mrs. B. Suddenly, the old woman is alert and she thinks of a cat stalking its prey. And it's no everyday housecat. For all her bony, frail exterior, Janice knows she is dealing with a big cat. Maybe not a lioness, but a stealthy, dangerous predator, like a jaguar.

"You were saying?" Mrs. B asks with unusual politeness.

"I was saying the trip was very nice," Janice concludes and heads off to clean the bathroom.

As she is about to leave, Mrs. B takes up her story as if there has been no break in their conversation. By now she is sitting in her usual armchair by the electric fire. "Becky's baby brother was the pride and joy of his parents. However tired they were from their day's work, he could not fail to lift their spirits. Some babies are just like that. Their happiness seems to come from an external source, unconnected with their family or physical circumstances. And these children spread joy like a light shone into a dark corner. When her parents were at work, Becky, as the eldest child, had the responsibility of looking after her brother. She was fonder of him than anyone else in her family but by the time he was four the appeal was beginning to wane. She was a girl who wanted to explore the city and create alternative, more exciting worlds for herself in her head. Which is why she was looking out of an upstairs window dreaming of rich dresses and carriages, rather than minding him, when a large delivery van swung into their narrow street and smashed into her brother, throwing him into the gutter."

Janice has one arm into her jacket. "What happened to him?"

There is no answer from Mrs. B and she thinks she hasn't heard her. "Mrs. B, did he die?" There is still no reply, but a gentle snore issues from the armchair. Janice cannot decide if Mrs. B is faking it, but she closes the front door quietly after herself, all the same.

On the bus on the way home, for once, she has no time for story collecting. What had happened to Becky's brother? She is assuming it is not good news, but she would still like to know for certain. Did the parents blame Becky? How old had she been? She recalls this doesn't really matter when you are a child, as you don't ever think of yourself as young. You are just you, and will take up guilt and responsibility without noticing that they are far too large for you and that they are really things an adult should be wearing.

But she wasn't like Becky, was she? She had protected her sister, hadn't she? She keeps coming back to that thought and something else. It is an incident that happened at the end of her stay in Canada, and, she reflects, it *had* been a good stay. On the last night, her sister had pulled out an old fountain pen from her desk and had written on a clean white piece of paper so Janice could clearly read it,

I remember what you did.

Then she had put her pen away and got up from the desk and made them both supper.

THIRTEEN

Every Story Ends in Death

"So, what happened to Becky's brother, Mrs. B?"

Janice is taking off her coat in the hallway after stopping off to collect Mrs. B's post from the Porter's Lodge. She also picked up a piece of information that she thinks Mrs. B will find interesting—but that can wait. First, she wants to know about the little boy. She is not expecting good news.

Mrs. B doesn't say anything and continues scanning yesterday's *Times*, which she has open on the table in front of her. Janice has not made a start on the many piles of books around the room but she has cleared the large oak table by the window so Mrs. B now has somewhere to sit and eat—and read the paper.

Still nothing but silence from Mrs. B.

Janice waits.

Thinking back to her last visit, she is less and less convinced that Mrs. B had really been sleeping and is now pretty sure she had heard her previous inquiry about Becky's brother. She certainly does not think Mrs. B is hard of hearing or lacking in understanding.

Still nothing.

Janice is getting irritated; a deal is a deal. "Mrs. B, you promised. You promised you would tell me Becky's story."

"I did not promise, and please do not talk to me as if you were six; we are not in a playground." She spits this out and Janice is once more reminded of the woman in purple. "However," she continues more moderately, "I told you I would tell you about Becky and I will."

She adds, as if the words are being dragged from her, "I passed an indifferent night and am in some pain from my back and legs. So I shall tell you later when the painkillers have started to take effect." She looks back down at her paper. "I also had the shits, so you may want to change my bed." She turns another page of her paper, but Janice is not fooled. Mrs. B is blushing.

"I'll get you a hot-water bottle." Janice had spotted one of these in the airing cupboard. "Then I'll sort the bed out and get a wash on."

Mrs. B *hmph*s at her without looking up.

Janice quickly creates order in the garret bedroom, where it looks like Mrs. B has tried to clean up—although stripping the bed was clearly beyond her. It is very smelly, but she has dealt with worse. She once looked after Geordie when he had a stomach upset. Mrs. B hardly eats enough to keep a sparrow alive, whereas Geordie . . .

After putting the sheets in the washing machine, Janice returns to Mrs. B, who is now sitting in her usual armchair, and she offers to make her a cup of chamomile tea. Mrs. B accepts this with a subdued, "Thank you, Janice."

Janice is starting to get concerned. She is unsure whether Mrs. B is really ill and she should ring for a doctor, or whether she is just embarrassed. When she brings her the tea, she decides to try an experiment. "I was in the Porter's Lodge chatting to Stan, and he tells me your son has submitted some plans to the local planning department for converting your house into a multi-media virtual-reality interactive space. I think I have that right," she says, watching the frail old lady carefully. "I believe it is to, 'create a symbiosis of old and new learning, preserving the external structure but bringing enlightenment to the inner.' Stan gave me a look at the bursar's copy of the proposal."

It is as if Mrs. B has been electrified. "He's done what? I should have drowned him at birth!"

Janice's obvious shock seems to register with the old lady, who is now sitting bolt upright in her chair.

"It's a figure of speech, Janice. I would not in any circumstance put my son in a sack with a pile of bricks and throw him in the River Cam."

From the way she says this, Janice can't help feeling she is deriving considerable satisfaction from considering the prospect.

"I don't know what offends me more. The fact he is working behind my back or his use of such atrocious language. Well, that was a few hundred thousand wasted on his education. How can the boy have so little soul? When I think of his father . . ." Mrs. B is silent for some moments. "I shall have to give this some thought. Thank you for bringing it to my attention. Now, I suppose you want to hear about Becky's brother."

Janice settles down to tidy a cupboard just beside Mrs. B's chair. Over the years it seems to have been the depository for stray screws, flashlights, keys, old postcards, and every other type of clutter. Janice has a drawer in her kitchen that contains the things that, "might be useful one day." Mrs. B has a whole cupboard of them.

"Of course, he died," Mrs. B declares matter-of-factly.

Janice looks up from her sorting. "I thought he was going to."

"Yes, every story ends in death. And I'm afraid his story was a very short one."

"What about Becky?"

Mrs. B relaxes once more into her chair and pulls the hot-water bottle around so she is hugging it to her stomach. "I think the question is, what about his parents? His father, his mother . . . the loss of a child is a terrible thing and the loss of one like that . . . well, it can hardly be imagined. Don't you agree, Janice?"

Janice turns around, surprised she is asking her opinion. Then it strikes her that Mrs. B wants to see her face, that she is checking whether those words about losing a child are striking a chord. The crafty old bat. Janice turns back. She knows Mrs. B will see nothing there. But she's been warned. "Yes, I would agree," she says briefly.

Mrs. B sniffs and continues. "Becky's parents were poor, ill-educated Parisians, but that was no barrier to their love. They didn't love the boy less because their lives were hard, and they had seen death and destitution walk past their door before. They loved him more because he had, for a brief moment, illuminated their lives with a special kind of glow. It had given them a glimpse of what was golden and good and cast the rest of their wretched existence into the shadows. Without their beloved son, everything was stripped bare in the shattering, unforgiving light of reality. And everywhere they looked, there was Becky. Very much alive."

"So what did they do?"

"When they could not stand the sight of her any longer, they sent her away to the nuns. Do you have any experience with the Sisters of Mercy, Janice?"

This time Janice does not turn around to answer. "Enough," is all she offers.

"Exactly. A bigger bunch of pious, hypocritical old shrews would be hard to find."

This does make Janice turn around. She feels she owes it to Sister Bernadette to say, "They're not all bad."

Mrs. B studies her face for a while. "You are quite right, and it is intellectually slovenly to give in to generalizations. But I think for the purposes of our story we can assume that the nuns who were entrusted with Becky's care were a right bunch of old bitches."

Mrs. B chuckles. "Years later she walked past the building that had housed the convent she had been sent to. It was now a garage. She derived considerable satisfaction from walking in and asking to test drive their largest and most expensive red motor car."

"How long was she in the convent for?"

"Oh, many years, and during that time the nuns did all they could to make Becky's life a misery. At every opportunity, they reminded the child that she had the blood of her brother on her hands and that she was unworthy to walk this earth. She was a creature beyond redemption. Only hell was waiting for her. It is also true to say that Becky did what she could during those years to make the nuns' lives a misery in return. We must not forget this is Becky we are talking about after all.

"When her fifteenth birthday came, she was sent packing. As you can imagine, the idea of Becky staying on and taking vows was not one that anyone seriously considered. If the nuns had been women with a sense of humor, they would have slapped their thighs and roared at the very idea. As it was, they deposited Becky onto the street and shut the heavy wooden door behind her; then they went into the chapel, dropped to their knees, and offered up a prayer of thanks. I like to think that it was on this spot that the red motor car would later sit in all its vulgar glory. But here, I suspect, I am being fanciful. However, I do believe that from their stations in the chapel, heads bent in prayer, they would have heard Becky's laughter from the other side of the door."

"What happened to her then?"

"She entered the home of a wealthy and aristocratic family. And now we have a marvelous example of the stories that Becky was able to weave. I wonder what she actually came to believe herself in the end? Was she a valued member of the family beloved by all, especially by the younger son (in Becky's stories there was often an infatuated younger son)? Or was she the upstairs maid, emptying the family's stinking chamber pots? Whichever it was, it did not last long and before much time had passed, our now sixteen-year-old Becky was knocking at her parents' door."

"Were they still living in the same place?"

"They were, and at her knock, her mother came down and opened the door to her . . ."

"And?" Janice has now finished sorting but doesn't want to move. She thinks they must look like an odd couple: a tiny old woman swallowed up by a battered leather chair and a dumpy woman in a faded wrap-around apron sitting expectantly at her feet.

"Her mother took one long look at her, offered up a prayer to Our Lady, and crossed herself."

"After all that time? Could she not find it in herself to forgive her?"

"What you cannot see is the thing that was immediately obvious to Becky's mother: that her eldest daughter was heavily pregnant."

"Aah."

"Her mother grabbed her daughter by the hand and marched her back to the Sisters of Mercy, but they would not open the door to her. I believe they drowned out the sounds of her knocking with a rousing chorus of 'Sileat Omnis Caro Mortalis' which, if your Latin is a little rusty, Janice, translates as, 'Let all mortal flesh keep silence.'"

"Who was the father?"

"I don't think we will ever know. I do not credit Becky's suggestion that it was an aristocratic younger son. But I think we must not forget, in our appreciation of the fanciful stories Becky was able to tell, that we are talking about a girl who was little more than a child. Someone who had been abandoned by her family, abused by the nuns, and thrown friendless onto the street. I very much expect Becky had been raped. After all, she had no one to protect her. I suspect, in reality, had we heard the young Becky telling her grandiose stories, we would have felt very little urge to laugh."

"What did her mother do next?"

"What would any mother do in those circumstances? What would your mother have done had you come home pregnant?"

Janice wonders if her mother would even have noticed. Of course she does not say this to Mrs. B. She has no desire to discuss her mother with her. She heaves herself to her feet and decides it is time to throw in a curveball of her own. "How did you and your husband meet?"

Mrs. B looks up in surprise, but Janice knows she has her. It is like watching a cat with a ball of string; Mrs. B cannot resist it.

"I will never forget the first time I saw Augustus . . ."

Augustus, Tiberius, Decius—Janice can see a pattern emerging.

"I had just arrived in Moscow and I was to meet my contact in a tea room near the river. I had never experienced cold like it and for a while when I entered the café I was just aware of the humid warmth on my face. I could see nothing through the steam from the samovars, except for the glint of their red and gold enameled surfaces reflected in the gilded mirror behind the counter. And then I saw him. And in that instant, I knew."

"Straight away?" Janice is temporarily side-tracked from the fact that this woman was actually a spy.

"Yes. Why? Do you not believe in love at first sight, Janice?"

Maybe, possibly. But not for her. What can she say? "I think I must do . . ." She is about to add that it features often enough in the stories in her collection but stops herself in time. "What were you doing in Moscow?"

"What do you think, Janice? You are an intelligent woman, despite your best efforts to appear the opposite."

Bit cruel, Janice thinks, but at least Mrs. B doesn't think she's a fool.

"I imagine you know my husband became head of MI6. We met when he was my handler in Russia. I had studied French and Russian at Cambridge after the war, and I was recruited to play a minor role in our operation in Moscow. Women, then as now, are often underestimated. But I do like to think that, in a small way, I made a difference."

She then spoils this dignified but rather pompous speech by adding, gleefully, "And it was exceptionally exciting. I have never felt so alive."

"How long were you in Moscow for?"

"Five years in all, then Augustus and I married. And that was the end of that; I was no longer allowed to work, not in the way I would have liked. As he progressed in the service, we were posted to many countries around the world, and I had certain duties associated with that. Not ones I really relished though. Still, I never regretted marrying him for one single instant. And he said it was the same for him when he saw me emerging out of the steam in that tearoom," Mrs. B adds, rather self-consciously. "I was a very different woman back then, Janice. I was never what you would call a beauty, but Augustus always said I had great presence."

"Well, that hasn't changed," Janice says, looking down at her.

Mrs. B looks up at her in surprise and says softly, "Thank you, dear."

Janice turns away to hide her feelings. She is surprised and touched, and it confirms to her once again that it is in people's stories that you really get to know them. But what is Mrs. B's story? Is it a spy story? A story of a woman who was a frustrated spy for all but five years of her life? Or is Mrs. B's tale a simple love story? She suspects it is the latter. She wonders if, in the intensity of that love, there was much room for Tiberius.

The talk of her husband and spying brings something else to Janice's mind—all thoughts of Becky temporarily forgotten. "Mrs. B, you and your husband must have the most amazing network of contacts. Are you getting proper advice about the college's plans?"

"I am not an idiot," Mrs. B barks at her, obviously regretting her earlier moment of softness. "Naturally I have sought legal advice, but it is all, 'on the one hand this, on the other hand that.' The thing is, when you get to my age, most of the friends you could have asked are dead." She starts to drum her fingers on the arm of her chair. "Of course, there is always Mycroft."

"Who's Mycroft?"

Mrs. B gives a crack of laughter. "It's what Augustus always called him. His actual name is Fred Spink, but Augustus always said he was the brightest man he knew. A small, unremarkable man, but he served for many years as legal counsel within MI5. He's been retired for years, of course, but I believe he's still with us. I would have read his obituary in *The Times* if he'd died. Yes, I might give Mycroft a call." Mrs. B smiles. "I rather think he had a soft spot for me." She then looks like she wishes she hadn't shared this, and Janice isn't surprised when she says, irritably, "Are you just going to stand there, or do you think you might actually do some cleaning?"

There is no further talk of spying or Becky as Janice sets about polishing the wooden floor. When she is just about to leave, Mrs. B waylays her. "I've been giving this some thought, and it is very useful that the porter, what did you say his name was, Stan? Well, that Stan would confide in you."

Janice is wondering what's coming next, and how Mrs. B can have lived here for so long and not known Stan's name—he has worked here as man and boy.

"It occurred to me that you are in a unique position to find out information . . ."

"As I have been doing," Janice cannot help pointing out.

"Yes, dear, as you have been doing."

Janice is not taken in. That was a very considered "dear," not the impulsive, gentle "dear" of earlier. The old bat wants something.

"It struck me that you clean for Tiberius and might very well overhear or come across—as you are dusting and so forth—information that could be useful."

"No!" As a bark, it is worthy of Mrs. B herself. "I have very strict rules about cleaning, and I will not spy on your son." She almost adds, "Shame on you!" But she sees there is no need; Mrs. B is blushing quite as much as she did when she shat the bed.

FOURTEEN

One Perfect Moment

"Oh, it's you."

The words are out there, and she cannot put them back in her mouth. She imagines the three individual words hanging above the bus driver's head, like washing on a line. She thinks of Geordie and wishes, like him, she could pluck them down and peg up something old and worn instead. Anything. "Single to Riverside," would do. After all, that's where she wants to go to pick up Decius and meet up with Adam. She just hadn't been expecting the geography teacher, as she had been thinking of something completely different—a pregnant Becky. For some reason, it seems like this is Mrs. B's fault. It's not fair. She hadn't been thinking of him. It's not his normal route and it's midafternoon.

"Can I help you?" He is smiling at her, and she finds it unnerving. How long has she been standing there? She hears a, "Come on, get a move on," from behind her, and the spell is broken. She taps her card against the ticket machine and takes a seat as far back as she can on the bus. Her heart is going like a piston engine.

After the second stop, she moves forward. He cannot see her, she is pretty sure of that, but she can now see his left shoulder. At the next stop, she moves another row forward. Still out of sight, but from here she can take in most of his back.

She looks around the bus, suddenly conscious that people might be looking at her. No one is. She thinks of Mrs. B emerging through the steam in a Moscow tearoom. A spy meeting a spy. That is a story steeped in romance. But this? What's just happened to her? It's a dull, cold Thursday afternoon, and she stepped onto a corporation bus and made a fool of herself.

She suddenly remembers one of her stories that always leaves her with a dilemma. She enjoys it—after all, it has a happy ending—but there is always a question mark at the end. Something that threatens to upset her system.

Arthur Leader is a man in his eighties. She occasionally cleans for him when his regular cleaner, Angela, is on holiday. He is a man who likes order and routine; she doesn't blame him—she does too. One day (as she was ironing his shirts) he told her the story of how he met his wife.

The future Mrs. Leader had been out to the cinema with a boyfriend and, on returning to his car, they realized it had been broken into and the boyfriend's raincoat had been stolen. They debated whether they should go to the police and in the end thought they would call in at the local station. The young policeman on the desk was one Detective Constable Leader. He had looked at the woman in front of him (he barely noticed the man) and liked what he saw—an attractive brunette in a crisp white dress, with blue candy stripes. He started to take down the particulars, explaining to the boyfriend that they would be keeping his car so the forensic team could examine it. As Janice had maneuvered the shoulder of Arthur's shirt onto the ironing board she could not help smiling—oh, how things had changed.

Arthur then told Janice how he had taken the brunette's hand in his and helped her as he took her fingerprints—for elimination purposes. As he pressed her inky fingers onto the card, he realized—that was it. A done deal as far as his heart was concerned. When the statements had been faithfully recorded—Detective Constable Leader was always thorough, and though he didn't know it then, he was going to rise up the ranks until he was Chief Constable—he ordered a car to take the brunette (along with his heart) home. He made sure the PC who was driving the police car made a careful note of where she lived. It was always his boast afterward that he got the raincoat back but stole the girl. It was only at his wife's funeral, many years later, that her sister told him she had come back that evening and said she could not emigrate to Australia with her as planned, as she had just met the man she was going to marry.

And the dilemma that this story leaves Janice with is this: maybe sometimes life is not about having a story; maybe it's about finding one perfect moment. That moment in a Bournemouth police station. That freezing afternoon in a Russian tearoom. She pictures her words hanging in the air—"Oh, it's you"—and then the smile. He did smile at her. She doesn't kid herself that it was a perfect moment. But it was a moment, nonetheless. It's only as she's walking up the path to collect Decius that she remembers to remind herself that she is a married woman.

When she gets to the front door it is ajar and her first thought is that Decius could have got out and onto the road. She steps quickly inside and looks around, then sinks down onto her knees in relief as she hears the *tip, tip, tip* of his claws on the wooden floor and then spots him emerging from the kitchen. He runs toward her, his small legs flicking forward in his ballerina-style goose-step that never fails to make her smile.

He looks at her and then up at the open door behind her, as if to say, *"What? You think I'm an idiot?"*

As she strokes his curly head and reassures him, she hears voices emanating from the open-plan sitting room.

"Well, I don't know why you're blaming me."

Definitely Mrs. YeahYeahYeah.

"It's not a matter of blaming anyone . . ." An irritated Tiberius (she wishes she could still think of him as Mr. NoNoNotNow but that is a thing of the past). ". . . It just makes it more complicated."

"But you said get her some help in the house," Mrs. YeahYeahYeah says, sounding petulant.

"I know I did, but I didn't think anyone would actually take the job, especially not Mrs. P. I mean, she's such a . . . well, a quiet nothing. And you know what *she's* like. I thought Mummy would chew her up and spit her out."

Janice is reeling. How dare he! And he calls his mother "Mummy"?!

"But Tibs, do you want her to have help or not?"

Tibs?!

"What I want is to get her out of that house. She's not safe in there on her own. You know she can barely walk. Those stairs are an accident waiting to happen."

"We could put in a stair lift, I suppose?"

"Don't be ridiculous!" Tiberius barks, and Janice is left in no doubt whose son he is. "It's a listed building."

"Well, I just thought—"

"Well, I wish you wouldn't. I've got to think of a way out of this. That space should be used for academic purposes; it's what Daddy would have wanted. And it's not about the money. She needn't think that."

Janice is past being surprised by the "Daddy"; she's still too angry about the "quiet nothing." And what's with "the money"? She can't take it all in.

Tiberius is on a roll now. "You have that incredible space, and the college can do nothing with it. She's rattling around on her own in there. I wouldn't be surprised if one night something got caught in that electric fire of hers and she burnt the whole bloody place down. I know she's my mother but she's a fucking nightmare."

Perhaps this is where Decius gets it from?

Tiberius, in a more moderate tone, adds, "I'd better get going. I don't want to miss the train."

In one swift movement, Janice is on her feet and back out the door. She shuts the door quietly on a *WTF* look from Decius and rings the doorbell. Her hand is shaking.

Walking across the fields with Adam later, she is unusually quiet—not that she thinks Adam notices. He's too busy racing Decius and creating obstacles for him to jump over like he's about to enter him for the fox terrier gymkhana. Her heart lifts as she listens to his running commentary; oh, such a boy still. And for this half an hour at least, she genuinely believes he has shaken off his terrible burden. She watches as he wallops through the undergrowth, springing off logs, shouting encouragement to Decius to get a clear round. In a small, unexpected way, it is a perfect moment.

She keeps watching the boy and dog playing as she reviews the conversation she's just heard. She can't kid herself—that definitely *was* eavesdropping. She's glad Adam is so preoccupied as she needs time to think. Was Tiberius right? Is it safe for Mrs. B to live there on her own? And really, shouldn't the space be for students, not one cranky old woman? She hates to admit it, but maybe her son has a point. What would her husband have thought? She only has Mrs. B's view on that. And what did he mean about the money? What money? And if there is money, wouldn't she be able to afford something nice and much more suitable? Images of Mrs. B being thrown out of her home by her son into a smelly care home are fading fast.

Her mind starts to drift elsewhere. That smile on the bus. She can't help returning to that. It was a nice smile, a friendly smile. She may have felt a fool but she doesn't think the bus driver who looks like a geography teacher was laughing at her. It was much more like he was sharing something with her. It's just she has no idea what.

FIFTEEN

The Oldest Story in the World

Mike is off unexpectedly early, waving a handful of folders under her nose as he passes her on the landing. "People to go, places to see."

Janice smiles perfunctorily at the oft-repeated joke. She still has no idea what he's up to but she presumes he must be getting some interviews (at the very least), as he keeps disappearing off for meetings. She's glad when he's gone as she wants the bedroom to herself so she can choose what to wear in peace.

Her brief is a difficult one. She needs an outfit that is suitable for wearing when you have your head down other people's toilets, but that also—on the off chance you should bump into a bus driver who looks like a geography teacher—says: *I am a friendly woman*; *I am never going to be beautiful but hopefully I'm not past praying for*; *I am the sort of woman who likes to walk and I might manage Snowdon if you didn't go too fast*; and *I am definitely not a woman who blurts things out without thinking.* And all this, without looking like mutton dressed as lamb, or as if she has gone to too much effort.

Carrie-Louise greets her with, "Now . . . tell me, darling . . . I can see you have done . . . something. Is it your hair? Well, whatever it is . . . I approve!" Janice would like to hug her. The bus had been driven this morning by the Hells Angel—"Mornin', love"—and she hadn't known whether to be disappointed or relieved. However, for now, she has other things to think of: Mavis is due for coffee, and she needs to get baking.

Janice puts down her tack hammer and pulls the fabric tighter on the footstool she is repairing for Carrie-Louise. She is working in the dining area and although the partition doors are closed into the drawing room, she can still hear Carrie-Louise and Mavis's conversation quite clearly. She has been thoroughly enjoying it but if she's honest she does think Mavis might be winning on points. Despite the delivery of homemade Florentines on the best tray, Mavis has managed to flaunt a forthcoming trip on the Orient Express, a visit to Glyndebourne, and her dance mobility class in Carrie-Louise's face. Carrie-Louise had countered with, "Oh my . . . five days on a train with George . . . No, no . . . it will be marvelous . . . darling." But then Mavis played her trump card and drew her new smartphone from her handbag. Carrie-Louise is fearful of most forms of technology and Mavis was soon talking to her about apps and the joy of Audible. "That would be so good for you, now you can't get out so much."

Mavis's phone has just sounded ("Ring My Bell" by Anita Ward).

"Oh, Josh is such a card; he keeps changing my ringtone." This is a slam-dunk as far as Mavis is concerned; her grandchildren live in Worthing, whereas Carrie-Louise's grandchildren are 10,000 miles away in Melbourne. Mavis spends some time on the phone chatting away to her daughter. Bit rude, Janice thinks, and she wonders about putting on her white apron and going in with more coffee. She might even bob Carrie-Louise a curtsey to cheer her up.

She needn't have worried. Mavis ends her call and Carrie-Louise gets started. "Darling . . . you . . . sounded so . . . different."

"What do you mean?"

"Just then . . . on your . . . new phone."

"Oh, really?" Mavis asks, sounding unsure.

"Yes . . . so, so . . . different."

"How do you mean?"

"You know . . . just different . . . when you were talking to your daughter."

"Well how, how was I different?"

"Oh, I don't know . . . darling . . . just *different*," Carrie-Louise says, vaguely this time:

"Yes, but what do you mean, *different*?" Mavis says again, getting slightly shirty.

"Well . . . you sounded . . ."

"Yes?" Mavis is getting more impatient.

"Well . . . you sounded . . . really, really . . . lovely."

Janice starts hammering again to mask her laughter. There is no doubt about it; that is a late knock-out by Carrie-Louise.

Janice arrives early at Mrs. B's, giving her a chance to call in to the Porter's Lodge to see Stan. She has brought him some of the Florentines from Carrie-Louise's. First, they cover a few generalities over a coffee: how Arsenal did last night against Liverpool, whether they are going to have a bit of snow, and who will be dancing the lead in *Les Sylphides* when Stan goes to Covent Garden this weekend. He and his wife, Gallina, are very fond of the ballet. Janice then brings up the subject of Mr. B.

"You must have known him when he was Master here?"

"Certainly did. He was here for quite a few years. A nice man. Private, mind. But I suppose that comes with having done the job he did. We had to have all sorts of extra security when he was in the college."

"But he lived here, where she is now?" She nods in the general direction of Mrs. B's accommodation. She can't quite bring herself to call her "Lady," but feels it would be disrespectful to call her "Mrs. B" to Stan.

Stan nods. "That's right, just the two of them. It's funny, she wasn't half so bad back then. Still a bit uppity but they were one of those couples . . . you know . . ."

Janice waits.

"I don't think they felt the need for other people."

Janice keeps quiet; she feels there is more.

"Always felt a bit sorry for their son. I mean, he's a right twat, but sometimes I think they barely noticed he was there."

"Do you know anything about the arrangement with the house, how it was left when he died?"

"Ooh, can't help you there, love. I think it was pretty complicated, something to do with a will or covenant? But that's all I know, really."

There is one final thing Janice wants to check. "When I'm not here, I mean the rest of the week, do other people look in on her?"

"Not really. Her son comes over every couple of weeks. His wife used to, but her ladyship gave her one hell of a time and she stopped coming."

"And if something happened, there are fire alarms and . . . you know . . . ?"

Stan nods. "Goodness, yes, there are very strict rules on health and safety with buildings of this age. It's the same with most of the colleges." He coughs and shifts in his seat. "She has no idea I do it, but I always check on her on my rounds. Just a quick look in the window to make sure she hasn't fallen or anything like that. So you mustn't worry too much." She has the feeling he's going to reach out and pat her hand, but he ends up vigorously rubbing his hands together. "I tell you what though, she seems to have perked up a bit since you've started coming by. Maybe the old girl was lonely."

Janice wonders what Mrs. B has done to deserve such kindness from a man whose name she cannot be bothered to remember. As she gets up to leave, she comes to a decision. "Thanks for the coffee, Stan. You'll be seeing a bit more of me, I'm afraid. I've decided to split my hours so I come in two or three times a week, rather than once. It will suit me better."

Stan looks at her from under his brows but says nothing.

As Janice works her way around the upper gallery dusting the shelves, she replays the conversation she overheard between Tiberius and his wife in her head. Mrs. B is particularly grumpy today and is reading in her usual chair below. Janice wonders if she's had another bad night. Maybe this place is too much for her? Perhaps her son is right? But how could she ever talk about it to her when she's made it perfectly clear she wouldn't report back on anything she overheard at her son's? Mrs. B would be bound to know something has changed and might even think she had been talking to her son about her behind her back.

As she moves down to the ground floor and starts dusting

there, she can feel Mrs. B's eyes on her. After a while she proclaims, "You look different."

Janice keeps on dusting but doesn't say anything.

When she is closer to her chair, Mrs. B says slyly, "So, all dressed up to meet your husband later? I expect you'll be going to the bingo and then to the pub for 'Steak Night.'"

Janice knows she is trying to get a rise out of her. She will not give her the satisfaction.

"I believe it's two-for-one on a Thursday."

Janice just keeps on dusting. But something in her face, something in her demeanor, must have alerted Mrs. B—the predator.

"Ah, so not your husband. Like that, is it?"

All the joy is stripped from her day. She is left feeling sordid and cheap, a ridiculous woman in a red sweater and jeans, a feather duster in her hand.

"I'm going to clean the bathroom," is all she says.

When she returns to the main room to start organizing the piles of books, Mrs. B has made her a hot chocolate. She has spilled most of it getting it to the table. Janice cannot bring herself to touch it.

"So, Becky is about to become a mother," Mrs. B starts. Janice knows she is watching her, but she will not look at the old woman who has just stolen one of the few bits of happiness that belonged solely to her.

Mrs. B's voice is unusually quiet when she begins. "I cannot imagine the birth was a pleasant experience . . . if they ever are . . . Becky gave birth in one of the worst hospitals in Paris. I imagine if Charles Dickens had seen sixteen-year-old Becky struggling through the doors he might have rubbed his hands together and picked up his quill. But of course, this was 1907 and Charles had been dead for nearly forty years."

Janice can't help noticing that Mrs. B talks about Charles Dickens like he's a personal friend. She moves down the room to work; she does not want to get drawn in further.

Mrs. B's voice becomes louder, "I do wonder if her father drove her to the hospital in his Hackney cab. Who can guess what would have been going through his mind? However, the point is that Becky gave birth to a healthy baby girl. I wonder, if it had been a boy, would things have been different? Yes, a golden, curly-haired grandson might have found a place in that home. But Becky gave birth to a girl, and we can imagine what her parents thought of having another miniature Becky in the house. So it was not long before the baby and Becky's shame were hidden away, out of sight, on a farm in the country well away from Paris. Becky, they threw out onto the street."

Mrs. B leans down and turns on her electric fire. "I think at this point it would be hard not to feel sorry for Becky. But as they say, what doesn't kill you only makes you stronger. Becky took up the only profession open to her, the oldest one in the world: she started working the streets of Paris. To muscle her way in among the other whores, to arrange herself in that dark doorway, to take her first customer . . . and to do all this with a smile on her face—I think we can assume she would not have let the other whores see her cry—well, that must have taken great strength. Maybe the nuns had contributed something useful to her education after all—as I said, what doesn't kill you only makes you stronger.

"It wasn't long before Becky came to understand that there was a definite hierarchy within the world she had entered, and, being Becky, she was keen to climb the ladder. And as luck would have it, there were always women—Madams, shall we say—who trawled the underworld looking for enterprising girls like Becky. These were the girls who would move from being *la prostituée professionnelle*, to *la fille d'occasion*, until ultimately they became la crème de la crème; *la courtisane*."

Janice wants to ask the difference between the three but won't.

Mrs. B pauses expectantly, before continuing. "Once recruited by the Madam, Becky's education began in earnest. Within an elegant, discreet establishment in the Sixteenth Arrondissement, Becky began her lessons. And no, not the education in sexual practices that you are considering, Janice, although no doubt that was included too."

Janice slams a book down on top of the pile she has been sorting.

"Her main education involved elocution lessons, how to dress, dancing classes, and how to wear her hair so she appeared to her best advantage. She learned which heeled and jeweled shoes drew the eye to the ankle and which exotic fragrances best suited different occasions—and where on her body to wear them. Becky reveled in this new and unfamiliar role; for the first time in her life, she was the most gifted and valued student in the class. She quickly advanced in her studies, uncovering the mysteries of her new profession: the perfect timing of a slow lowering of the lashes, how to languidly extend a hand to show the flash of the underside of a snow-white wrist, when to tilt her chin in just such a way to give a laughing, sideways glance. Oh, Becky loved learning it all. The only thing her new Madam did not have to teach her was how to sing; the nuns *had* taken care of that, and Becky had a beautiful voice.

"Now, a girl like Becky working as a *fille d'occasion*, was expected to 'entertain' the clients of the house, but that was not the limit of her world. She might choose to grace Les Folies Bergère with her presence—the management always encouraged girls like Becky to mingle with their customers. And we need to remember that the Beckys of this Parisian world were not hidden away in some shameful corner; the men they associated with wanted to flaunt them in front of the world. And that suited Becky just fine. A typical day for her might start with riding in the Bois de Boulogne (Becky was extremely fond of horses), then lunch at the Café de Paris, before heading off to the races. Becky had never had so much fun in her entire life. By the late afternoon, Becky would be available for 'work' at the discreet house in the Sixteenth Arrondissement; after all, she was *une cinq à sept*."

Mrs. B stops talking. Janice stops dusting. Janice wants to know what this means. She knows Mrs. B wants to tell her. They are back playing chicken. But Janice's heart isn't in the game.

"Would you rather be a prostitute or a cleaner?" Mrs. B suddenly demands.

She wonders if sometimes there is much difference. No, she is being ludicrous and self-pitying—cleaning up after people is not the same as selling your body. She doesn't want the next thought, but it comes anyway. Is it worse to sell your body than to have it picked up and put down by a man reaching for something convenient to relieve himself into? She cannot bear to think of this anymore, to remember last night's quick grapple in the dark. She knows Mrs. B is watching her but, like Becky, she will not let anyone, especially this woman, see her cry. She looks away from her, still not answering her question.

"You do know, Janice, that you are an exceptional woman."

This does make her look back, this time in surprise.

"I do not know you, so to make cheap assumptions about your life was wrong of me and I apologize. However, what I can do is talk about facts. And the fact is that you are an exceptional cleaner. I believe you to be an exceptional woman too. But for now, let us deal with factually recorded evidence." She adds dryly, "I believe you underestimate yourself, but I'm not sure you will listen to my opinion. After all, I have proved myself to be a crass and thoughtless old woman, so, as I say, I shall just deal with recorded evidence rather than my opinion. These are the facts: you are an excellent cleaner who also bakes to a very high standard; you can and do use a soldering iron, a multi-purpose power tool, and, I believe, a chainsaw was even mentioned. You know the rudiments of upholstery and make your own cleaning equipment—although why you are cleaning a doll's house is beyond me. Even my daughter-in-law is impressed by your ability to dismantle and clean all the working parts of her outlandish coffee machine—something that is well beyond herself and Tiberius. One of your employers mentioned your ability to put all sorts of people at their ease and made specific references to your ability to break up fights. I will not embarrass you by repeating the many things that were also recorded about your extraordinary sensitivity and kindness."

"But where's this all coming from?" Janice exclaims.

"My husband was head of MI6. I myself for a time worked in covert operations. You did not think I would take up references and investigate a relative stranger who I was going to let into my home?"

Janice cannot help it—she doesn't want to, but she smiles at Mrs. B.

"Really, Janice, I may rate you as a cleaner, but sometimes I do wonder about your intelligence." But Mrs. B's tell-tale muscle is twitching on the side of her face as she says this.

"Would you like a hot chocolate?" It is all Janice can think of to say; she certainly doesn't feel able to digest all the things her employers have said about her.

"Yes, I would, and please make yourself one. I did try to fix you one earlier but I seem to have thrown most of it on the floor."

Once Janice is sitting at the table sipping her hot chocolate she asks, "So, come on, what is *une cinq à sept*?"

"This was one of the ways Becky would have been described. This is because it was between these hours, five to seven, that men would call at the discreet house in the Sixteenth Arrondissement and consider which girl they would like to spend the early evening with. I believe there were photographic albums depicting the various girls, and by their stance in the photograph a client could appreciate, shall we say, their preferences. Then a message would be sent to the girl of their choice, and they would arrive to entertain their guest."

"A bit like ordering from Argos," Janice can't help interrupting.

"Argos? Oh, is that the store that sells things from a catalog? Yes, just like Argos. I believe Becky's images within this particular catalog suggested a fondness for lesbianism and bondage—although who was being bound, her or her client, I cannot say."

Mrs. B stops suddenly and looks thoughtful. "Or maybe I can," she says slowly. "I believe she liked to dominate other people." She looks at Janice and says enigmatically, "Remember that, Janice. It will come into our story later."

Mrs. B sips her hot chocolate. "Now we come on to Becky's transition from *la fille d'occasion* to *la courtisane*. As *la fille d'occasion*, she was linked to a house, but the aim was to become an independent—*la courtisane*. However, there was rarely a clean switching of roles; it was a gradual process. A man might take more than a passing interest in a girl like Becky. He would want to be seen with her—often after the *cinq à sept* hours; he would take her to dinner, to the opera perhaps. It might be that he would see her more often, take her to lunch, to the races, even set her up in her own apartment. He would become a 'significant man' for her. However, these relationships were rarely exclusive, and even when a woman was a fully independent courtesan—not linked to any one man or Madam—she might pop back to her old 'house' now and then and do a bit of, what we could call 'overtime.'"

"So, did Becky meet a 'significant man'?"

"Oh, many such men. She was rarely exclusive, but at times some were more prominent than others. I can give you an example of one such man who she met early on in her transition to *la courtisane*. He was forty years old, a married man, obviously very wealthy. His family had made their money as wine merchants, and I understand provided the wine for the Vatican. I am sure that made Becky smile, and, oh how those nuns would have choked on the blessed sacrament had they but known. This man set her up in one of his sumptuous villas where he had a fine stable of horses—I remember telling you that Becky had a great fondness for riding. He took her with him on trips to Morocco and Venice. I believe I also said earlier that men derived considerable prestige from being seen with a magnificent courtesan. Becky had lustrous auburn hair, a sensuous mouth and figure that would make young men openly blush and their mothers cross themselves. She was not a beauty as such, but . . ."

"She had great presence," Janice cannot resist contributing.

Mrs. B gives her a double look. "As I was saying, she was an extraordinarily attractive woman. But before we paint a portrait of a paragon that any man would desire, we must remind ourselves that this is Becky. She had a filthy temper and was ruled by one single obsession: herself."

"What happened to the wine man?"

"Theirs was a very tempestuous relationship. They were known to strike each other in public and on one occasion he was so angry with her he locked her in the villa. Becky got the last laugh though; she let all his horses out of the stables and let them run through the house. I can picture her in a beautiful silk gown, laughing as she chased them through the rooms. I wonder if she rode one through the villa? I rather like the idea of her clearing a Louis XV chiffonier as if it were a fence. In the end, her temper was too much for him and they parted company. I believe he paid her a handsome pension."

"Even though he'd had enough of her?"

"Yes, and this, like the bondage, will come into our story later. It is important to note that there were strict rules around these types of relationships."

A bit like cleaning, Janice can't help thinking.

"A gentleman, if he had formed a significant connection with one such as Becky, was expected to behave generously toward her when they parted."

So, not like cleaning.

"Now, for the time being, we must leave Becky as the talk of Paris. Best to leave her there in blissful ignorance because, unbeknownst to Becky, storm clouds are gathering. A war is coming. It is also well past the time you should be leaving. You must go or you might miss your bus."

Janice glances at her watch; she can't believe what time it is.

"I hope you don't expect me to pay you for that last hour?" Mrs. B is back to barking.

"Oh no, I would never expect that, Mrs. B."

She can see the tell-tale muscle start to twitch. "Are you quite sure I can't call you Mrs. P? It has such a ring to it. I believe it suits you."

Janice doesn't grace this with an answer.

As she goes to collect her coat, Mrs. B announces, "I did manage to telephone Mycroft and he's coming to see me the week after next. I think you will enjoy meeting him."

Oh, so she is meant to be there. War is coming here too and Mrs. B wants her as part of her war committee.

Janice puts on her coat and collects her money. As she closes the door behind her, she thinks of Tiberius and of his, probably valid, concerns about his mother alone in this house, and of the woman who, today, had humiliated her and also touched her to the core. She wonders, if it comes to war, whose side will she be on?

SIXTEEN

There May Be Trouble Ahead

The post has arrived early and there are a number of letters on the doormat: the usual array of bills, which leaves Janice with a sinking feeling somewhere below her ribs; a catalog depicting an old lady on a stair lift, which makes her smile as she can't help thinking of Becky; and a postcard from her sister. She puts the other mail aside and sits down on the bottom stair holding the postcard. It's from Antigua, and her sister and husband appear to be having a wonderful time. Her eyes follow the familiar loops and sweeps of her sister's handwriting and, rather than the lines that tell of a diving trip and rum punches, all she can picture are the words, *I remember what you did.*

She is still sitting there, frowning, when Mike comes down the stairs. "Shall we have a coffee together before we both head off?"

She translates this as, "I'll have mine white with two sugars, and whilst you're at it pop a couple of biscuits on the side." What she can't interpret is what is behind him suggesting they have a coffee together. She can't remember the last time they had a chat over a coffee or a drink. A new job maybe? She looks at the bills still sitting on the small table by the front door and fervently hopes so. And also that his new employers don't take the Mrs. B approach when it comes to interrogating references.

What follows is one of the most bizarre conversations she has ever had with her husband. Although, as she finds very little to contribute, she thinks it might be more correct to call it a monologue.

Mike: "You know I've always admired how you've tackled your cleaning career."

Career? Since when has it been a career? And admired me? Most of the time you're embarrassed I'm a cleaner and I rarely go to the pub with you because after a few pints you make that quite obvious by making not-very-funny jokes at my expense.

Mike: "You're very professional and I think that's important when it comes to the domestic arena."

What are you on about? The "domestic arena"?

Mike: "In some ways, you're like the perfect brand: always reliable, always the same."

Have you been drinking?

At this point she manages to say, "Mike, what are you on about?"

Mike: "It will become clear."

Janice: "When?"

Mike: "You may have wondered about the meetings I've been going to."

Janice: "Well, I was hoping they were about a job." (*But I'm now thinking AA*)

Mike (grabbing his coffee and two biscuits and heading for the kitchen door): "Just be patient, I've got a few more meetings to go to yet. I may be late a couple of nights this week."

She wants to ask if he's having an affair but doesn't know how to say it without sounding hopeful.

Mike (now in the hallway but peering back around the kitchen door): "I'm glad we've had this chat. You've always been very supportive, I know that, and I like to think we make a good team."

She doesn't even know where to begin with this one. It sounds like something from a bad motivational speaker. Perhaps that's what the meetings are about? Oh, please God, don't let it be that, Mike is going to set himself up as a motivational speaker. It's one of the few avenues he hasn't tried yet. The man of a thousand jobs? It doesn't bear thinking about. She imagines seeing his face on posters stuck to lampposts and empty shop-fronts inviting people to hear him speak in community halls and libraries. Then she imagines herself following the same route with Decius, trying to take them all down.

She walks to the bus stop wondering if she could talk some sense into him if this is really what he's got in mind. Would he even listen to her? He certainly hasn't in the past.

"Oh, it's you."

She's been so lost in thought she doesn't realize it's the geography teacher driving until he's talking to her. He repeats, "Oh, it's you," whilst smiling at her in a way that makes her stomach drop through the floor of the bus.

"Yes, about that . . ." she starts to say.

And then from behind her comes the inevitable, "Come on!"

"Right-o!" is all she manages, before moving into the body of the bus and sitting down. What was she thinking of? Right-o? No one says "Right-o!" unless it's Captain Hastings in some made-for-TV Agatha Christie. She wishes she had Decius by her side so he could look up at her with that "*What the fuck were you thinking of, woman?*" look in his eyes.

And what's she going to do now? Should she try and say something as she gets off? But that would mean going to the front door of the bus rather than the side door where people normally disembark. Should she just wave from the side door and hope he turns around and sees her? But will he know what stop she's getting off at? She tries to think what Decius would advise, and even though he is miles away, she finds she can imagine the expression on his face. And it is very clearly saying, "*Carpe Diem,*" which is quite profound for him—but then, he is named after a Roman emperor.

She gets up at the last minute, just before her stop; she's going to do this quickly and has decided on a pleasant, "Have a good day." When she gets to the front door of the bus he looks up and smiles. Before she can get the words out, she realizes she's staring in horror at a bank of CCTV images that show the driver the inside of the bus. She points at them, and all she can say is, "But you can see."

"Yep." He nods.

"You saw me last time."

"Yep."

"Moving up the bus and watching you."

"Yep."

She turns to leave, all shreds of dignity gone.

"It made my week," he says quietly.

She glances back at him, not sure she's heard right.

"Actually, it made my year," he says, more firmly. She notices he has a slight accent—Scottish?—and his eyes, which seem to be sharing some joke with her, are greeny-gray. She wonders if as well as being a man that likes walking up Snowdon, whether he might like dancing. Then he steals her line, which makes her wonder if he's been thinking about what to say too.

"Have a good day."

She can't remember the walk to collect Decius and has no recollection of her conversation with Mrs. YeahYeahYeah. She knows she wouldn't actually have said *whatever* to her face, but she's pretty certain she was thinking it. By the time she gets to Fiona and Adam's house, she has herself more in hand. Decius, she notices, is particularly bouncy today, and while they wait for Adam to appear he is like a dog on a spring. Each time he hits the ground he looks up at her and his face seems to be smiling. If a fox terrier can laugh she thinks maybe this is it. She knows how he feels; she wants to laugh too.

Fiona and Adam both come to the door, and as Adam and Decius chase around each other, Fiona taps Janice on the arm. "Would you mind if Adam took Decius around the block on his own? He won't go far. I thought it would be nice to have a coffee."

Janice wonders what Fiona wants to say to her. She knows there is something, but she also knows it can't be as weird as Mike's conversation this morning.

"That's fine," she says, adding, "but I think he needs to be kept on the lead." She doesn't want to be explaining to Tiberius that his pedigree dog has gone missing. She knows she can trust him but says to Adam, "It's not that I don't trust you, Adam, it's just he's not my dog and I can't let anything happen to him." To try and lighten this, she adds, with a laugh, "I just couldn't bear it."

He looks at her, and she suspects it is the same look that he gave his "twat" counselor. "And you think I could?" He walks away, Decius's lead firmly wrapped around his hand.

Fiona has the coffee already made in a cafetière and biscuits laid out on a plate. She's been planning this, Janice thinks and wonders what's coming next.

Fiona fiddles with her glasses in her lap for a while. "I was going to build up to this gradually . . ." She looks up and smiles crookedly. "You know, chat about the weather. But what I want to know is . . ." She looks out of the window, in the direction that Adam and Decius have gone. ". . . Do you think he's doing okay?" She rushes on, oblivious to the fact she hasn't poured either of them a coffee. "It's just that he seems so happy when Decius is coming over and for a while after he gets back, he's like the old Adam. And I wondered if he ever says anything? And I know I shouldn't ask. He would hate me for it. But I'm so worried about him. I mean, he's doing okay at school, and they've been really good. He has a couple of friends from football, but I don't think they're that close. I've said he should ask them over and all he said was, 'What, on a playdate?' and stomped off to his room." Fiona is crying by now. Not with big noisy sobs but with tears that run in a stream down her face like they already know the way. "And the one person I could talk to, the one who loved him like I do, fucking left him. And I don't know what to do."

Janice is on her knees in front of the chair with both of Fiona's hands in hers. "He has you," is all she can think of to say. "He has a mother who loves him and is always there for him." She sits back slightly but still holds on to Fiona's hands. "I don't know what you should do either." She instinctively adds, "I'm just the cleaner," and she sees her instinct is right. Fiona gives a half-laugh. "Thanks for the reference by the way."

"You're welcome. She was a bit of a battle-axe on the phone. Are you sure you want to work for her?"

Janice is not, but says by way of explanation, "She was a spy."

"Oh." Fiona nods as if this makes perfect sense, which Janice knows it doesn't. She sits back in her chair and pours them both a coffee. Fiona reaches for one of the tissues she keeps ready in a box for the recently bereaved. "Convenient," she says, pulling one out.

Janice has literally no idea what to say, so rather than think about it she just talks. "When we go walking, I think Adam has moments when he is just a twelve-year-old boy playing with a dog. You said you didn't want him to be defined by John's death. I don't know the answer to that one, whether we can choose our own story or not. But I can tell you that in the fields playing with Decius—"

"Bloody stupid name for a dog," Fiona interrupts.

"His owner is called Tiberius."

"Blimey! I don't know who I feel more sorry for."

Janice does but does not offer this up. "What I was going to say is that there are times when Adam is playing, I can see he isn't defined by his dad killing himself." She says this bluntly because she knows this is not the time for "passed on" or "no longer with us." "He hasn't forgotten it of course; it's probably part of him like the blood running through his veins, but he finds some peace whilst living with it—if that makes any sense."

Fiona nods.

"I don't have any answers. I wonder who does. But when I see that boy, I really do think he will be okay. There will be more and more times like that in his life." She adds, "You should come out with us sometimes."

Fiona sighs like she is suddenly very tired. "I'd like that."

Janice wants to say one more thing.

"When I was Adam's age, my mum wasn't really around, and I would have done anything to have had a mum like you."

"Ah, thanks," Fiona says. But Janice understands that she has no idea what she's talking about, in the same way as Janice can never really know what it's like to have been married to a man who killed himself.

When she returns Decius back to his home, Mrs. YeahYeahYeah is waiting for her just inside the back door. Janice is absolutely exhausted but is immediately wary. She tries to look like a "quiet nothing." She senses it is better to be underestimated in whatever is to follow.

For once she wishes Decius wouldn't sit so close to her. He has his bottom parked on her left boot.

"He's very fond of you," Mrs. YeahYeahYeah says in a puzzled voice.

"Oh, I think that's because I feed him," Janice says, then immediately regrets it.

"But he has a special vegan diet. I hope you're not giving him treats?" Mrs. YeahYeahYeah is suspicious.

"No, I just meant on the days when you've been out." Janice tries to look as slow and nothingy as possible. She also lifts her foot so Decius will get the idea and trot off to his bed in the kitchen.

He settles his bottom a bit higher up her boot.

"It's very good of you to take on my mother-in-law like this. I know she's not an easy woman . . ." Mrs. YeahYeahYeah leaves an encouraging pause.

For some reason, a loud announcement of, "Mind the Gap," sounds in Janice's head. "That's okay. I'd really better get going," she says as brightly as she can.

Mrs. YeahYeahYeah stalls her, stepping closer to the back door. "There's a lot going on at the moment with my mother-in-law and the college; it's complicated. We don't want her to be worried about it, so if you should ever hear anything that seems to upset her—I mean, you know what old people are like; they can get the wrong end of the stick—you would be doing the right thing in telling my husband about it. He really is the one dealing with it all, you know, power of attorney, her legal affairs, organizing everything for her as she's not really keeping up with it all . . ."

Janice tries hard not to stare at her in disbelief and focuses her gaze as blankly as she can on her left ear.

Mrs. YeahYeahYeah fiddles with one of the many urine-colored zips on her dress coat (emerald-green today and inserts printed with dead pheasants) "Yes, Mrs. P, he is absolutely the one to talk to." She adds with slow significance, "I know you'd find him *very* grateful."

Janice doesn't know where to look; she just knows she can't keep looking at this appalling woman. She glances down at Decius and what he thinks of Mrs. YeahYeahYeah is clearly written all over his face, "*You cu—*"

"No!" Janice roars before she can stop herself. She cannot bear that word.

Mrs. YeahYeahYeah steps back as if she's been slapped.

In the stunned silence that follows, the two women stare at each other. Belatedly, Janice drops to her knees and starts fishing about in Decius's mouth. *Just go with it*, she silently begs him. With her other hand she surreptitiously pulls a tissue from her coat pocket and then stands up with a flourish like a very bad conjurer. "So sorry about that, I thought I saw he had something in his mouth."

Decius sneezes in apparent disgust and trots away. She doesn't blame him. "I didn't want him to choke," Janice says lamely.

Later, standing outside in the road, Janice calls for a taxi. She doesn't care what it costs, she just knows she needs to get home quickly. She prays Mike is out at one of his "motivational meetings" and that she will have the house to herself. Whilst standing there waiting for the car to arrive, it starts to snow. She looks up and lets her vision blur as she watches the sleety flakes in the glow of the streetlamp. She wishes she could do the same with her emotions. Today she seems to have covered all the extremes, and it has left her totally spent. As she tries to empty her mind, one thought keeps intruding. She is pretty certain Mrs. YeahYeahYeah will be telling "Tibs" tonight that maybe Mrs. P is not such a "*quiet* nothing" after all. She wishes this thought didn't make her quite so uneasy.

SEVENTEEN

Stories Have to Be Told or They Die

"Don't you have another jumper?"

Even her husband has noticed she's been wearing her favorite red jumper every day for over a week. She washes it every other night and hangs it on the hot towel rail in the bathroom to get it dry for the morning. When it is still damp, she puts it on anyway (their towel rail has never really worked, despite her replacing the bleed valve). There has been no sign of the geography teacher, but this morning the Hells Angel said cryptically, "Brecon Beacons, love."

She had taken a seat at the back of the bus, her face burning. Did everyone know what she's been thinking—that maybe the geography teacher is on holiday? Was she making, as Sister Bernadette would say, "a complete show of herself?" Or, was the Hells Angel the geography teacher's friend and he had asked him to say something to her?

She's still wondering about this as she brings another pile of books to the table. She is at Mrs. B's and is halfway through organizing her library. Over the past few visits, they seem to have established a companionable co-existence that she would not have thought possible when the door had first been opened by the woman in purple. Mrs. B has asked her to create a catalog of her and her husband's books. Mrs. B does not own a computer and has no intention of learning how to use one, so instead, Janice is working on an old-fashioned card index. This involves sitting at the large oak table on an original (as it turns out) Chippendale chair, examining each book in turn. Mrs. B encourages her to be thorough. "How can you possibly catalog them correctly if you have no idea of their contents?"

So, after the small bit of cleaning that is needed to keep on top of things, Janice makes them both a coffee or hot chocolate, as the mood takes them, and she starts to read. Mrs. B in turn sits in her favorite armchair reading *The Times*, occasionally letting out a loud snort or expletive if the article she is reading demands it. Janice loves not only examining the words and illustrations within the library but the feel of each book in her hands. Every one is different: the book's DNA told through the weight, feel, and smell of the paper; the color and texture of the endpapers; the way the spine is flat to the touch or rounded like a razor shell; how each bit of embossing and printing feels different under her fingertips; and how every book falls open in a different way, revealing the secret of a favorite story, artist, or recipe. From her seat she can see out to the grass quadrangle beyond and watch the students come and go. Stan waves as he goes past on his rounds and as she waves back, she realizes these hours are without doubt the happiest of her week. She quickly amends this as she pictures Decius's face ("*Charming!*")—her joint happiest hours.

Today, the light is streaming through the latticed glass, the sun creating patterns on her jumper as it dries and warms the wool next to her skin. She has just found a story that she wants to share with Mrs. B. This has become part of the routine too—she reads particular pieces aloud; they have to be stories and they have to be based on truth. (In keeping with what Janice believes is expected of a story collector.)

"I think you'll like this one, Mrs. B. The main character reminds me of you."

"What are you on about?" Mrs. B barks and Janice thinks, some things will never change.

"It's here in a history of Perthshire. Was your husband Scottish? There seem to be a lot of books about Scotland . . ."

"He was no more Scottish than you are. He came from the home counties." She adds grudgingly, "But his family did have a shooting lodge in the Highlands."

"Ah, I see."

"Go on, get on with it. I don't have time to waste. It may have escaped your notice, but I'm not getting any younger."

Janice smiles and begins. "The story is of an earl who married a showgirl. She was what would have been called, at the time, 'a flashy piece.' She was well past her prime, but he loved her. And she loved him."

Janice has discovered a new story-collector guideline for best practice (now that she is prepared to share some of her stories). They have to be retold in a certain way. Almost as if she were reading it aloud from an enormous storybook.

"And tell me, am I the earl or the strumpet in this delightful tale?"

"Oh, definitely the strumpet. She was not a beauty, but I believe she had great presence."

Janice thinks for a moment that Mrs. B is going to choke on her hot chocolate.

"The local people didn't take to their new countess, and I am sad to say they didn't make her very welcome. They found the sight of her frankly embarrassing. She made no attempt to dress like the dowager countess or like the earl's sisters, but instead chose theatrical-style costumes which, now she had more pin money, could be that much brighter and jollier than ever before. Her husband's family and the local gentry turned their noses up at her and the villagers laughed at her behind her back and quite often in front of her face too. The more they laughed, the more she delighted in shocking them. She had her coach painted bright pink and, instead of harnessing to it the chestnut bays, which her husband had bought her as a wedding gift, she persuaded a friend who ran a traveling circus to lend her his zebras. And this is what she rode to church in, with the earl happily sitting alongside her. When the vicar delivered a moralizing sermon on the dangers of vulgar ostentation, she went back to her friend at the circus and borrowed a tiger, which late one night she tied to the church doors so the poor man could not get into his church."

"I don't know why you call him 'poor man.' Sounds like he deserved it to me."

"I thought you'd like her." Janice grins at Mrs. B. "Her finest hour came when the vicar and the parish realized that the main church window needed some very expensive renovation work. One of the stained-glass windows depicting the Virgin Mary needed replacing. As this was beyond the means of the local diocese, they naturally turned to the earl, who had always had a great sense of civic duty. He said that he would fund the window on the proviso that his wife was on the committee. The vicar could hardly refuse and accepted the offer of funds. Further, the earl mentioned in closing, his wife's role on the committee was to be that of overseeing the creative design. Which is why, three months later, when the residents of the county turned out for the unveiling of the window, they found themselves gazing at a stained-glass image of the voluptuous and colorful countess, not the Virgin Mary."

Mrs. B gives a crow of laughter. "Now, that *is* a good one for your collection."

Janice can't recall ever telling Mrs. B that she is a story collector—but it seems there is no need to.

Later, as Janice is making some soup, Mrs. B hobbles over and positions herself on a stool at her elbow.

"Are we ready for Becky's war years?"

"Oh, I think so," Janice says, reaching for the onions and chopping board.

"I think for today we will concentrate on the early war years, as it is in the latter part of the war that the foreign prince enters, stage left."

"I'd forgotten about him." Janice then adds, "And are we talking about the real prince? I think you said there were two of them?"

"Yes, a real prince who was to become a king."

It strikes Janice as she starts to chop the onions that this is beginning to sound more and more like a fairy tale. "This is a true story?" she asks uncertainly.

"Indeed."

"So, the war? We're talking about the First World War?"

"The nuns should be so proud to know that their education wasn't wasted," Mrs. B says with heavy irony.

"I never said I was educated by nuns."

"Didn't you?" Mrs. B says vaguely. And Janice is reminded once more that she is tricky—one to be watched.

"So where was Becky when the war broke out?" Janice asks.

"Still having a marvelous time in Paris. For those with money and influence, life in war times could be surprisingly enjoyable. Although, I do believe at one time during the war the tango was banned."

"How wretched for them," Janice says, aping Mrs. B's irony.

"Pretty soon Becky decided to join in the war effort, helping a baroness who was organizing transport for doctors to and from hospitals. I think Becky must have liked working with a woman who, in normal circumstances, would have looked straight through her. By now our Becky owned a smart new Renault—I wonder if she bought it from the garage that was on the site of the convent? I do hope so. Whatever the case, she offered her services and off she went gallantly chauffeuring the doctors."

"Was she anywhere near the fighting?"

"I very much doubt it. Remember the first rule for Becky: look after number one. I know she took her personal chef and Vietnamese maid with her. So we can presume she did not face too much hardship."

Mrs. B breaks off in the middle of her recital, looking thoughtful. "I wonder if that is one way our Becky was different from Becky Sharp? I cannot recall Becky Sharp ever taking an interest in her servants, can you?"

Janice shakes her head and starts chopping carrots.

"It is strange, but Becky's servants rarely had a bad word to say about her, and often quite the opposite. To them, at least, she seems to have behaved well. I find that interesting."

"What, that anyone could behave well to their staff?" Janice cannot resist asking.

"You know, you are getting more like Becky Sharp and less like Amelia every day."

Janice is silenced and they both know that Mrs. B has won that round.

Mrs. B sounds perkier as she continues. "I'm afraid to say the ministering-angel persona soon wore thin, and when the weather turned colder Becky looked for an excuse to leave the baroness and her good works behind. I strongly suspect she invented an illness as an excuse because suddenly we find a young doctor telling her that for the sake of her health, she must leave the cold and move to the fashionable city of Cairo—which just so happened to be exactly where she wanted to go."

"I wonder how she persuaded him?"

"One can only imagine. Once in Cairo, Becky took up with another 'significant man.' Married, of course, this time to one of the Egyptian royal family. I am not sure if he had a stable of horses, but her Egyptian friend did have a stable of Rolls Royces—which, in some way, will have made up for Becky's disappointment at not being able to continue with her war work." Mrs. B's words drip with sarcasm. She continues. "And here we come to another event which sheds an interesting light on Becky and on things yet to come."

Mrs. B stops, suddenly changing the subject. "Are you really going to make that soup without stock?"

"Yes, trust me. I'm a cleaner." Janice grins. "So, what was the event?"

"The event took place in a souk in Cairo. She was out with her Egyptian friend and there was an assassination attempt made on his life—one of many such attempts, I believe. As the would-be assassin rushed toward her friend, Becky threw herself bodily in the way and saved him."

"She must have loved him," Janice suggests.

"Well, that's just it. I believe that Becky—and this is just my opinion—formed better relationships with some men as friends than she ever did with them as lovers. I think this was an act of friendship rather than love. She did have men in her life of whom that could be said."

"What, friends rather than lovers?"

"Yes. But I think the event is significant because it is clear she held her Egyptian friend in high regard—and again, I would suggest you remember that as our tale unfolds."

"Mrs. B, you sound like something out of *Arabian Nights*." Janice laughs.

It is a throwaway comment but Mrs. B's reaction is extraordinary. She spins around on her stool and fixes Janice with a penetrating look. "How do you mean?"

Mrs. B sounds so suspicious and for the life of her Janice cannot work out why. She lets it go, as another thought strikes her. "Of course, Becky could have been gay, and sex with men was just her professional choice rather than her personal preference?"

Mrs. B appears to relax. "This is true; we mustn't forget the catalog. And there were more albums or catalogs to follow—in which I believe sodomy was added to her portfolio along with lesbianism and performing as a dominatrix."

"Was this in Cairo?"

"No, come the unbearably hot Egyptian summer, Becky returned to Paris."

"Her health, I expect," Janice says, grinning.

"Indeed. Once back in Paris, Becky broke with her original Madam and formed a relationship with another—one who ran a very high-class establishment, perhaps the finest in Paris. Becky also set up her own apartment and salon. As I said earlier, the move from employee to entrepreneur was often a complicated journey. It was in this arena that Becky was able to start consorting with titled men as well as those with great wealth. And sometimes she was lucky enough to find men who had both." Mrs. B looked at her watch. "And that, as time is getting on, is where we will leave her."

"Mrs. B, I keep meaning to ask about Becky's daughter. What happened to her?"

"Still living on the farm."

"Did Becky go and visit her often?"

"Never."

Janice slowly stirs the soup.

"What are you thinking?" Mrs. B demands.

"So, in all this time she didn't see her? And she was wealthy, wasn't she?"

"She was certainly amassing a considerable amount of money and possessions." Mrs. B nods, not taking her eyes off Janice. "Why does this bother you so much?"

What can she say? It changes everything? She feels like she has been watching a film, seeing Becky's life as pure entertainment and now she is brought up short. She had even laughed at the tango being banned, when mere miles away men were being slaughtered in their thousands.

And all the time that Becky is off being Becky, there is a daughter there, a living, breathing child, who wants her mother. How could someone ignore a child? It is a question she has asked herself many times before. She can feel Mrs. B's eyes on her. All she can manage to say is, "I think I was forgetting this was real and that there was a darker side to Becky."

"What were you expecting? You wanted a true story. People are complicated. It is never as simple as black and white. What is it you want?" Mrs. B sounds impatient.

Janice feels like there is something she wants to say, but that it is just out of her reach. It's not about her own mother; she knows she needs to keep that buried where it is. But there is something else much closer to the here and now that's eating away at her. She tries again. "In my stories, and I do collect stories . . ." She feels a sense of relief at saying this out loud.

"I love that normal people do the unexpected, that they are courageous, funny, kind . . . selfless. I know these people have faults—of course, that's life." She starts to pace around the kitchen, trying to articulate, to catch at the thing she is trying to say. "But there is comfort in finding goodness and joy in their stories. People who are run-of-the-mill, people just trying to get on and do their best. What you're talking about is taking someone who is completely selfish, who should be the villain and you're saying, 'But hey, they can be all these good things too.'" Janice clenches her fists as she paces.

"It works both ways, Janice, don't be naive. Bad people, or whatever you want to call them, are never all bad." Mrs. B is now sounding angry. "Tell me what it is *you* want to say," she then repeats, more earnestly.

Janice looks at her with something like horror. She feels agitated and unsettled, like something is crawling under her skin. Then the words are suddenly spilling out of her. "I know what you say should make me feel doubly happy—'oh look, bad people can be good too.' But somehow, I don't want to hear it. When it's in a book I can go with it—enjoy Becky Sharp being feisty and awful, with a few redeeming features." Once she's started, Janice finds she cannot stop. "But when it's a true story, I feel like I just can't bear to listen to someone saying, 'But they're not all bad.' Because in real life, yes, that's it, in *my* life, I have to live with what is bad, day in, day out."

Her heart is racing, and she can hear a pounding in her ears, urging her on, "And I have spent years and years saying to myself, 'Oh, look, it's not black and white. So, he's deluded, he hurts people, he's selfish, he lets people down, he's a bad father, he lies, he exaggerates, he wastes the money that I go out scrubbing floors to earn and then he looks down on me for what I do.' And I have spent all this time saying to myself, 'Ah, but it's not all bad,' looking for the good in him. 'He keeps getting new jobs, he is not out of work for long, he doesn't beat me, he doesn't chase other women, we've had some family days out, he's quite cheerful, his friends seem to like him in the pub, and he puts the bins out if I ask him.' And do you know what?"

Janice knows she is now shouting this. "It is not enough. It's not fucking enough. So when you say, 'It's about balance' and 'Hey, look, this person you thought was crap actually has some good points,' I can't bear it because I have spent *years* trying to be reasonable, doing what you're asking me to do now. 'Oh, it's not black and white, Janice.' But sometimes when you've spent all your energy trying to see both sodding sides of it, trying to find the good in your shit situation, you don't want some old woman who doesn't know you telling you to get it in proportion. Sometimes you want to stand on the roof and scream that it is completely fucking awful, and you can't do it anymore."

She is shaking uncontrollably and for a second thinks she's going to be sick in the sink. Then she turns in a circle like a trapped animal and crouches onto her haunches. She doesn't think she is crying but she can feel her face is wet and there is snot above her upper lip. She dashes a hand across her face and thinks of Fiona, but won't let her in. If she does, she knows she will be filled with guilt, as things are so much worse for her; compared to that, why should she be crying? And she can't do that either, can't just keep on telling herself, "Well, other people have it worse."

She finds she would like to curl up in a ball by the sink and put her head on the cold floor, so she does just that.

She feels a bony hand on her shoulder and hears a voice that is so unlike Mrs. B's that she thinks it is someone else. It's saying, "Come and sit in the chair by the fire and I am getting you a brandy." She wonders briefly where this person got the big blue blanket from and realizes that it *is* Mrs. B and she must have made it up the spiral stairs and back. When she looks at Mrs. B, her face is white with pain. "We will make it several doubles and we will both have them," Mrs. B declares.

Janice is not sure who helps who, but they get themselves to the fire and Mrs. B pushes her into her husband's old chair and wraps the blanket around her. She then sinks into her own chair and pulls a Sainsbury's bag toward her, from which she produces two mugs and a bottle of brandy. "I hope you don't mind it from a mug. I thought I might break the glasses if I tried to carry them in there with the bottle."

"I'd drink it from the bottle," Janice says, with perfect truth. She has stopped shaking but she feels like she has been dragged from a car wreck.

Mrs. B hands her a mug full of brandy. "Well, that was something different," she says.

And Janice starts to laugh and Mrs. B does too, but she cannot really work out if they are laughing or crying.

EIGHTEEN

Home Is Where the Heart Is

She wakes up staring at an unfamiliar cream ceiling. There is a strange gurgling from the hot-water pipes, and she turns her head toward the sound. Glancing at her phone, she sees it is 7:14 a.m. She is in one of the college's guest rooms, a twin room with furniture reminiscent of a British Heart Foundation charity shop. Dated, but still with some life left in it. The bed she is lying in is hard and narrow, but there is nowhere she would rather be.

Mrs. B had organized the accommodation for her last night, summoning Stan (and remembering his name) and commandeering the use of one of the guest rooms—for which she said she would pay. Janice had seen Stan give her a worried look, as she huddled in Mr. B's chair wrapped in a blue blanket.

"Janice has had a bit of a turn," Mrs. B had offered.

Janice had tried not to giggle at this; it sounded so bizarre, and the brandy was having its inevitable effect.

Stan had wanted to call an ambulance or a doctor, but Mrs. B had mouthed at him—well within Janice's hearing—"Time of the month."

His reaction had made her want to laugh too. He couldn't get out of the room fast enough. After Stan had fled, Mrs. B told Janice that this had been a fail-safe ploy during her short career as a spy. "And it's amazing what you can hide in a sanitary towel. Of course, they used to be so much bigger back then," she added, with obvious regret.

This had made them both laugh, and Mrs. B had poured them another couple of brandies.

Mrs. B had not asked Janice about her husband or her outburst, but she had insisted that it was she who called Mike to let him know of his wife's whereabouts. Janice had pulled the blanket around her more securely as Mrs. B took her phone. If she could have put her fingers in her ears without feeling even more foolish than she already did, she would have done so.

She'd watched as the frail woman with rolled-up trousers delivered her instructions. She swung her tiny feet back and forth as she spoke, and Janice knew she was enjoying herself. Mrs. B's performance would have been worthy of a grand duchess, and every word she uttered could have cut glass. She'd brooked no argument and barely allowed Mike to open his mouth.

His wife had felt a little faint, nothing to worry about, maybe she had been overdoing it. She would be staying in the college as her guest to save Janice traveling home by bus. No, there would be no need for him to come over by car to collect her; she would not put him to the trouble.

Janice had known her husband would be impressed by his conversation with Mrs. B, and by the time Mike was down the pub that evening it would have evolved into being, "a lengthy chat with her ladyship." She wouldn't be surprised to hear that they were spending Christmas with her this year.

Only as Janice had got up to go to bed did Mrs. B ask her a question.

"Do you mind me inquiring, Janice, why you do not leave your husband? If you view this as an impertinence, please tell me so."

What could she say? Pity? Atonement for colluding in sending Simon away to school? She was not sure either of those held much water. So she had just said, "I don't mind you asking, and if I knew I might even tell you." At the door she had turned and said, "Thank you, Lady B."

Mrs. B had barked back at her. "Call me that again and I *shall* call you Mrs. P."

Lying in her college bed, staring at the ceiling, Janice cannot pin down why it is she doesn't leave Mike. Because if there is one thing that came out of last night's outburst, it is her clear conviction that this is what she wants to do. Instead of standing astride a massive seesaw trying to keep her life in balance, she has jumped off and let one side bang, with an ear-shattering clang, onto the ground. There is some relief in that.

She doesn't think she is staying out of pity. That well has run dry. Simon is a grown man, not a young boy. If she's going to do anything in atonement, she should reach out to him, not stay where she is, staring at Mike. There are the finances, of course. Mike had once remortgaged their house without telling her, so there are still quite a few years to go on that, but they have some savings. Not a lot, because, once again, Mike has a way of dipping into them, but she has steadily built up a few thousand pounds. But where would she go? There isn't enough money for mortgage *and* rent. The few friends she has can't afford to help her—and she wouldn't ask it of them. She could get a live-in job as a housekeeper but is that really what she wants? To be at the beck and call of someone like Mrs. YeahYeahYeah, twenty-four hours a day? And how could she leave Decius? Even the thought of it makes her feel panicky. Then there's Fiona and Adam. Doesn't she want to stay in touch with them too? Not forgetting Mrs. B, and people like Carrie-Louise and Geordie.

By the end of an hour, her head aches from problems that just seem to run in endless circles without ever getting closer to an answer. She doesn't think the brandy from yesterday is helping either. She looks back to the conversation with Mrs. B that started it all. Had Mrs. B known something needed to give? Had she purposefully poked her bony finger into one of the loose bricks holding up Janice's badly constructed world? Janice wouldn't put it past her.

And what about Mrs. B's world? Didn't she have a dilemma all of her own? Was Tiberius a man with some hidden virtues? She still cannot contemplate telling Mrs. B about the conversation she'd overheard. For all his NoNoNotNow arrogance, maybe he really cares what his father wanted and does want to create an educational legacy in his name? Perhaps he lies awake at night worrying his mother is going to fall and kill herself? Is Mrs. B being selfish in not considering another option? Again, Janice's mind runs in circles—with no conceivable resolution in sight.

When she emerges from the room, Mike is waiting for her with Stan in the Porter's Lodge. They are chatting about football, and she can imagine next time she visits, Stan telling her that her husband is a good bloke. She finds herself hoping that Stan has a friend at the college where Mike briefly had a job as a porter. This might save her from a conversation in which she has to be enthusiastic and positive about her husband, when she really just wants to say, "I'm sorry Stan, but you have absolutely no idea what you're talking about."

"Come on, Jan, let's get you back home." Mike is all concern and ushers her to the car, taking her bag from her. She knows at this moment he is genuine and without even noticing it, she is back up on that seesaw. He's not that bad; some men would leave her to get the bus back on her own. She has to forcibly remind herself that it is her money that pays for the car and puts petrol in it. But that doesn't really help as she is then telling herself she is being selfish; she shouldn't be keeping score as marriages are meant to be a team effort.

She gets in the car and leans against the cold glass of the window. Her head is splitting and she feels totally drained. She closes her eyes and lets Mike's talk wash over her. He puts his hand out and touches her shoulder. "That's it, you get some sleep." Then he turns on the radio and puts the cricket commentary on—loud.

When they are home, she says she is going to go out. She feels nothing is going to get her through the front door, not even a push in the middle of her back to propel her over the doorstep. "I thought I'd get some fresh air and go and walk that dog." With Mike she calls Decius, "that dog." This is so Mike does not laugh at his name and Decius does not become the butt of an oft-repeated joke down the pub. She hopes Decius would forgive her.

"We're not even going to have a coffee?"

No, Mike, make your own bloody coffee. She doesn't say this out loud and wonders why she can no longer verbalize her rage. It is seeping out of her. All she wants to do is lie down in the middle of the path and be left alone. Instead, she takes the keys from him, gets in the car, and drives away.

What Janice loves about dogs, well, Decius really, is that they are amazing barometers of mood. Today he doesn't bounce once, nor does he chase after tantalizing smells. He walks to heel by her side as if these other things are beneath him. He looks up to check on her occasionally and she knows from his lopsided mouth and the tilt of his head that he is trying to make her laugh. *Stick with me, kid, and I'll get you in the movies.* When this doesn't work and she sits down, exhausted, on a bench overlooking the river, he climbs up on her lap (without even trying to investigate her pocket for snacks) and lets her bury her face in his fur.

When she drops Decius back home, she prays Mrs. Yeah-YeahYeah will be out. She is, but Tiberius is in the kitchen drinking coffee and reading from his tablet. "Nice walk?" he says, looking up at her before going back to the screen. It is the first time he has spoken to her in four years. She feels like he has put his foot out to trip her up and only just remembers to grunt "Yes, thanks" as she leaves. She used to think it would be nice if sometimes he exchanged some pleasantries with her, now she wishes that she was still invisible.

On the way home, she pulls over into a turnout and spends she has no idea how long staring at the windshield, seeing nothing but the individual drops of rain that are gathering there. She does not want to go home but knows there is nowhere else she can go. So she sits on, watching the drips on the glass until a bus drives past, throwing up water onto the side of the car. She thinks about the geography teacher for a second but only feels the bleak disappointment of a child who has been told too early that fairy stories are just childish nonsense.

Eventually, she pulls into the drive and Mike is waiting for her. She can see in his face he is worried, and she is back to feeling guilty. As she steps out of the car, she realizes this has been the main preoccupation of her life: guilt.

Mike watches her as she walks up to the door. He doesn't ask why she has been so long, and she can tell she is unnerving him. He doesn't even ask, "What's for dinner?"

As she hangs her coat up, she says, "I'm going upstairs. I'm not feeling too good."

"Don't worry about dinner," he says, like this might be her main concern. "I'll get us a takeaway."

She contemplates saying, "We can't afford it—neither the takeaway nor your pints in the pub on your way to collect it." But she really is past caring.

She runs a bath and sinks into the hot water. For a minute, she submerges her whole body and head in the warmth and finds some comfort in the way the water muffles all other sound. She hears Mike close the front door and start the car as if he is several streets away. She re-emerges and puts her head back. She is searching for a story that will help her. Eventually, she chooses one. She wants one that takes her far away from this house. She lowers her shoulders, so they are under the warm water and imagines herself telling it to Mrs. B.

This is the story of a man who made airplanes. He knew this was not what he really did, but it was what his children said when they went to school and the class was asked to take turns and to talk about their dads. And later it is what his grandchildren said when they were asked if they were related to him. "Yes, he's Gramps, and he makes airplanes." He had an unusual name and was now a Business Czar who was featured in the news, so it was a question they were used to answering.

The man who did not make airplanes made a very small part that went into most airplanes. It kept the planes up in the sky for longer, using less fuel, and as a result of this, he sold an enormous number of them and became very rich. What most people did not know, and he did not tell them, was that he was frightened of flying. This is the reason he had invented the part in the first place—to make planes safer. If he traveled, he liked to go by boat, and many people thought he did this because he wanted to save the planet. He did (and he was proud his invention helped cut emissions), but this was not the main reason for his love of boats.

Many journalists who wrote about this man believed airplanes and conservation were the dual stories of his life. As he was such a rich and successful man it was felt that he should be allowed two stories.

However, his real story was that he was a man who loved birdsong. It was what made him happiest, and he wanted to listen to as many birds as he possibly could. Therefore, he did not spend his money on enormous mansions and fast cars (and certainly not on private jets). He used his money to buy all the recordings of birdsong that he could, and when an old and extensive archive of British birdsong came up for auction, he canceled two board meetings and lunch with the Minister of Transport to be there to buy it.

Having bought the rare recordings (no one else stood a chance), he then spent almost as much money making sure they were remastered to provide the optimum sound. After that, he bought himself a large pleasure boat and fitted it with speakers. He then invited anyone who cared to join him to spend their Sundays sailing around the lake near his house listening to the sounds of the birds.

Janice falls asleep in the bath, imagining the call of birds and the wash of water against the side of a boat.

She is awoken when the bathroom door bursts open and Mike peers in. "How you doing?" he asks cheerily; she can smell the beer from here. “Feeling better?” He doesn't wait for an answer but pushes into the bathroom and balances a cup of coffee on the side of the bath. “I thought you might like this.”

He waits expectantly.

“Thanks,” she says, taking a sip.

Milk and two sugars, just the way Mike likes it.

NINETEEN

Never Tell a Story to a Deaf Man

The following days move in a repetitive cycle: up early, out of the house early to avoid Mike, and a walk to catch the bus—she no longer looks for the geography teacher; early coffee in a café then as many cleaning jobs as she can fit in; a walk with Decius—the thought of which drags her through the day—then it is back to the house—late. Into bed in the spare room—early. Repeat. She is not yet due back at Mrs. B's but she thinks of her often. Mike comes and goes, and when he is in the house with her he is alternately hearty or sullen. She can't decide which depresses her more. She knows she should feel sorry for him, talk to him, even, but she keeps thinking of a saying she came across whilst cataloging Mrs. B's books: "Never tell your story to a deaf man." She has never been able to tell Mike her story.

Thursday has come around again. As always, the bus doors open with a sigh, as if exhaling, and they shudder closed behind her. Today's driver was a young Asian woman with two long plaits tied with orange bows. As the bus pulls away, Janice is left looking up at the block of well-maintained, Art Deco–style flats on the other side of the road. Déjà vu. Except, she reminds herself, she has seen this many times before.

But she has never seen that before. Standing in front of the main doors that open into the foyer is the geography teacher. The lights from the building illuminate him as if he was on a stage. He is wearing dark trousers and brown trainer-like shoes. His jacket (which looks like it would be good for climbing Snowdon in) is navy and in his hand, he is carrying a cycle helmet. He is worrying the strap of this between his thumb and forefinger. He half raises his other hand to her before letting it fall. Even from this distance, she can see he is trying to smile but that it's not really working. A sudden blast of wind moves his cycle helmet so it swings in front of him, but does not move the gray hair that is cut close to his head—just like a geography teacher would wear it.

Janice takes all this in in a few seconds but it feels like she has been standing on the opposite side of the road for hours. She is going to have to cross the road. She tries to concentrate. This is how accidents happen. People are distracted—they step out in the road and . . . bang! She has an image of a bus knocking her comically up into the air and killing her before she even gets to speak to the bus driver, and she can't help herself but now she is laughing. He must see this as he stands a little straighter and smiles back at her. She looks carefully right, then left, and crosses the road. The short path to the front door feels like a catwalk—but it is the catwalk that features in her dreams, where she is pushed out in the middle of a fashion show and has no option but to walk down the catwalk carrying her mop and bucket. In her dreams, she is always wearing her worst clothes and never her red jumper.

These thoughts get her to the front door and because she cannot think of anything else to say, and because she hopes it will make him smile (he is looking worried again), and because she thinks of it as theirs, she says, "Oh, it's you."

He does smile and says tentatively—and it *is* a slight Scottish accent—"I hope you don't mind?"

"But how did you know I would be here?"

"I'm a bus driver."

"I know you're a bus driver." She wants to ask if he was ever a geography teacher but now's not the time. "But how did you know I'd be here today?"

"It's Thursday," he says, as if this explains it all.

She looks blankly at him.

He is back to looking worried again. "I'm not a stalker or anything strange like that. I'm just good with timetables. I guess it comes with the job." He hesitates, then adds, "And I have been driving you for the past seven months."

"Have you?" She looks at him in genuine surprise.

He laughs. "Didn't think you'd noticed me."

But she's thinking, *seven months? How can I not have spotted this lovely man?* Instead, she offers, "I'm a cleaner," and then wonders *why* did she say that? She knows if Decius were here he would be looking at her with his *"Get a fucking grip, woman"* expression.

The geography teacher says simply, "Yes, I know."

"How do you know?"

"I'm a bus driver."

He is really, *really* nice, but this is getting weird.

He laughs, seeing the expression on her face. "You hear all sorts driving a bus. It's one of the things I like about it. People always surprise you. I guess it's like driving a black cab, just bigger, and you don't have to tell people what you think about everything. I've heard at least two people say you are the best cleaner in Cambridge." He suddenly looks sheepish. "I noticed your name on your bus pass. But I haven't been looking up your address and driving my bus past your house, or anything like that."

She knows he means this as a joke but it brings reality down like the February rain. It is Thursday, it is bloody freezing standing here, the wind is whipping her hair about her face, and she is married to the man of a thousand jobs. And she cannot see a way out. Despite her outburst with Mrs. B, despite how she was feeling two seconds ago, she knows part of her is still wedged in there in Mike's alternative universe. In his world, she should be grateful to be with him and she should enjoy being the butt of his jokes. "You're taking it too seriously, Jan, come on, lighten up. Where's your sense of humor?" She wonders if she would have some hope of escape if she wasn't also chained to a memory that says, far more loudly than Mike ever could, she does not deserve better. And it makes her want to cry because she likes looking at this man, but the truth is it is just a fairy story.

"I was wondering if we might have a cup of tea together sometime?" He says it like he expects her to say no.

And maybe it is that, maybe it is the anxiety in his eyes, but she hears herself saying, "Yes, I'd like that."

He looks genuinely shocked. "Great, well . . . great!"

She has said "yes," and meant it, but she feels she needs to qualify it.

"It's complicated . . . I'm married." Now it is out there. She can't bring herself to say the clichés: "But we sleep in separate rooms" or, "My husband doesn't understand me." So, she finds herself repeating, "It's complicated." She adds, "I'm sorry."

"Okay," he says slowly, looking at the cycle helmet in his hand. "Look, we can just be friends meeting for tea." He adds, "And it will be fine, you mustn't worry. I'm not a real ladies' man."

Oh, he's gay. She definitely didn't see that coming.

He reads her look. "No, no, I'm not gay." He half laughs. "It is just I do have quite a few female friends . . . well, like you say, it's complicated." He brightens. "I could tell you about it over tea." He adds, "I just wanted you to know I'm not some sleazy oddball."

"Just a bus driver," she says.

He nods. "Who would like to have tea with a cleaner."

It is only when she is opening the door to Carrie-Louise's flat that she realizes she does not know the geography teacher's name.

TWENTY

The Thick and the Thin of It

Adam is telling her about a sci-fi comic series he is collecting. She is touched he talks to her like she might actually have some idea of what he is on about and she hopes her replies don't give her away. She thinks she is doing quite well until he says impatiently, "No, he's in *Descender*. You're thinking of *Mass Effect*." She had actually been thinking about where the geography teacher might suggest for tea and what she would wear. She tries to look suitably contrite and inquires a bit more about *Descender*.

Adam suddenly laughs and shakes his head. "You're just like Mum. I bet you watch *Midsomer Murders* like she does too." It is not said in anger, just the bewilderment of youth that old people could actually like that sort of stuff. He runs off to find a stick for Decius, who looks at her with his *"About blooming time"* expression and chases after him. She is glad that Decius moderates his language around Adam.

As Adam races ahead, she thinks of Simon. With him it had been *Star Wars*. It amazes her how young boys can get wrapped up in the minutiae of the worlds they choose to become obsessed about—which she realizes is a bit rich coming from a woman who collects stories and keeps an extensive library of them in her head. On an impulse, she pulls out her phone and calls her son's number.

"Hi, Mum."

She can't read his tone. Is he pleased to hear from her? This leads her to her default position—guilt—as it is some weeks since she has phoned him.

"How are things? I was just thinking about *Star Wars* for some reason, and you popped into my mind."

She is glad to hear the smile in his voice as he says, "Now what brought that into your head, 'Yousa thinking yousa people ganna die?'"

She has no idea what he is talking about. She never did when he started quoting from the films, but rather like when she chats to Adam, it doesn't seem to matter what he is saying; just that they are talking is enough. It amazes her that this fact seems to have passed her by.

"Look, I'm sorry I haven't called . . ." she starts.

"Don't worry about it, Mum. It's not like I've been great at keeping in touch. Look, I can't really talk now, I've got to head out to a meeting."

Janice can't help feeling awkward and disappointed. "Of course, you're at work. I should have texted."

"No, it's fine. Are you around at the weekend? I could call and have a catch-up then."

She feels her spirits rocket. "Yes, that would be great, anytime you like."

Suddenly remembering the atmosphere at home, she adds, "Call me on my mobile."

As she hangs up and walks on, she watches Adam, who is now wrestling Decius for a large branch. She feels a huge wave of affection for him. So, it has taken a twelve-year-old boy to remind her that we should just keep talking to our children.

Since their conversation over coffee, Fiona has come out with them on a few walks and Janice is pleased to see the change in her as she watches Adam. To start with, Fiona bombarded her son with questions. She seemed to feel the need to keep up a constant flow of conversation—a bit like she's just been doing with Adam, Janice realizes. Then, over time, a more natural order has been established; she and Fiona chat and lag behind, and Adam and Decius run ahead. Gradually, she has seen Fiona's shoulders drop and she notices she has stopped watching Adam's every move. She thinks Fiona has seen what she sees: a twelve-year-old boy happily playing with a dog. Of course, it doesn't give the full picture of how Adam is doing, but she thinks it gives his mother hope.

The only thing that mars her memory of these walks is something that she knows is entirely her fault. And it is a thing she cannot explain to Fiona and Adam. Decius the circus dog had been balancing on Adam's knees and then on his two feet (briefly) as Adam lay on his back on his coat on the grass. Fiona and Janice were the audience on a bench nearby, and applauded as required, in between chatting about new additions to the loft in the doll's house. Janice had seen Adam pull a packet from his pocket and reach in for a reward for Decius. She can't remember actually jumping up from the bench, but suddenly she was in front of Adam, dashing the packet from his hand, screaming at him, "Get it out of his mouth, has he eaten any?" She had pulled Decius away from Adam and frantically checked the dog's mouth.

Then Fiona was by her side, and she had a hand on her shoulder. "It's okay Janice. They're dog treats. I said it was okay for Adam to buy them. Is Decius allergic to something we don't know about?" Janice had looked at Adam's white face and Fiona's calm one, and had kept saying, "Dogs can't eat chocolate. They mustn't, they really can't." Fiona had kept her hand on Janice's shoulder and said, as if to calm a small child. "It's okay Janice. It's not chocolate. It's okay."

Later she had apologized to them both but did not expand on why it had upset her so much. How could she? The following walk had been a bit more stilted and awkward than before—but soon, in their joint admiration of Decius the wonder dog, the atmosphere had eased and nothing more was said about it.

After dropping Decius back home, Janice decides to go into the center of Cambridge. She still has a reasonable amount left on the John Lewis voucher Simon sent her for Christmas and she would like to look for something new to wear for when the geography teacher calls her about tea. She did manage to remember to give him her mobile number, even though she forgot to ask his name.

She has been thinking about this all day and has decided she would like to wear a skirt. She rarely wears one and she doesn't want to turn up wearing anything that reminds her she scrubs toilets for a living. She has a couple of skirts in her wardrobe that are quite flattering and not too dressy. Her leather jacket should look okay with one of them—she could even wear her red jumper. But she is not at all sure about the shoes she has. She thinks her John Lewis voucher might stretch to a pair of black boots if she chooses carefully.

The woman who comes to help her is in her early thirties and soon points out some knee boots that might work and that won't break the bank. As she returns with a pile of boxes, the assistant is waylaid by a short woman in her forties, who is carrying around a sample boot—similar to one of the ones Janice has chosen. The woman is pin-thin and dressed entirely in black. This immediately makes Janice nervous—she has had problems getting boots to fit around her calves before. On one occasion a young male assistant had dropped to a lying position to try and get the zip up a leg that was never going to fit in the tiny bit of leather he was trying to wrap around it. He seemed to take it as a personal challenge—one he lost. He was oblivious of the searing embarrassment Janice felt standing in the middle of the showroom like an Ugly Sister. Oh God, is this going to happen again? If the boots do fit the thin, very posh-looking woman, they are never going to get around Janice's legs.

The other customer reminds her of Mrs. YeahYeahYeah. She has already tried to pinch the assistant who is helping her—as if Janice did not even exist.

She tries again. "You! Can you come over here." It isn't a question.

Janice nearly hugs the assistant when she politely refuses. "I will be with you in a moment, madam, I am just serving this customer."

Unable to get her physical presence, this does not stop the woman from calling across the shop to her. "But you have to tell me. Will they flop? Will these boots flop? I have bought others before, Italian leather, and my legs are so slim they just will not hold up."

Janice smiles at the young assistant who is helping her into a rather nice pair of black leather and suede boots. "Not a problem I can say I've ever had."

"Me neither," the girl admits, grinning.

Janice can feel their shared bond as the thin woman shouts across the department. "Would you say my legs are very slim? Is that the issue? Because I do not want the boots to *flop*."

"I will be with you in a moment, madam," the assistant says and winks at Janice.

Janice thinks she loves this girl. She has already found her a great pair of boots that are in the sale, and she has not been lured away by this more demanding and, she suspects, very much richer customer. As they manage to pull up the zip of the boot Janice is trying on—snug, but okay—she shares her story of the young man lying at her feet.

The young assistant suddenly bounces to her feet, and this appears to set off the other customer again. "Tell me, you. You! Are these Italian leather?"

The assistant turns in the woman's direction but keeps her attention on Janice. "I have the same problem you have with boots." And with this she lunges forward. Janice sits back in surprise.

"I used to play a lot of squash," she explains, striking another pose. She now looks like a player reaching for a tricky shot. She comes back to a standing position. "You get very fit but you do get enormous legs. It's all that lunging."

Janice laughs. "I can certainly understand that. But what's my excuse?"

The girl smiles down at her. "I think those boots look great." She then adds quietly, "I used to play squash for England."

"Now, madam," she says, turning away from Janice. "How can I help you?"

As Janice leaves John Lewis with her boots *and* a story, she can still hear the other customer's querulous voice. "But you are sure they won't *flop*?"

TWENTY-ONE

When Push Comes to Shove

Janice gets through the front door faster than she has done in years. She wants to get her box containing her new boots out of sight. As she runs up the stairs—no sign of Mike—she thinks of the young woman in the shoe department of John Lewis. Maybe life is not about having a story? Perhaps it is about having done one thing that you can look back on with pride? That you feel defines you. She thinks of her neighbor, Mr. Mukherjee. He runs a dry cleaners, but he also played cricket for India when he was sixteen. Does the young woman smile and remember playing squash for her country and think, "Yes, *I* did that"? She hopes this thought sustained her when she was dealing with Mrs. Floppy-Boots.

She hears Mike coming out of the sitting room and quickly steps into the spare room. She only gets a few inches beyond the door. There are large brown cardboard boxes everywhere. They are piled on the bed, on the chest of drawers, and on the floor. She can see her books, headphones, and jumpers have been dropped in a heap by the side of the bed.

"Hi, love. Jan, you need to come down here. I've got

something to tell you. Don't worry about all the boxes, I can explain."

She picks up her belongings and places them neatly on top of her box of boots, which she then stacks on one of the large boxes. She knows the simple task of tidying is giving her mind time to catch up. Perhaps Mike has got a sales job and this is the stock? Maybe that's what the meetings were about, all that motivational talk was sales speak? Her heart sinks—he has tried sales before. But whatever happens, these boxes are not staying here. This is *her* room. She may not be able to leave him but she will never go back into their bedroom, into that bed.

"Come on, Jan. It's exciting news. Just the fresh start we need. A new adventure."

Perhaps he wants them to emigrate? He could go on his own. She could stay here. She knows it's too much to hope for, but now she needs to find out.

Mike has a box beside him in the sitting room, but she cannot see what's inside. She sits down on the sofa. Perhaps he has started packing already?

She is suddenly conscious of not having eaten or drunk anything for hours. "Before you start, Mike, I would *love* a cup of tea."

"You can get us one in a bit. Or better still, we can go to the pub to celebrate."

She hopes he is going to New Zealand. It is about as far away as she can think of.

"I know you've been a bit run down lately," he starts. "Well, I've been working on something that I think will give you the boost you need. I have been brainstorming with a team who show how franchising can really put you at the heart of any community and of course, once you're bedded in, sales opportunities naturally follow. If you build on this by expanding your product portfolio, you then have classic exponential growth."

Okay, so not motivational speaking, but still making no sense. Some sort of franchise? Hopes of Mike in the Antipodes are fading fast. She looks up toward the ceiling, thinking of all the boxes; this sounds like it could cost them money.

"What's in the boxes, Mike?"

"Let me finish." He is now sullen, but she watches as he takes a big breath, and the cheery Mike resurfaces. "It's really you who showed me the way and I think you should take some credit for that."

She knows she is staring at him blankly.

"The domestic arena . . ." he continues, then laughs. "Sorry, too much jargon. One of the things they kept repeating was, 'Keep it simple, Mike.'"

The thought is there before she can stop it. *Keep it. Simple Mike.*

"So, put simply, I am going to start a great new business and it is one that will combine our talents."

He sits down next to her. He tries to take her hand, but she is too quick for him.

"What's in the box, Mike?" It is all she can think of to say.

"Right, yes, maybe best to start there. Let's not waste time when we have the real thing in front of us."

He opens up the box and pulls out a number of cleaning products. It is a brand she has never heard of.

"What are those?" she asks, with a sinking heart. She can see where this is heading.

"This is an integrated range of premium quality cleaning products . . ." He rushes on, seeing her face. "It's not what you think . . ."

He has no idea what she thinks. If he did, she wouldn't be sitting here listening to this shit.

"I've not only bought into the ingredients that constitute,

let's say, the raw materials of the cleaning trade, but have given considerable thought to the value-added end: the tools of the trade. Then when I expand on this area through franchising, that's where the real money lies."

He now pulls from the box a hold-all made from neon floral fabric. The pattern reminds her of one of the inserts in Mrs. YeahYeahYeah's hideous dress coats. He unzips the bag and brings it over. It contains what looks like five enormous electric toothbrushes, each with a different-sized head. The bodies of the brushes are in the same vivid floral design as the bag.

"So?" she says, uneasily.

"This comprehensive range of electronic brushes works alongside our cleaning products to revolutionize housework."

She has no idea where to start. She plumps for her biggest concern. The cleaning products looked really cheap; these brushes look like they could have cost a lot more. "What have you done, Mike? How much did that lot cost?"

"I knew you'd be negative. You can never see the bigger picture." He takes out one of the brushes as if he is going to try and pass it to her but obviously thinks better of it.

"How much, Mike?"

"The cleaning range was on sale and has meant an initial investment of only £750, and we will recoup that many times over." He is now sounding petulant. "The brushes are my own design, so they inevitably needed greater investment."

"How much, Mike?"

"Each pack retails at £59.99 and so the income from them will far outstrip the outlay. We will more than double our money."

"How much, Mike?" She feels no emotion, just very cold.

"Obviously I had to order in bulk but I beat the price down to £29."

"How much, Mike?" She has an image of herself stuck on this cheap leather sofa, a Miss Havisham, surrounded by cleaning products, saying to the end of her days, "How much, Mike?"

"The initial outlay was £29,000 . . ."

"Jesus Christ, Mike! That's all our savings. How *could* you?" She is starting to tremble. All that work, all those hours. And he didn't even discuss it with her.

"You're just not looking at this right, Janice. Rather than see that investment as a net negative transaction, you need to view it as a net gain of over £30,000."

She asks urgently, "Can you return them and get our money back?"

"Get in the real world, Janice. Business doesn't work like that. I have imported them in bulk and if you were not just a . . ." He stops himself before he says, "just a cleaner." He continues. "If you were business-minded, you would appreciate that to get the best price you pay upfront, prior to shipping. This is not something you pop down to Tesco to buy."

"I know you can't buy them in Tesco."

"What?" He looks confused, and then more hopeful. "So you're beginning to see, Jan. I thought it would take time, but I knew you'd get there—"

"But you can buy them in Lidl."

"What?"

"It's where I bought the set I've got. The gray-and-white set I keep under the stairs. They cost me £7.99. And they *can* be useful, not for everything, but they are great for getting limescale off the shower attachment."

But Mike doesn't seem that interested in the shower attachment. He looks stunned. But she has to give it to Mike, he always bounces back.

"I don't think you've grasped, Janice, that these are far better quality. And most importantly are in colors that ladies will like. And," he adds, gathering confidence, "the most important feature that you're overlooking is the convenient and attractive carry bag."

"What are you on about? Nobody takes their cleaning equipment out with them."

He looks up at her with a strange triumph in his eyes. "That's not true. You do sometimes."

"Mike, I'm a sodding cleaner." She now realizes the feeling of cold she was experiencing is actually icy rage.

"I know you're a bloody cleaner," he shouts back, all cheeriness gone. "Do you think I like having a wife who's a skivvy? You treat me like I wouldn't have thought this through . . ."

She looks at him in disbelief. "But you didn't."

"I did my research and I can see there is real potential. I even thought—more fool me—that we could work on this together. Can't you see that with your cleaning contacts we could be selling my range into all the places you go and into your clients' networks?"

Mike is now pacing the room. He is a big man, and the room suddenly seems very small. He kicks the box of cleaning products out of his way.

"So yes, I did my research! I called some of your clients and sounded them out. They weren't as negative about my idea as you are, let me tell you."

"You did *what*?!"

The tone of her voice stops him dead in his tracks. It is unlike anything he has ever heard from his wife.

Now her rage feels like it is forming ice splinters that she fears will pierce through her skin. She stands up and Mike takes an involuntary step backward. She catches sight of them both in the mirror: Mike, tall and faltering; herself, small and taut, every muscle clenched. "*Who* did you speak to?" She has to know, even if she has to beat it out of him.

He sees just by one look at her that he has to tell her.

"It was the first four on your list, the list in your phone." Now he is speaking he seems to gain more courage. He pulls himself up to his full height. "I don't know why you're making such a fuss—"

But her look stops him.

"Mike, I am leaving you."

And now it is out, she is suddenly calm. No matter what happens next, she will be free of this. She would rather sleep under a hedge than stay another moment with this man.

She leaves the room and collects a suitcase from under the stairs. Moving from room to room, she quickly and efficiently makes her choices and packs them. Upstairs, she selects a large suitcase from the wardrobe and does the same there with her clothes and toiletries. The only problem occurs with the books. It is difficult to know which to choose, and she cannot take them all. She fills an old wine box with her favorites. She can collect the rest later. She tries not to think about where on earth she will be taking her bags and this box. She has the small amount of money in her current account and that is it.

Mike appears at the bottom of the stairs.

"Now, come on, Jan. You're not serious. We can talk this through. Maybe the idea needs adjusting, but you'll see I'm right about it."

She does not answer; she is tuning him out as she makes her final selection of what to take.

"Look, come on, let's have a coffee together."

This does permeate her new calm.

"Mike, make your own bloody coffee." For once she says this out loud. "And I don't have sugar in my coffee and never have done."

"Jesus, Janice, is that what this is all about? Just because I got your coffee wrong?" He is staring up the stairs at her.

"It is not about the *fucking* coffee!" And this she roars. She thinks she has at long last found her inner lioness. And she hasn't even needed her music and headphones. "What it *is* about is always letting me and Simon down. It is about making me feel that every mistake you make is somehow my fault, that I am nothing and should be lucky to have a husband like you. I have done everything I can think of to keep things going for us while you flit from job to job. Christ, Mike, do you think I didn't want more? But I just got on with it and yet however hard I work, you always make me feel like I should be ashamed, that I am 'just a cleaner.'"

"But you *are* just a cleaner."

She doesn't think he says this to hurt her; she thinks it is actually what he thinks of her, and she wonders why it has taken her so long to see it. The calm is returning. Her son has never made her feel like she is "just a cleaner." For all his expensive school and posh friends, he has never done that. And she suddenly remembers there is a bus driver out there who wants to have tea with a cleaner.

She repeats, with a calm certainty, "I am leaving you, Mike."

"But you can't." He is coming up the stairs two at a time.

And suddenly she is afraid—terrified—with a fear that robs her of breath and speech. She cowers before him.

Her expression makes him stop and he looks genuinely bemused. He says gruffly, "Jan, I wasn't going to hit you. You know I'd never do that."

She stands up straight; her heart is racing. She manages to whisper, "I know that."

"What is it, Jan? Look, we can work this out." He is pleading with her.

She suddenly feels more tired than she has ever done before in her life.

"No, we can't, Mike. I *am* leaving you."

She gathers her things and walks them awkwardly down the stairs. Mike sits at the top watching her go. The last thing she does is pick up the postcard from her sister that is still sitting on the hall table.

TWENTY-TWO

A Traveler's Tale

Janice drives around the villages outside Cambridge for an hour. She does not follow any planned route, she just turns alternately left and then right until she is completely lost. Lost is good. As yet, she cannot tackle any of the practical considerations, like where she is going to spend the night. She has very little money. Maybe in the car? Could she find a really cheap B&B?

When she sees a wide turn into a huddle of deserted barns, she pulls over and parks. How could Mike have done it? What must her employers have thought of him—of her? This upsets her far more than the money. It was her world, and it was private. She thinks of Sister Bernadette and wishes she could hear her now, whispering in her ear, but there is just the sound of the wind on the car and the creaking of the fences by the barns. It occurs to her that Mrs. B reminds her of Sister Bernadette—the tiny, often irascible nun. She thinks of the blue blanket Mrs. B wrapped around her. Could she go to her? But that is the problem with the private world she has constructed for herself, the world that Mike has now violated. In it, she *is* just a cleaner.

And now there is no inner lioness telling her she is more than that and no Sister Bernadette suggesting she could turn to them for help. In fact, she has to make herself look at the record of her employers—the list Mike stole—and then she has to ring them and apologize for what he has done. She imagines him rooting around in her bag to find her phone and copying the numbers while she was, what? Cooking? Putting the washing in? She stares at the dark shapes of the farm buildings and listens to the wind. She thinks if ever, *ever* her pathetic, guilt-ridden, mouse-self tries to talk her into going back to Mike, she will just need to remember this moment sitting in a car, in the dark by the deserted barns. She knows it will be enough.

She reaches for her phone. She has to do this sooner or later. Mike had said the first four names. All she begs is that Mrs. YeahYeahYeah isn't one of them. She thinks she can bear anything except having to make that call. She touches the screen and her phone lights up.

It is bad, but not as bad as she feared. However, her anger rekindles as she looks at the names. This makes it sickeningly real. On the list are: Major Allen, Mrs. B, Dr. Huang, and Geordie. Oh, Mike would have loved that last conversation. She cannot bear to think of her husband's sycophantic overtures to the world-famous star. She will leave Geordie to last.

She rings Mrs. B first. At least she believes Mrs. B has the measure of her husband. She wonders if he rang her before or after her outburst. Mrs. B gave no indication that Mike had been in touch trying to rustle up interest in his cleaning products. But then, she was a spy and is used to keeping things close to her chest. She can feel her hands growing clammy as she presses the number. The phone rings out, but no one answers. She begins to feel anxious—then remembers Mrs. B sometimes doesn't answer her phone. She will leave it until she sees her in person.

The call to Major Allen actually makes her laugh. Before she gets far into her excruciating explanation, he stops her.

"No need to say more, Janice. I was on to it straight away. My son has warned me about this type of thing and it is often reported on in *The Telegraph*. I believe it's called phishing. Knew he was dodgy as soon as I heard him. Put the phone on the side and went and made myself some tea. Thought I'd let him build up his phone bill. Have you been hacked, dear, is that it? Might want to change the password on your phone. My son says that usually does the trick." Janice says she will do just that and hangs up.

Major Allen's story is what she calls a story half-told. In Major Allen's spare room, he has 214 boxes of shoes. She knows this because she has counted them. Inside each box is a pair of beautiful women's shoes. He encourages her to look at them and admire them. They are all size three (Major Allen is size eleven) and none of them have ever been worn. So far he has not volunteered why he collects these shoes (in size three) and she hasn't asked. That is not how story collecting works. The story has to be freely given. The exceptions to this are the stories she collects on a bus, or in a café. As these usually include an element of her own imagination (and are filed between fiction and nonfiction), she allows them to fall outside her normal rules.

Next is Dr. Huang. This is more awkward. Janice can hear in her tone that she thinks Mike's call was impertinent and offensive, and that she thinks poorly of Janice for allowing her husband access to her number. Janice doesn't blame her. She thinks it is only the fact that Dr. Huang has only recently joined her cleaning list (after waiting for several months) that stops her from firing her. She has yet to discover Dr. Huang's story, but she thinks it may have something to do with the beautiful orchids that she grows in her conservatory—time will tell.

When Janice gets to Geordie's name, she finds she is cold and shivering. She puts the heating on and pulls a warmer coat from the back seat. But it makes little difference. Geordie answers on the first ring but then sounds preoccupied and she wonders if he is busy or if maybe he cannot hear her clearly. She wishes she could see the funny side of it—sitting in her old car, by a barn, shouting out her apologies to a world-famous tenor. But as she talks, she can hear her voice is breaking. She thinks Geordie hears this too because he loses his air of preoccupation. "Don't worry, pet, you get plenty of butt-kissers in my line." Which only makes it worse as it confirms that Mike's call was fawning, as well as objectionable and inappropriate.

The line is quiet and Janice wonders if she can breathe in without Geordie realizing it is a sob.

"Are you still there, pet?"

She nods even though she knows he can't see her. She doesn't trust her voice.

There is silence, then she hears Geordie's booming, reassuring voice. "You could really help me out, Janice. What are you up to now, lass?"

"I'm in the car." She manages to say this without crying but it comes out as a whisper. She isn't even sure Geordie hears it.

"Would you consider doing me a bit of a good turn? I'm just waiting for me man to bring the taxi round. I'm heading to Canada. We start the tour on Saturday . . ."

She hears him call to someone in the distance. "In here, man. Be with you in a sec.

"I could do with someone keeping an eye on this place. Would you consider house-sitting for me, Janice? It would be for three weeks. If that's not too much to ask? You know Annie and her plants; she'd never forgive me if I let them die."

Janice doesn't think it is the thought of his dead wife's plants that is prompting him to make this offer. After all, they both know Janice pops in and keeps an eye on things when he goes away on these trips.

Now she can't stop crying and she knows—and she thinks Geordie knows too—he has just thrown her a lifeline. But then, he is the man who as a boy walked to London, who was helped by a tramp who walked by his side.

When she stops sobbing and can form some words, she manages, "Have a good trip. My sister lives in Canada."

"Whereabouts?"

"She's in Toronto."

"That's great. She could come and see us. Let me have her email and I'll get them to send her a couple of tickets. And tell her to call by and say hello afterward, mind."

"I will," Janice manages. "And thank you, Geordie."

"Will you get away, you're doing me the favor. You've got your key. Help yourself to anything you need."

And then he is gone, and she is sitting in the car shaking with cold and exhaustion and relief.

When she reaches Geordie's house, the light is on in the porch and there is a note for her stuck on the hall mirror.

Bed made up for you in the front guest room. Bottle of something for you in the fridge. See you in 3 weeks. G x

Janice brings her bags and box of books in from the car and leaves them in the hall. She closes the door after her and listens to the quiet of the house. The mellow tick of the grandfather clock, the slight creak of the pipes (Geordie has left the heating on), and best of all, mixing gently in with these, the soft silence. Janice sits on the chair in the hall, savoring the delicious quiet. She thinks of the man who did not make airplanes and knows at this moment she would not swap this quiet for the most beautiful birdsong in the world.

After a while, she wanders into the kitchen, a large room painted a faded gold color. The units are made from old pine and on the dresser are the red and blue plates that Annie used to collect. There are also numerous colorful pots containing plants. She recalls Annie telling her that she and Geordie had bought many of these on a trip to Mexico. She looks at the photo of Annie on the middle shelf, a tall, attractive woman with long, dark hair. Geordie had met Annie on a singing tour of America where she had been working on the publicity for his concerts. Annie had once told Janice she had spent her early life in an orphanage and knew little of her heritage, "But look at this hair, Janice, that's got to be pure Cherokee." Janice wondered whether being an orphan was the reason she and Geordie had decided to have such a large family. They have six children, all scattered around the globe. Janice studies the photograph of the much-loved wife and mother who died of cancer, one day before her sixtieth birthday. "Thank you, Annie," she says quietly.

She suddenly realizes the noise she can hear is not the central heating pipes but her stomach. She is starving. She looks in the fridge but there is little there apart from some jars of pickles, butter, jams, half a carton of milk, and a bottle of Champagne. This last item has a sticky note with her name on it. She closes the door. Maybe a cup of tea. She's not sure she feels like celebrating. She checks the freezer and sees Geordie has a stash of M&S ready meals. She will microwave one of these in a minute; she can always replace it tomorrow. As she waits for the kettle to boil, she checks on Annie's plants, although she knows they will all be fine. Geordie works at keeping these plants alive with the same passionate love he demonstrated when trying to save their green-fingered owner. Janice knows Geordie will not allow anything else to die in this house.

"Unless it's me, lass. And then . . ."

"I know, Geordie," Janice often finishes for him. "They will find the score for *La Bohème* wrapped around your heart." Privately, she thinks it will be tied there with a strand of his wife's beautiful hair.

On the dresser beside the spider plant is an old-fashioned CD player. Annie's favorites are stacked up beside it. Her taste ran to mellow, soothing sounds—performers such as Frank Sinatra, Nina Simone, Ella Fitzgerald, and Louis Armstrong. Janice doesn't think she is ready for dancing but feels she could listen to this. She selects a CD at random; it is a compilation of old songs.

Janice sits in Geordie's large, worn pine chair by the Aga and sips her tea. She can't help smiling as Frank Sinatra announces, "He's leaving today." Okay, he's off to New York, not to a rambling house in a Cambridge suburb, but she gets the idea. "You and me both, Frank," she says and feels more settled when she hears her voice come out stronger, less like a woman who is going to cry.

When the next song comes on, she puts her tea down and walks with a slight sway toward the freezer—she'll choose one of the ready meals. But the music is too enticing. Before she reaches the door, she spins on the ball of her foot and sidesteps across the kitchen. After all, as Nat King Cole points out, there may be trouble ahead, but she could always face the music and dance.

TWENTY-THREE

In Search of Scheherazade

She wakes to the sound of a text arriving. For a moment she cannot gather her thoughts. The light is different. There is a soft, peachy glow coming through the curtains. She must have slept really late. When she focuses on the fabric, it looks like someone has painted peonies and peach blossoms on it. Ah, Annie's choice, and it comes back to her. The bed is so soft. The mattress seems to fold around her, and she remembers the hard bed in the guest room at the college. Complete opposites except for that feeling she is where she wants to be.

The thought of the text breaks through her drowsy reflections. Mike? Is this what it's going to be like from now on? Every time her phone alert sounds, she's going to wonder if it's him and then feel slightly sick? She's heard you can personalize incoming alerts so you know who's sending them. Perhaps Adam would show her how to do this. She snuggles down into the warmth, trying to decide what sound she would choose for her husband. In the end, she concludes that most of her ideas are a bit too cruel, and a fart wouldn't really work because people might think it was her. As she is now laughing, she decides to reach for the phone; best to get this over with whilst she is still smiling.

> How about The Copper Kettle
> opposite King's College, tomorrow
> at noon?
>
> The Bus Driver AKA Euan.

Oh my God! *So* much to think about.

Is she free? She will make sure she is. She'll start really early. She pictures Major Allen still in bed as she vacuums around him. This makes her smile some more—and she is already grinning.

Next: she likes the choice of café. Nice view.

Noon? Is he thinking coffee or lunch? Maybe he's playing it safe—start with coffee and see how it goes?

Did she remember to bring her new boots? Yes, they're in the car.

Skirt, red jumper, and jacket? In the bag at the bottom of the bed.

Likes the fact he uses proper punctuation in his texts.

Perhaps he likes books too?

No kiss at the end of the message? Sensible, would have scared her.

She leaves the obvious one to last: Euan? How does she feel about that? She thinks it's rather nice. Euan is a man who would like country walks and know the names of all the trees. He may even have once taught geography.

She quickly texts back.

> Yes, that would be great. Janice
> AKA The Cleaner.

Now she can't lie still. She has to get up and do something. She doesn't have any work on today (two of the families she cleans for have gone skiing). She doesn't want to think about practical things like, what is Mike up to? What about the rest of her things? What on earth is she going to do when Geordie comes back? These can all wait. For now, she is going to have a long soak in the bath with a book and a cup of coffee—made just the way she likes it. She offers up yet another silent message of thanks to Geordie.

Then she remembers Simon; she should thank him for the boots. She hopes they will speak at the weekend—although heaven only knows what she will say. For the time being, she sends a text.

Just used your John Lewis voucher. Was saving it for something special. Bought some great black boots with it—so a big thank you. Mum xx

Glad you got something nice. Simon x

And *there* is a kiss she is not scared of receiving. She wonders if she is going to cry again.

Her phone rings as she is stepping out of the bath. It's Stan. Despite the warmth from the bath, she suddenly feels cold.

"I think you'd better come."

"Oh no, Stan! What is it?"

Not that, please, not that. She should have kept calling last night.

It seems that Stan can hear the panic in her voice. "No nothing like that . . . it's just . . . well, I think it would be best if you came over. I couldn't think who else to ring."

It's only as Janice is getting in the car, hair still wet from the bath, that she wonders why Stan didn't call Mrs. B's son.

Stan escorts her quickly to Mrs. B's door, the small wooden one that opens into the quadrangle. He doesn't shed any light on what's been going on. All he will say is, "I can't get anything out of her, she just tells me to fuck off."

Janice hurries alone into the main living area.

"And you can fuck off too." There is a pause. "Oh, it's you."

At first Janice can't see Mrs. B. Then she realizes she is sitting under the oak table. Her back is against the central support and her legs are poking out in front of her. She looks like a very tiny and untidy doll that someone has propped there. Her sticks are on the other side of the room. It looks like this may be where they landed when she threw them.

"Oh, Mrs. B, let me help you up. You can't sit there like that."

"I don't want to tell you to fuck off, Janice. In fact, you are one of the very few people of whom that can be said, but would you please just leave me in peace."

"But you're not in peace. Something has happened. Can't I help you up and . . . I could . . . I don't know, I could make some hot chocolate?" She had been about to say, "And you can tell me all about it," but she worries that Mrs. B might find this patronizing and she doesn't want to risk her status as a person Mrs. B doesn't want to swear at. She is rather proud of that.

"Oh, sod off, Janice."

So that didn't last long then.

"Hot chocolate? What am I? A toddler? I am a ninety-two-year-old woman, with one of the highest first-class degrees this college has ever awarded. It might interest you to know it was my contacts that got my husband this position here, not his. I can speak four languages, I have an exceptionally high IQ, and I once killed a man by strangling him with a belt, prior to which I disabled his associate who was trying, in turn, to kill me. I did this by administering a narcotic. So, Nanny giving me a nice hot chocolate is not going to make a sodding bit of difference."

Janice is caught completely off guard. She has no idea what to say. So Mrs. B killed a man.

Mrs. B slumps further under the table and appears to be talking to herself. All Janice can hear is a jumble of, "A bloody big sack would have done it . . . how dare he . . . little runt . . ."

This reminds her of the night she stayed in the college. Perhaps Mrs. B is drunk? She asks, in a lighter tone, "Mrs. B have you been at the brandy again?"

"How dare you, Janice! How fucking dare you! Not you as well." Mrs. B is spitting with rage and is pushing at the floor with her hands, trying to get her body so it is sitting more upright.

Despite the tirade, Janice can't bear it; she wants to help her, and she takes a step closer.

"Do not come any closer. Why I didn't keep one of Augustus's guns is beyond me. I'd like to lock the doors and shoot the fucking lot of you." And with this, she suddenly bursts into tears.

The sobs rack her thin body, and she puts her chin to her chest and lets her hands fall to the floor. She looks completely defeated.

Janice turns and flies up the spiral staircase and grabs the blue blanket and a box of tissues from the side of the bed. In a few seconds, she is kneeling beside Mrs. B under the table, leaning her forward—like she is a doll—and wrapping the blanket around her. She leaves the tissues by Mrs. B's side and then pulls two cushions off the armchair, which she then props around her. For a second, she thinks about lifting her bodily into the armchair, but instinct tells her Mrs. B would find this demeaning. But at least she can make her more comfortable.

Janice sits there for some time, propped up under the table beside her, holding Mrs. B's hand. The old lady does not snatch it away and after a while, she returns the pressure slightly.

"Tissue?" Janice says, offering Mrs. B the box.

"Oh, sod off, Janice," Mrs. B replies, but takes one and blows her nose.

Eventually, Janice asks, "Did you lob your sticks all the way over there?"

"Might have done."

"Do you hold a world record for javelin as well? Did you miss that one off the list?"

Mrs. B snorts, then cannot resist adding, "Actually, I was a hurdler."

"You going to tell me what happened?"

Mrs. B closes her eyes and sighs. "I suppose, if I must." She then adds in a softer voice, "Do you mind if we stay down here under the table? I find it strangely soothing."

Janice does too; she has never noticed before how the light from the old glass in the main window throws shadows over the wall and bookcases in the upper gallery. It's a bit like looking at them from underwater.

Mrs. B begins, still holding Janice's hand. "My husband, Augustus, was very fond of good wine and during our years traveling, we curated—I believe you could call it that—a small but interesting cellar. It represents the countries we have lived in, and different bottles and vintages mark specific events that have been important to us. We keep, or I should say, kept, it in the large cupboard off the hallway."

Janice knows part of this as she has been in the cupboard but was told by Mrs. B, in no uncertain terms, not to dust in there.

"Today my son, Tiberius . . ." Here, Mrs. B closes her eyes as if she is struggling to say his name. "He came and took all the wine away."

"Oh, Mrs. B," Janice can't help saying.

"He did this because he believes, or rather *says* he believes me to have a drink problem. He found the empty brandy bottle and mugs in the supermarket carrier bag, and on investigation, also found a bottle of wine in my bedroom."

Janice has a mental picture of Tiberius rampaging around the house, with Mrs. B physically helpless. It is not a pretty picture. "But you're not a drinker, Mrs. B. I could explain to him about the mugs, and I clean your room; I know you never normally have wine up there."

"No, you are right. I took a special bottle up to bed with me because yesterday was our wedding anniversary. It was a red wine we had bought together on a trip to Bordeaux."

Janice presses her hand briefly to her mouth. She can feel what it is costing Mrs. B to reveal these personal details. "You don't have to say any more, if you don't want to. Surely there must be something you can do to get them back?" But as she is saying it, Janice is wondering how. Mrs. B cannot physically go and get them. Could she help in some way?

"The thing is, Janice, it's not really about whether I drink. Quite frankly, at ninety-two, if I wanted to drink a couple of bottles a day it would be nobody's business but my own. All this represents is a ploy on my son's part to have me removed from the college. *My* college."

Decius. What would happen about Decius? This sudden thought fills her with horror. Two minutes ago, she had been ready to stride into Tiberius's house and demand the wine back. She had even imagined loading it into her car when Mrs. YeahYeahYeah was out somewhere with her husband. But now? She pictures Decius's funny tip-toe walk, his scruffy, quirky eyebrows, and recalls the comfort she derives from burying her face in his fur. How could she leave him? She knows if Tiberius were to get wind of her conspiring with his mother, he *would* fire her. She feels she should, once again, offer to talk to him about the empty brandy bottle—that really is all her fault. But she just can't bring herself to, in case Mrs. B takes her up on it.

Mrs. B pats her hand, as if to comfort her—which only makes her feel ten times worse. "You're not to worry about it, Janice. This is between me and my son. And we mustn't forget Mycroft."

"Mycroft?" She has forgotten him. "Oh, Mycroft."

"Yes, he's coming to visit the day after next and I would consider it a favor if you would be here. I also believe by then we will have a better idea of what my son is planning regarding my home. I have recruited a double agent."

The thought of this seems to perk Mrs. B up and she sits up straighter under the table.

"Who?" Janice asks, and she knows she sounds incredulous.

"Mr. Stanley Torpeth."

"Who?" Janice repeats, but light is beginning to dawn. "Oh, Stan." She cannot resist adding, "You didn't even know his name."

"A great oversight on my part," Mrs. B says, a little guiltily. "I must remember to apologize for swearing at him. Although"—she brightens up—"that's nothing compared to what he's used to."

"Now you have completely lost me."

"Stanley's wife Gallina is Russian. He has promised to bring her to meet me one day. That will be such a treat. Apparently, she has a magnificent temper. You know the Russian language is very expressive—there are so many ways to blaspheme and marvelous nuances that can be brought into play."

Janice leans her head back onto the support in the middle of the table. "You really are a class act, Mrs. B. Oh, by the way, I've left my husband."

"That does not surprise me in the least, my dear. When he called me on the phone, I was in no doubt that was what you would do. But sometimes these things need to go at their own pace; they cannot be rushed, whatever outsiders may think."

"Is that why you didn't say anything?"

"I didn't mention it, Janice, because I do not believe a woman is represented by the conduct or morals displayed by her husband. Augustus and I were always very clear about that. It was true we loved each other dearly but we were very independent people. *You* certainly do not have anything to apologize for. Whether I believe your husband to be deserving of being whipped through the streets on bended knee wearing a hair shirt is another matter altogether."

Janice would like to kiss the old lady sitting beside her, but instead, she gives her hand a last squeeze and offers her a hot chocolate.

"Yes, I think that would be excellent, and we might move to the armchairs now. I believe my arse is completely without feeling."

Janice collects her sticks and helps her to her feet. When she is settled in the chair, Janice heads to the kitchen. "Is there no drink at all, Mrs. B? I think you could do with a splash of brandy in this; you've had a shock."

"I am afraid not. Tiberius was tediously thorough in removing all the alcohol from the premises. I do not believe it helped matters that he found some of it under the sink. He certainly did not appear to credit my explanation that I kept it there as many of the other cupboards are too high for me to reach."

"But Mrs. B, why shouldn't you keep your drink wherever you want to? It is absolutely nobody's business."

"I am afraid Tiberius is trying to make it other people's business. As he is having little success getting me removed from here on the grounds of being infirm, he is now going to paint me as a drunkard. Still, we do have Stanley keeping an ear out and there is always Mycroft."

Janice is tempted to offer to pop out and replenish supplies and get some brandy for Mrs. B's hot chocolate. But what if Tiberius came back? What if he caught her? When Mrs. B says, "You must not be involved in this Janice. I do not want you to jeopardize your position," Janice thinks she now knows how Judas felt.

When they are sitting in the armchairs by the fire, Mrs. B asks, "So, would you be interested in hearing more about Becky—perhaps not today, but on your next visit? Or do you feel she is such a flawed character that she is no longer of interest?"

"Oh, Mrs. B, it's not like that. You know why I felt like I did."

"In part I do, but I do believe there's a lot that you're not telling me."

Janice looks at Mrs. B over the rim of her hot chocolate mug. "I know exactly what you're doing."

"And what might that be?" Mrs. B replies, trying to look the picture of innocence.

"You didn't think I would come back and clean for you, did you, so you've been feeding me a story, Becky's story, thinking I will want to hear more?"

"Well, it worked, didn't it?" Mrs. B positively chortles.

"Scheherazade!" Janice declares, playing her trump card. "I spotted you were uncomfortable when I mentioned *Arabian Nights*. So I looked up the book of *One Thousand and One Nights*."

"And the story is?"

"It's about a Sultan who was so devastated when his first wife betrayed him, that he killed her. After that he took a new virgin bride for one night only, and the following morning killed her too. All so he would not be hurt again. When Scheherazade was unfortunate enough to be chosen as a bride, she spent the night telling the Sultan a fabulous tale. He was so engrossed in the story he did not kill her as he wanted her to continue the tale the following night. Which she did, and the night after that, until—as in all good stories—they fell in love and lived happily ever after." Janice cannot help feeling a little smug.

"So I am Scheherazade?" Mrs. B inquires, smiling at her.

Janice cannot quite read the look, but she knows Mrs. B is building up to something.

"Oh, how the nuns would be blushing now." Mrs. B shakes her head.

"What?" Janice says suspiciously. She doesn't trust this woman—too tricky by half.

"You really need to be more rigorous in your investigations," declares the ex-spy with a first-class honors degree. "Scheherazade did not tell the Sultan the same story every night. She told him a different tale and it is this compilation of beautiful and mystical stories that constitutes what, in the English translation, is known as *The Arabian Nights*."

Mrs. B is swinging her small feet back and forward—a sure sign she is enjoying herself enormously.

"Scheherazade was a storyteller, but foremost she was a collector of stories." Mrs. B turns a bright eye on Janice.

"You, Janice, are without doubt, Scheherazade."

TWENTY-FOUR

An Island of Books

Major Allen does not appear to mind in the least that Janice is making an early start and when she arrives, he is already on his second cup of coffee and tackling the *Telegraph* crossword.

"Always awake by six a.m., up by six thirty a.m. at the latest. Comes from years in the army. On exercise we trained our men the same way. Bowel movement at seven a.m. and on with the day." He coughs and returns to the crossword and Janice wonders if he is regretting sharing the last part.

She is quick but thorough with the cleaning. She reflects that this comes from years of experience. As she bundles up the sheets she has stripped from the major's bed and carries them to the utility room, she thinks about Scheherazade. So, she was a collector of stories. Well, Janice knows she is a serious collector too and now, it seems, a storyteller. Hasn't she been sharing some of her stories with Mrs. B? But . . . Scheherazade? It is such a beautiful name, exotic and thrilling. Whereas she is a woman putting a load of washing on before picking up a mop to tackle the spilled tea and porridge stains on the kitchen floor. Scheherazade? Hardly.

She thinks back to Mrs. B's comment about Janice not telling her everything. Of course this is true. Mrs. B knows it, and she knows it. Did Janice ever really believe she was the woman with no story? After all, she is Scheherazade (she is warming to this idea), and she would appreciate that *everyone* has a story to tell. But can you choose your story? She thinks about Adam. She hopes he can choose a different story for himself. And if he can, isn't there a chance she could too?

She pictures Adam running around the field yesterday with Decius. It doesn't bring with it the normal feeling of joy. There is something lurking—a gnawing fear that these precious moments are under threat.

Decius had been particularly bouncy as she walked with him back to his house. For once he seemed oblivious of her mood. On the doorstep, as she unclipped his lead, he had turned his head and licked her hand. His expression seemed to say, "You and me. Dream team." She could barely bring herself to look him in the face. In the same way, as she could not look at all the wine boxes stacked in the hallway by the entrance to Tiberius's office. For a split second, she had thought about going up and picking out a bottle to take to Mrs. B—surely, he wouldn't notice one missing? But then she heard the familiar *tip, tip, tip*, on the wooden floor and remembered what was at stake and had turned and raced from the house.

She arrives at the café at 12:05 p.m. She has been loitering further up the street, by the market, to time her arrival at exactly this moment. Not too late, but not too early. Five minutes late shows she is not too eager, but that she is not a careless, unpunctual person. Euan is already at a table by the window and is halfway through a cup of tea. She takes this in in a few seconds, plus the dark trousers—similar to before but khaki rather than brown—and a nice jumper, black with a zip. He stands up and smiles—and there her stomach goes again. She is so glad she bought the boots. She reminds herself she was sold them by a woman who played squash for England. The thought sustains her as she crosses the room.

The first bit is easy: what coffee would she like, anything to eat, isn't the view wonderful across to King's, so many bicycles, did he bike here today, no, so you came on the bus (joke about did he drive it), they establish he lives near Ely.

Then silence. She stirs her coffee. He looks into his empty mug. She thinks it should be easier than this; she is approaching fifty and he looks about fifty-five. It seems so unfair that now, when they should have moved beyond all that, their inner teenagers have decided to wake up, stretch, and say, *"God, this is SO embarrassing!"*

Get a fucking grip, woman. She thinks of the fox terrier she loves. And didn't one of the people Mrs. B get a reference from say she could put people at their ease? Perhaps she can—herself included.

"Is that a Scottish accent?" she tries.

"I guess 'Euan's' a bit of a giveaway too." He looks up and is smiling again. "My family are originally from Aberdeen, but we moved when I was seven and I grew up in the Wye valley, not far from Hay-on-Wye. Have you ever been there?"

"No, but I've always wanted to." This is getting easier. And she actually wants to ask the next thing; she isn't just trying to make polite conversation. "I've read about the book festival there. Have you been?"

Please, please, please say you like books.

"I used to help out there when I was a lad, doing the parking . . ."

Yes, but do you like books?

". . . and now I go back most years for it. It's a good chance to catch up with old mates and . . ." He spots her coffee cup is now empty. "Would you like another?"

"Yes, please." But all she is thinking is, *do you go for the books or the mates?*

He gets the waitress's attention and orders more coffee and tea. When he looks back at her, she knows she is sitting there expectantly. She imagines she has the same look Decius has on his face when he is hoping she has brought the chicken snacks with her.

"What were we saying? Oh, the festival. It's a great boost for the town, live music, food and drink stalls. Feels a bit like a party. Some people hate it and rent their houses out and go away . . ." He pauses as a young girl comes to clear their table. He hands her the empty cups. "Yes, some people head for the hills, but I like it. But then I've always loved books. Got the shit beaten out of me at school for it, of course, but hey!" He shrugs, adding, "My dad would always patch me up though, you know, make a fuss of me. Perhaps he felt guilty." Euan smiles. "After all, he's the one that got me in trouble in the first place. He ran a bookshop."

Janice pictures herself standing up, leaning across the table, putting her hands either side of this glorious man's face, pulling him toward her, and kissing him full on the mouth. Instead, she asks him what he likes to read.

The next hour flies by and coffee merges into lunch. She finds out he loves Hemingway but struggles with Fitzgerald—the writing is beautiful but are the stories believable? She almost tells him that she collects stories—almost, but not quite. She discovers he is currently reading a lot from a Mexican writer, and she thinks of Annie and her plant pots. By pudding (yes, of course, they should both have some), they are discussing whether it is better to be a good and prolific author or to write one thing of outstanding beauty, like *To Kill a Mockingbird*.

Then they order coffee and the flow is interrupted. He checks his watch—yes, he has a bit more time. She visits the bathroom. When she comes back to the table, it feels like ordinary life is back pressing in on them, and she realizes she is sitting here with a relative stranger. She knows so little about him. She is suddenly very aware of her age, her build, her hands that look like cleaner's hands. And now her inner teenager is back, pulling up a chair and saying, *"Yeah . . . but, what do I say now?"*

She realizes that the talk of books gave them shared ground—an island on which to stroll—easy in each other's company. But they can't stay there forever. And now she doesn't know where to go next. She feels stranded and she knows to ask him some more about books will only accentuate this feeling.

"I've left my husband."

Why did she say that? What was she thinking of? It's like she's leaped off their island and plunged into ice-cold water.

"Right . . . right . . . are you okay?"

She can see he has no idea what to do with this. Why would he? All they have established is that they would be friends meeting for tea—or lunch, as it turns out. She sees his internal struggle and it's painful to watch. Can he ask? Should he ask? Will she mind? In the end, he looks up and does what she did when they first met: he reaches for safe small talk.

"What about you? Where did you grow up?"

She relaxes; she can do this. Or some of it. "I grew up in Northampton; we moved to the UK when I was seven."

He nods, acknowledging the small, shared similarity in their histories—the same age he was when he moved to Hay-on-Wye.

"I was born in Tanzania but we moved to Durham when my dad got a professorship in the Archaeology Department at Durham University. They were very interested in his work on the Olduvai Gorge."

"I've read about that. Isn't it the site of one of the earliest records of man?"

She nods, thinking that his love of the gorge, rather than teaching in Durham, was at the heart of her father's story.

"But you ended up in Northampton?"

She looks out of the window at something far beyond the bicycles and buildings. "My dad died when I was ten; he had pancreatic cancer." She adds, "It was very quick." She never knows whether this was a good or bad thing. She looks back at Euan. She's glad he hasn't said the traditional, knee-jerk, "I'm sorry." She knows she is sorry enough for both of them.

"We moved to Northampton because my mother decided she wanted us to stay in the UK and she has a sister there."

"Is she still there?"

"No, she died about fifteen years ago."

Now he does offer, "I'm sorry."

He can have that one. She is not sorry. She knows this is a terrible thing, and with it comes a mountain of guilt. Luckily, she has already laid a foundation—a massive bedrock of guilt to place it upon.

She realizes whereas their previous conversation had been carried on at a normal volume, now they seem to be talking in hushed tones. She had thought she could do this, but she can't.

"Do you have any brothers or sisters?" he asks.

She manages to say, "I have a sister," but now she wants to leave. There is no point in this. It's never going to work. She stands, and a second later he does too. He half puts a hand out toward her, as if he is going to, what? Stop her leaving? Take her hand? But then his hand drops to his side. She can only glance at him, but in that look, she can see he is frowning and concerned.

"I must go," she says, turning to collect her bag off the back of the chair.

"Look, Janice," and now he does put his hand out. He doesn't touch her but his hand hovers somewhere between them. "Could we start again? We don't have to talk about families. We could talk about books. We could stick to that."

She thinks of the island made out of books that they found themselves on, and more than anything she wants to go back there. To her surprise, she finds herself saying, "I collect stories. I don't mean stories in books—although I have a few of those—more, the stories of people. Just people." She does not know how to explain it more than this.

"I collect conversations." He sounds embarrassed, as if he has bought a packet of store-bought biscuits to a homemade cake sale. "They're not real stories as such. Just things I overhear that make me think, or laugh . . ." His voice peters out.

He tries again. "We could talk books and swap stories . . . Well, mine are . . . not really—"

Because of the struggle and because she realizes she cannot bear the thought of never seeing him again, she interrupts, "I'd like that."

He sighs, exhausted, like a man who has climbed Snowdon.

As she walks away, she can't help wondering what Euan's story is. She hopes he will tell her when they next meet. However, if he does, she knows it will not be a fair trade, because she is never going to tell him hers.

TWENTY-FIVE

Reading between the Lines

Mrs. B is sitting at the oak table beside a small, rotund man. His face is wrinkled like an apple that has been left too long in the fruit bowl. He is plainly dressed and if Janice had to guess what his profession had been, she would say that he came from a very long line of plumbers.

"This is Mycroft," Mrs. B declares to Janice, beckoning her to join them. "And *this* is Janice," she says, tilting her head toward her.

The small man jumps to his feet—he is surprisingly sprightly for his age. He extends a hand to Janice. "Fred, please. No need for that. I'm Fred Spink. Very pleased to meet you, Janice."

He doesn't say, "I've heard a lot about you," but it hangs unsaid in the air and Janice is now sure they were talking about her just before she came in. She can't help wondering what Mrs. B said.

Mrs. B cuts across her thoughts. "Nonsense, Fred, you will *always* be Mycroft to me."

With a jolt, Janice realizes Mrs. B is flirting. How unbelievably frivolous of her.

Mycroft chortles and reddens, looking more and more like an apple every minute. "Now, you behave yourself, Rosie. Or I shall spill the beans to Janice about that time in Madagascar."

Rosie?! Janice pulls a chair up to the table. She wishes they had some wine in the house. She would very much like to hear about "that time in Madagascar" over a glass or two. But, of course, they have no wine. The memory of the lost wine does much to sober her mood, as does Mycroft's next statement.

"Now, before we get carried away, I suggest we tackle the issue in hand." He draws some papers toward him that are lying on the table and puts on a pair of silver-rimmed glasses. "I have spoken to Stanley at some length, and have read all the documentation you sent me, Rosie."

Janice can't help it; she is distracted, again. She tries to imagine herself calling Mrs. B "Rosie," and fails. She has never thought of her as a woman with a first name—and certainly not such a little girl's name. If she had to pick a name, she would have gone for something like Drusilla, or Medusa—was that the woman with snakes for hair? But Rosie? Rosie is not a woman who kills a man.

"Janice, are you actually going to grace us with your attention? Would that be too much to ask?" Mrs. B is back to barking at her.

Mycroft continues. "I have also had some success in viewing the documentation held by the college and shall we say . . ." Here, his gaze travels up to the furthest corner of the room. "I *may* have been fortunate enough to get a glimpse of the email correspondence between the interested parties." He looks even more vague than he did a few seconds ago.

"So you hacked into their system," Mrs. B states, and her feet start to swing merrily back and forth under the table.

"Oh, that is something far outside of my capabilities and I

would vehemently deny the inference were it to be suggested," Mycroft says, peering over his glasses and moving his head from side to side to look at both of them.

Mrs. B's feet are still swinging. "But you know a man who can."

"Again, you are suggesting something that is well beyond me. I am, after all, just a retired civil servant, living quietly with my wife in Sevenoaks. The most exciting thing I do these days is attend the monthly meeting of our local ornithological society. Did you know we recently saw a desert warbler at Sheerness that had been blown off its migratory path?"

But Mrs. B is not fooled. "So what did the emails say?"

"Yes, do you have copies we could read?" Janice inquires.

In unison, Mrs. B and Mycroft's heads snap round so they are facing Janice.

Mycroft reaches out and pats her hand. "Oh, my dear, you never write anything down." He shakes his head at her in gentle reproof. "I will summarize. The main facts are these: Augustus, in his capacity as chair of an educational fund started by his great-grandfather, made a substantial donation on behalf of the trust to the college during his time here as Master." He pauses and looks at Janice. "You may or may not be aware, Janice, that Augustus's family income derived from the importation and distribution of spirits and other intoxicating beverages. A very lucrative undertaking, particularly in the closing part of the eighteenth century. However, Augustus's great-grandfather had a 'Road to Damascus' moment when he was arrested—no doubt as an innocent bystander . . ." Here, Mycroft once again studies the rafters at the far end of the room. ". . . During what was to become known as the Cleveland Street Scandal. The police raided a male brothel and arrested a number of extremely well-connected men, including, I believe, a duke. Augustus's great-grandfather was never charged with any wrongdoing, but his name was whispered around the clubs of London. It was at this point he launched a very public campaign against the causes of vice, in particular the inequities of drink—"

Mrs. B interrupts. "Augustus always said he went down as the most imbecilic of his ancestors. Not for his predilections but for attacking the very business on which his wealth was founded."

"What happened?" Janice wants to know.

Mycroft continues. "He invested an enormous sum into an education fund. In the early days, this was directed at promoting a teetotal lifestyle, but over time this was relaxed to include many forms of education. Luckily for the family, Augustus's great-grandfather died soon after from a stroke, thereby ensuring that no further money could be diverted away from the family."

"So how much did the fund give to the college?"

Mrs. B answers this for Janice. "Forty million pounds, give or take."

"Whoa!" Janice exclaims.

Mycroft leans forward and puts the tips of his fingers together. "And here is where Augustus showed his skill as a diplomat and negotiator." He turns to Mrs. B. "He really was a remarkable man, my dear."

"I know, Fred," Mrs. B says softly.

Mycroft coughs and takes up the story. "Within the terms of the endowment no reference is overtly made to this property . . ."

Never write anything down. Janice is learning fast.

"However, certain wording suggests there were, shall we say, strings attached. Reading between the lines, it seems the college was more than happy to accommodate these as the capital sum donated was so large and the 'strings' did not leave them out of pocket. The documentation refers to a further gift, a personal gift—or, I should say, loan. In this, Augustus allowed the college the income from a sum of £2 million that he placed within another trust. The implication is clear—although it has to be said, it is not explicit—that the income the college would receive would be recompense for allowing Rosie to live here to the end of her natural life. It was drawn up at the time Augustus received his final diagnosis of cancer—when he knew that this time it was terminal."

"Your husband was making sure you could stay here," Janice concludes.

Mrs. B just nods. It is clear she cannot say anything.

Janice looks at Mycroft. "So, she can definitely stay?" She realizes she is finding it hard to know what to call Mrs. B in front of her friend. So far she is opting for nothing, except the occasional "she." "Mrs. B" seems inappropriate and the thought of calling her "Rosie" seems farcical. She wonders how long she can keep this up.

Mycroft is once again studying the ceiling. "It is a question of abiding by the stipulations within the agreement. Within the terms she can certainly stay, but should she leave voluntarily, or because she is unfit to live here, the £2 million reverts to Augustus's estate. And that portion of the estate is willed to his son Tiberius."

"Tiberius wants to get his hands on the £2 million?" Janice is beginning to understand the reference Tiberius made to money. But hadn't he said it was *not* about the money? "Does he want the money to create some sort of legacy here to his father?"

Mycroft has never been more fascinated by the beams in the roof. "Ah, that is certainly what he wishes the college to believe. And the college is happy to fall in with this. After all, they would appreciate getting this building back plus gaining the suggested investment that Tiberius is indicating . . . however . . ." and the word hangs.

Mrs. B picks it up and throws it down on the table.

"*However*, you have found out that Tiberius has no intention of giving the money to the college and the plans he has drawn up are just a front to get their support."

He smiles a little sadly at his old friend's wife. "I believe as the popular saying goes, 'You may well think that, but I could not possibly comment.'"

Janice cannot see his eyes for the late afternoon sunlight that is reflected in the lenses of his spectacles.

All three of them sit back in their chairs.

"So what do we do?" she asks Mycroft, glancing at Mrs. B, who once again is silent. She wonders how her son's betrayal is affecting her. Did she know? Did she guess? So all that stuff she overheard about the building was rubbish. Or maybe her son would be happy for the college to have the building—just not any of his money. And what does he think his mother would do then? She certainly wouldn't be moving in with them, that's for sure.

Mycroft continues. "The information I have received from Stanley suggests that Tiberius is encouraging the college to gather information to prove you are not only infirm but constitute a risk to yourself and the college property you inhabit because of your addiction to alcohol. In this way, he is hoping to have you forcibly removed."

Mrs. B looks at them both and shakes her head. "I know to you I may seem like a very foolish woman for wanting to stay here . . ."

"Not at all, my dear." Mycroft takes off his glasses and rubs his eyes.

"You probably think my son is entitled to that money—"

"Rosie, let me interrupt you there. You recall I was one of Augustus's executors. We both know Tiberius was very well provided for."

"Yes, but he always had very expensive tastes . . ." She pauses and looks around the room at the shelves of books. She appears to be looking for something. "It's just that I do find I miss Augustus more with the passing of time, rather than less, and it is here where we were so happy and settled that I sometimes feel I find him. When I sit opposite his old chair, I can almost imagine he is still beside me and I fear that if I move from this place, he will be lost to me."

Janice sees that a tear is running slowly down the paper-thin skin of her cheek. In that moment, she chooses. If this is war, she knows whose side she is on. After all, Stan is already a double agent; she will be in good company. She will just have to be very careful. She tries not to think about Decius. She would like to be able to tell herself he is only a dog, but she knows that is never going to happen.

"What can I do to help?" she says, nailing her colors firmly to the mast.

Mycroft looks at his old friend and reaches out his left hand. He holds Mrs. B's hand in his. With his other hand, he pulls a pad of paper toward him and, picking up a pen, writes a few words on it. He passes this to Janice. "To get us started with our legal strategy, I suggest we take inspiration from this book. I imagine you will find a copy of it in this library."

Janice has organized well over two-thirds of Mrs. B's books and she is sure there are no law books in her collection. She glances at the paper and frowns when she sees the title written there. Then light dawns. Impulsively she reaches out, touches Mrs. B on the shoulder, and says, "Oh, you're going to like this." She is pleased to see a shadow of the old spirit in her eyes as Mrs. B looks up at her.

She will not say any more to Mrs. B until she has climbed the stairs to the upper gallery and found what she is looking for. She knows exactly where it is; she placed it there herself between *Barnaby Rudge* and *David Copperfield*. She returns with the leather-bound copy of *Bleak House* by Charles Dickens and gives it to Mycroft. She cannot resist commenting. "Jarndyce versus Jarndyce, I believe."

Mrs. B's rapier look flashes from Janice's face to Mycroft's and her feet start to swing to and fro. "So, that's the way, is it? I hope you won't be bankrupting me, Mycroft?"

"No, unlike the lawyers in *Bleak House*, who spent so many years fighting over the Jarndyce fortune that by the end of the case there was nothing left of it, I shall be providing my time free of charge."

"Oh, but you can't, Fred. You know Augustus would never have wanted that."

"I know he would certainly have been distressed that it was necessary to use such delaying tactics against his own son. However, I do believe he would have enjoyed the prospect of me leading the opposing counsel on such a tortuous journey that they no longer know whether they are coming or going. Oh yes, he would have liked that."

Janice thinks Mrs. B is possibly crying again, but she is also smiling. "Do you think there would be a way to get the wine back?" Janice asks.

"I am afraid to say I believe that may be a lost cause. We do not want to do anything, however small, to support their case that Rosie is an infirm old lady addicted to the bottle." Mycroft reaches into his jacket pocket for his wallet. "However, that is not to say we cannot think of other ways around this. Now, Janice, I wonder if I could trouble you to pop to the wine shop that I saw on the corner, and then we can toast our new coalition. I believe we should also invite Stanley to join us. I am not normally a man who experiences real wrath, but when I heard that Tiberius had taken Rosie and Augustus's precious wine—my wife will tell you—I turned the air positively blue."

Janice walks to the cupboard by the sink to collect what she needs.

"A bucket?" Mycroft queries.

"Well, there's no need for anyone else in the college to know what we're up to, and who looks twice at a middle-aged cleaner carrying a bucket?"

"Oh, we'll make a spy of you yet," Mrs. B declares, as Janice heads for the door.

TWENTY-SIX

The Foreign Prince

Mycroft is firm in refusing a second glass of wine.

"Only the one for me, thank you. I am driving and Elsie will worry if I don't set off soon."

A little later, he asks Janice if she would be kind enough to show him the way back to the visitor's parking. She senses there is more to it than this, and she is right.

"I hope you don't mind me taking you aside, Janice, I just wanted to say thank you for keeping an eye on Rosie. She is not as tough as she would have us all believe. Here are my details, should you need me." With this, he draws out a small, white card. Janice half-expects to see "Spink & Son, Family Plumbers. Est: 1910." Instead, there is simply a printed phone number, nothing else. Ah, never write anything down. As she accepts the card, she realizes she is having the same problem with Mycroft as she had earlier with Mrs. B. She cannot bring herself to say, "Mycroft" or "Fred" and yet, "Mr. Spink" seems absurd, so she is avoiding calling him anything.

"The sad thing is, Janice, that this action is causing Rosie unnecessary distress, when Tiberius and the college would be far better waiting quietly for a few more years for their money and building. I hope Rosie will live another five or more years, but we have to be realistic about these things. With that in mind, I have also ensured that my son, Andrew, who, I am proud to say, followed me into the legal profession, is fully conversant with the issues. He is happy to take up the case of . . . shall we say . . . Jarndyce versus Jarndyce, should I myself fall from my perch. He was very fond of Augustus and owes him a debt of gratitude for untangling a certain problem in Mongolia involving a pig and a stolen camel. Youthful high jinks, of course, but the authorities did not view it in the same light."

Janice (the collector of stories) wonders whether she will be able to persuade Mycroft to tell her his son's story one day.

Mycroft opens his car door. As he lowers his portly frame onto the seat, he turns. "I think what upsets me most about all of this is to see that such a strong woman can be bullied and lied to just because she is old. And that it should be her own son who does this grieves me more than I can say." He shakes his head and closes the door. It occurs to Janice that at least the problems she has with Simon stem from the distance that has grown between them, rather than them being rooted in dislike or deception.

As she returns past the Porter's Lodge, she spots that Stan is back in situ. He gives her a conspiratorial wink as she goes by. Rounding the corner into the quadrangle she checks her phone and sees she has missed four text messages from Mike. This adds to the further eight she has received earlier. These vary in tone from loving (*hi babe plz txt miss u*) to slightly annoyed (*rly need 2 c u this is not rite*) to demanding (*need car now!!!!*). She is surprised he hasn't texted, *wotz 4 dinner*? Apart from letting Mike know that she is safe and staying with a friend she has not replied to any of his messages. The car she will think about later. She feels mean depriving him of it, but she has had to do without it for so long she thinks there is no harm in him knowing what it feels like to wait for buses in the rain. There are two things she has made time for in relation to Mike. These are: calling the bank to make sure there is no chance he can set up overdrafts on their accounts and trying to contact their building society. This was less successful as the contact information on the website continually led her back to the frequently asked questions page, rather than identifying an actual phone number or email she could use. She wants to make sure Mike is not able to remortgage their house—again.

She has also received a text from Euan, and it has now been arranged that they will meet for a drink the following evening in a pub by the river. When she first read his text, she felt panic welling up within her, but she kept telling herself to just stick to books and stories and all will be well. It seems to be working because now she is really looking forward to it.

When she returns to Mrs. B's she finds her waiting expectantly by the fire. She has poured them both another glass of wine and Janice resigns herself to leaving her car overnight and getting the bus back. She wonders if Euan ever works a late shift.

"Are you ready for the next installment of Becky's story?" Mrs. B asks, settling herself more comfortably in her chair.

"Enter foreign prince, stage left?"

"Indeed."

"Mrs. B, before we start, are you all right?"

"So, I'm Mrs. B again, now am I? I noticed you didn't call me anything at all when Mycroft was here."

"I *was* thinking of trying 'Rosie.'"

Mrs. B ignores this and takes a sip of wine, but Janice can see the tell-tale muscle twitching in the side of her face.

"So we left Becky enjoying the delights of Paris which,

despite the war—this was 1917—was still a very pleasant place to be if you had the money and contacts, and Becky had both of these in abundance. We join her lunching in the Hotel Crillon, overlooking the Place de la Concorde. I picture her toying with a bit of lobster as she gazes over the square, where a century or so earlier Marie Antoinette was sent to the guillotine and relieved of her burden of worldly troubles."

"Why, Mrs. B, you're getting quite lyrical," Janice says, as she reaches for her wine.

"It comes from spending so much time in the company of Scheherazade."

It's Janice's turn to suppress a smile.

"Becky is joined at the table by an old friend who wishes to introduce someone to her. As you know, there were certain rules in her world, and this was also true regarding the etiquette surrounding introductions. A new 'suitor,' let us call it, required a third party to make the first advance. So Becky's friend made the introduction; his companion was a young man in his very early twenties, although Becky may have been forgiven for thinking he was even younger. A good-looking boy, slim and diffident. The foreign prince."

"Where was he from? Would I have heard of him?"

"We will come to that. He sat down beside her, and they started to talk. French was not a language he ever particularly enjoyed but he spoke it reasonably well. His German was much better. After a light lunch, there then followed what the prince was to describe as, 'three days of bliss.' They drove out in the afternoon into the sleepy, leafy countryside—far away from the fighting. They ate supper together in Montmartre, visited the cinema, and each morning would ride out on horses from Becky's own stable through the Bois de Boulogne. When they found that the nightclubs in central Paris were closing early, owing to the war, they, along with others, flocked to parties in remote houses on the outskirts of Paris, where they could drink and dance the night away. And of course, we must not forget the *cinq à sept*."

"So had the prince now taken over as a 'significant man'?"

Mrs. B nods. "And who can blame Becky? Not only was he young and attractive, he was a prince, and extremely rich. And here we come to another of the rules of *la courtisane*: a prince would not pay anything as sordid as cash for the services that Becky provided. However, there were other compensations. Prestige, of course, and a prince might give jewelry or clothes; he could order her flowers or send a bottle of expensive scent. And he might write to *Mon bébé*, as this young prince did, declaring his love, scattering the pages with childish endearments. In return, Becky would send chocolates that she knew he liked and erotic literature, which he would come to like very much indeed. But I am jumping ahead of myself. We are still in Paris, the couple has had three blissful days together, and now it is time for the prince to return to his duties."

"Where did he go? You said he spoke German well."

"I see you are imagining a young relative of Kaiser Wilhelm's, his black Germanic boots propped up on the sofa of the Hotel Crillon. You would be partly right—they were related. The prince's father, the king, was the Kaiser's cousin. The prince in our story is the Prince of Wales."

"You mean Edward, as in Edward and Mrs. Simpson?"

Mrs. B nods, looking extremely pleased with herself.

"You're kidding?"

Mrs. B just smiles at her, and Janice is reminded of Decius when he has brought her a particularly large stick.

"I guess I was thinking, when you said 'foreign,' that he might be Egyptian, like her previous lover."

"So an English man could not possibly be a foreigner? You do surprise me." Mrs. B raises a shaggy eyebrow at her.

"For goodness' sake, you know I'm never going to feel like that. I may have left Tanzania when I was very little, but I still remember the foreigners—the English visiting the dig with my father."

"So you are originally from Tanzania and your father was an archaeologist. The Olduvai Gorge perhaps?"

Janice can't believe she fell into Mrs. B's trap. Just further proof you should never underestimate an ex-spy with a first-class honors degree who once killed a man—however old they are.

She says it out loud. "You are tricky, Mrs. B. I knew you were trouble from the first time I met you in that ridiculous purple kimono."

Mrs. B smiles at her as if she has just paid her the biggest compliment. "Well, would you like to know more about Edward and Becky?"

"You know I would," Janice says, pouring out the last of the wine for them. "I didn't even know he had other mistresses. Although I suppose he must have done, but you only ever hear about Mrs. Simpson."

"Edward was what you might call a late developer. A few years before he met Becky, he had been sent to spend some time with a family in France. I believe the idea was that they would introduce him to a more sophisticated world, if I may describe it as that. I fear they found Edward very dull company: he went to bed early and his only real interest was sport—tennis, polo, riding, sailing, and golf. Plans to entice him into a world of wine, women, and song failed miserably, as did the family's attempts to introduce him to a more cultured society. Frankly, he found lunches with the great and the good exceptionally dull and he would far rather hit a ball around a court or course.

"However, along the road to his meeting Becky, he was brought together with an amenable woman who was encouraged to take the prince in hand. This she did and the result was quite remarkable. Edward decided that he liked women—even as much as sport—and he started making up for lost time. His enthusiasm for the opposite sex wasn't always in the best taste; he had no interest in those he described as 'ugly as sin,' and many of his comments about women were both demeaning and insulting. However, when he did meet a girl he found attractive, he could be charming and attentive. Interestingly, many who met him said he had a way of giving you his attention that could be most flattering. Those who knew him better understood that, in reality, the prince rarely remembered much from these encounters.

"Nonetheless, there is no doubt that his lunch with Becky did make a huge impression on him. He was emotionally immature and, compared to Becky, of course, he was a sexual novice. So it is perhaps not surprising that he fell for her hook, line, and sinker. I think it is true to say she was his first real passion. It is interesting that later he gravitated toward very dominant women, even asking them to give him 'a good hiding.' Who knows, perhaps Becky, in her persona as dominatrix, got the ball rolling, so to speak?"

"Are you *sure* this is all true, Mrs. B? I can't quite believe it."

"This is a story that has been recorded by many historians; I am merely presenting it to you in its best clothes."

Janice nods. She understands this; she herself is becoming a storyteller as well as a collector.

"Do you get an idea from all this what Edward was actually like?" Janice finds she is fascinated by the new character in the story.

"At this stage, he was probably at his most appealing: a

young boy—for all his twenty-three years—shy and rather gentle. As he developed into Edward the man, I think you would have found enough in him to make him the villain of any story. He was self-centered, vain, and greedy. Later, during the abdication, he was to lie about his wealth in an attempt to get the country to finance his new life. He could be petulant and form grudges against people he had taken against. He was also exceptionally stubborn; it was said of him that although he resembled a gazelle he was remarkably like a pig. Not even his best friends would have called him an intelligent man and, as I am sure you know, he later showed a rather unhealthy interest in the fascism developing in Germany and Italy. Racism and sexism became his old friends. Both his most experienced courtier and his prime minister would say they thought he would be a disaster as a king—and so it was proved. But like any character, any villain, there is always another side."

"So what was the other side?"

"I think the best thing is to tell you a story. During the First World War, Edward's role was primarily administrative and morale boosting. Most of this work he found extremely tedious, and as we shall see, he took every opportunity to escape to Paris or to wherever Becky was staying. However, on the morning of this particular story, he was due to visit soldiers who had been wounded in the fighting. Within the hospital were men who had received appalling injuries, some losing limbs, their sight, and others who had experienced the most horrific facial injuries. As Edward was walking through the wards, a throwaway comment by one of the doctors revealed that Edward was only being shown some of the patients. Those with the most horrendous facial wounds were being kept out of sight. Edward insisted on visiting these men and when he came upon a man who would barely look at him—a man almost unrecognizable as a human being—he leaned forward and kissed the man on what was left of his cheek."

Janice suddenly has to blink away tears. Mrs. B is watching her closely. "Exactly," is all she says. After a pause, she adds, "I know you like stories that reveal how, within the ordinary, there is often great talent, goodness, and courage. You have to allow me a few stories that give us hope that our villains are redeemable. I do like to hold on to that thought."

Janice wonders if she is thinking of her son. As she watches her friend's face—and it suddenly strikes her that Mrs. B *is* her friend—she can see the sadness etched into the lines there.

"As long as you don't expect me to go back to my husband and redeem him. That ain't ever going to happen." She says this to make Mrs. B smile—which it does—and because it is true.

Mrs. B pulls herself up straighter in her chair. "So, back to Becky and her new 'significant man.' What time they could they spent together, and it was generally acknowledged that Becky was the Prince of Wales's 'keep'—what we would call his mistress. When he was forced to spend time with the king and queen during their visit to France, he still found time to motor over to where Becky was now staying in Deauville, returning at dawn. If he was living farther afield, he wrote to her, letters crawling with baby-talk and endearments and littered with indiscretions—criticisms of the king and information regarding the state of the war."

Mrs. B shakes her head. "As I said, Edward was never the brightest of men."

"For all his redeeming features."

"Quite. And so it went on until Edward, who was really only on the cusp of exploring his sexuality, discovered another woman. This time it was an English woman he met in London who was married to a British MP. The badly written, self-absorbed, indiscreet letters now flowed in her direction and Becky was, in his mind, to be a thing of the past. He traveled to Paris after peace had been declared, and this time did not visit Becky, who was back living there. He made no attempt to contact her, did not conclude their business as a gentleman should. He did not treat her according to the rules of *la courtisane*."

"He treated her like a cleaner."

"Precisely. And this was a mistake, for as you and I know, Becky was a woman with a formidable temper." Mrs. B stifles a yawn. "And there we must leave Becky for the time being, rampaging through her apartment, throwing her Sèvres china at the walls, and tearing up a silk chemise that Edward gave her."

"But not ripping up Edward's letters?"

Mrs. B gives a small snort. "Of course not, for Becky was as astute as Edward was foolish."

Later, as Janice walks to check on her car before getting the bus, she thinks about Mrs. B's need for redeemable villains. She hates to acknowledge it, but she is a very old woman. Does she really want to end her days at loggerheads with her son? Janice can believe Mrs. B would forgive Tiberius for lying and scheming to get his hands on the money, but taking her precious wine, representing her as a drunk, and doing all of this because, he says, it is for his father, the man she adored? Janice finds it hard to get past that. She cannot imagine Tiberius kissing a man who has had half his face blown away. But Mrs. B clearly wants the hope of redemption for her villains.

And what does she herself want? She has no idea. Mrs. B's talk of foreigners reminds her of times she has felt like an alien in England—some memories more painful than others. But today? She has lived in and around Cambridge for nearly thirty years, and though she does not feel out of place because of her location, sometimes it feels like she is a foreigner in her own life.

She is trying to untangle this thought as she reaches the street where her car is parked. She needs to check if she should buy an additional parking ticket. She looks around to where her car was parked, but there is only a gap—her car is missing. Then she spots it. It is at the end of the street being driven away, and there is no mistaking the back of the driver's head: Mike.

TWENTY-SEVEN

A Drink Precedes a Story

Janice is late to meet Euan and not her five-minute, "I'm-not-being-too-eager late," but a full half an hour late. The type of late that shouts, "I expect she's stood me up. What was I thinking?" Without the car, she has had to rely on the bus, and she misread the timetable.

He is waiting for her at a table by the fire but stands up quickly when he sees her. Once apologies are made (her)—"don't worry, blame the bus driver" (him)—and drinks are ordered (him), they sit down. The fire feels hot after running from the bus stop and Janice can once again feel her inner teenager groaning and starting to wake up. *Oh God . . . SO embarrassing.* This time she has a weapon. She pulls a book from her handbag (slapping her teenage self around the side of the head as she does so) and she hands it to Euan. "You mentioned you hadn't read this, so I got you a copy when I was at the library."

"Thanks, that's brilliant."

She thinks this is a bold move on her part and hopes it makes up for being late. The inescapable conclusion is: yes, I was thinking about you; I went to some trouble to get you something I thought you might like; *and,* it is a library book, so we will have to meet again so you can return it to me. She hopes it is not too much, but Euan seems delighted. As they talk about books based on the Second World War—which is when this novel is set—she notices he strokes and pats the cover. She can't help wondering what it would feel like to be that book.

As they order more drinks, they decide to share a platter of meats and cheeses. So, not a vegetarian. You never know with these outdoor types that climb up mountains.

"Have you ever been a geography teacher?"

She thinks she may have drunk the first glass of wine too quickly.

He laughs. "Didn't see that one coming." He is smiling as he says, "Now, do I need to be a geography teacher, or do I remind you of a teacher you've always hated?"

Janice takes a big slug of wine; there is no way out now. "It's just, when I first saw you on the bus, I thought you looked like a geography teacher."

He is now laughing and shaking his head.

"I like geography teachers," she offers.

This makes him laugh even more. "What, all of them?" He looks at her and seems to come to a decision. "You said you collect people's stories. Would you like to hear one of mine?"

"How many have you got?" She is back in story-collector mode. One person, one story.

"I'd say about . . . four. But I'd quite like to make it five."

What does he mean? He can't have that many; that's breaking the rules. Then two thoughts tumble in on her: why does she need these rules in the first place? And, story number five, could that *possibly* have anything to do with her?

"So, go on, how many am I allowed? Doesn't everyone have more than one story?"

She can't think straight. One person, one story—that is the rule. But why? Is it so she can organize the stories in her head? Is it to keep the panic at bay? But now she has left Mike, is the panic still there? The answer is yes, sometimes, but not all the time. Yes, when she thinks about Geordie coming back before long. Yes, when Mrs. B pokes a bony finger into a particularly sensitive spot. Yes, when she thinks of her sister. But here, in this pub, with this man?

"You can have as many stories as you like." As she voices this rebellious new thought, she hears Sister Bernadette is back—she hasn't heard her whispering for a while. "Since you've been good, you help yourself to another, Janice." Another what? Drink? Surely not; Sister Bernadette was very clear about the evils of drink. Another story? And this is a truly revolutionary thought—rather than being the woman with no story (or the story she doesn't want to tell), maybe she could write herself a new story?

She looks at Euan, who is waiting expectantly. He has no idea what he has started.

"Ah, I can see what you're up to. You think if you keep quiet for long enough, I will tell you them all. Nice try. You don't get them all at once. You can have the one that is closest to me being a geography teacher, since you seem to have a soft spot for them. It's a good one, I think, in a small way. No sad ending."

"Do you have some with sad endings, then?" She knows she shouldn't ask, but she can't help herself.

"One," he says briefly, then he takes a pull from his pint. It is as if he is waiting, thinking. It seems he has come to a decision. Still looking into his drink, he says, "I do have one story that is sad. Maybe one day I'll tell you about it. I keep it as one of my four"—he glances up at her—"or possibly five, because it's an important part of me. But I've had other things in my life, stuff that's happened . . ." He stops and holds his glass in his hand, swilling the drink around slowly. He draws a deep breath and looks at her. "I used to be a coxswain on a lifeboat, working out of Ireland. Our family had always been in fishing, until Dad, well, he needed a change, so we moved. But after I left school, I ended up living in Ireland and I got back into boats. First, I was a volunteer with the RNLI and then I got a job as a coxswain on one of the bigger lifeboats. Loved it. So much about it: the light, the sea, the sheer scale of the waves and the horizons. And I had some great mates. But this day a storm came in, literally out of nowhere. Of course we'd been tracking it, but it spun and changed direction. We were out looking for a yacht that had gotten into trouble. Well, eventually we found it and—" He stops midsentence. "The thing is, we got the parents off and the little girl, but we lost the boy, their son. And something changed in me. I knew all of us had done our best. I guess it was just one death too many. When we landed, I walked away. That was eighteen years ago. I've never been to sea since."

Janice watches as Euan tilts his pint from side to side very slowly, letting the liquid sway in the glass. She thinks of the stories she collects and how normally she loves the unexpected. But here there is so much pain. Hasn't she devised her rules and categories to build a defense against the pain? But it's madness to think it can be avoided. She cannot file it away deep in the recesses of her library and only have stories with happy endings.

He looks up and half-smiles. "Look, I know we don't really know each other. I don't normally tell people that stuff, but if we're talking stories, I wanted to tell you because I will *not* have that as one of my stories. That doesn't mean I don't think about it, it's just I want some say in this. I don't know if that makes sense?"

"You think you can choose your story?" Janice asks for Adam, and she asks because she needs to know there is hope.

"Bloody hope so. And anyway, it's *stories* for me, not just the one, remember? And hey, I like being a bus driver. Though I am the fussiest bugger when it comes to safety—some of the other drivers call me 'Checkpoint Charlie.'"

Euan goes to the bar to get them more drinks and she studies his back, trying to imagine him at sea in charge of a boat, looking after a crew. She can easily picture it but can't put her finger on why. Stray thoughts float past as she watches him. Why was his dad the one who patched him up? Where was his mum? And what is the sad story that he does keep? She also tries to picture him as a little boy rummaging through his dad's bookshop.

Euan is back at the table and seems keen to leave the melancholy behind, so she smiles in sympathy with him as he sits down. "Right, you can have one of my stories, the one closest to me being a geography teacher." He pauses for effect. "I am the traveling bus driver."

Now her laughter is genuine. "Don't all bus drivers travel?"

"Not like this. I've never taught geography, but I do like maps, and I like to go to places I've never been before. Especially the ones I've come across in books I like. Now, you might not know this, but there is a shortage of bus drivers around the country. And if you have been driving for as long as I have, you can quite easily get taken on by a company that sends in drivers when bus companies need cover at short notice. I like to think of it as a traveling bus-driver superhero, but without the tights." He grins. "So I keep an eye out for this type of job and when I find one in an area I fancy, I load my bike on the train and off I go. The company puts me up in a pub or B&B and when I'm not driving, I go cycling and walking. I also visit places in the area I've been reading about. A few weeks ago, I was in the Brecon Beacons; last summer I was up in Northumberland exploring Hadrian's Wall." He takes another sip from his drink. "Is that okay as a story? Does that qualify?"

"It's a great story." She really means it. Without thinking, she asks, "You do this all on your own? I mean you're not married . . . or anything . . ." The inner teenager is back with a vengeance (probably payback for the swipe on the head). *Oh God! He'll know I'm interested . . . how embarrassing . . . he'll think I want to marry him.* It doesn't help that Sister Bernadette is also back whispering, "But you do, don't you, Janice?" She thinks of Mrs. B emerging through the steam of a Russian tearoom. Is this a "perfect moment" like that one? It can't be. That sounded so romantic; this is simply weird.

He's smiling at her like he's sharing some of what she's thinking, and she downs most of her new glass of wine.

"No, I've never been married. But that's mixed up with another story. For now, you can only have the one story. I'll tell you another the next time we meet."

Now she is thinking about Scheherazade, enticing you back with the promise of another story. If Mrs. B were here, Janice knows she would be snorting with laughter.

"So, go on. I've told you one of mine. You tell me your story." He is smiling at her and has no idea what he's done.

She looks down at her hands and realizes her fingers are clasped firmly together, as if, by one hand holding on tight to the other, she will be able to stop herself from falling. But it is no good. What had she been thinking? Despite her nails biting into her flesh, she is slipping.

His words reach out and catch her as she falls. "Janice, I'm sorry. Look, you don't need to tell me your story. Just tell me about one of the other ones, one of the stories you've collected. Could you do that?"

She looks at the book on the table and it steadies her. She reviews her library. She has a number of stories that begin their lives in the Second World War. She hopes Euan won't mind if she tells the story as if she were reading it from a large storybook—just the way she does for Mrs. B—as she knows it will help calm her.

She starts.

"This is the story of an Italian man who learned the secret of how to get spots of mold off just about everything." She adds, "It is a story any good cleaner would like." She says this to reassure him (and herself) that things are getting back on track—this is the cleaner and the bus driver having a drink and talking about books and stories.

"During the Second World War, the Italian was sent to fight in Africa, but he was not a very good soldier; before the war, he had been training to be a carpenter and he had been much better at that. He was soon captured and taken to England to a prisoner of war camp in the Lake District. From there he was sent out to work on local farms and in the surrounding woodlands. He felt disloyal to the land he had left behind, but the truth was he liked the countryside where he was now living. He loved the chameleon hills that changed color with the sun and the forests that whispered with the wind. And he liked the people he met—the farmers, villagers, shopkeepers, even the prison guards—and they liked him. He was the sort of man it would be hard not to like. He also made friends with the other Italian prisoners, some of whom, like him, found themselves at home at a time when they had thought they were lost.

"The people who liked him the best, however, were the people who could not see him. These were the children. Of course, they saw him walk past them on their way to school and caught sight of him striding up the hills among the sheep. But they never saw him when he was working on the presents he left for them in the forest. They never knew he was the person who carved animals for them out of old tree stumps and logs. All they saw were the badgers and foxes and rabbits that appeared as if by magic, to play with them in the woods.

"When the war was over, the man who ran the camp came to the Italian and asked him to help those who wanted to stay in England to find work. By now he knew most of the people who might offer these men jobs and he was trusted by both the Italians and the English. So this is what he did and he was very good at it—too good, as it turned out. At the end of several weeks, he had filled all the suitable jobs with all the suitable Italians. But he had forgotten one thing: he had not got a job for himself. The Italian did not want to leave what he now thought of as his home, so he looked every day in the paper for something that he might be able to do. Eventually, he saw an advert asking for applications for the role of Cleenyzee salesman. He did not know the first thing about cleaning and had never heard of the new Cleenyzee range of cleaning products, but he applied for the position, and he was given the job. Soon, he knew how to get sticky patches off the bottom of an iron and the best way to remove mold from just about anywhere. He was a quick learner.

"What the Italian liked most about his job was that he could travel around the countryside he loved, talking to the people he liked. Most of his customers asked him in for a cup of tea, especially those who were on their own and might not have had a visitor for days at a time. The Italian was happy to call by and also to run errands for them—and their houses had never looked so clean. One old lady he visited was too frail to use the excellent Cleenyzee products that she bought from him, so he gave her a demonstration, and in the process cleaned her entire house. The next week he came back and gave her the demonstration all over again. The following week he demonstrated how a curtain rail could be rehung when it has fallen down. And the following week he demonstrated how a leaky roof might be mended.

"When the old lady died, she left her house and land to the Italian and that is where he lived until he was eighty-five and he himself died. It was always said by people in the area that the Italian's house was the cleanest in the valley."

Janice looks around. She is slightly bemused to find herself sitting in a country pub. She is even more surprised to find that Euan has stopped patting the library book and is now holding her hand.

TWENTY-EIGHT

Never Write Anything Down

Janice is in the attic with Fiona looking at her current renovations to the doll's house.

"So, what do you think?" Fiona asks.

"I think it's wonderful . . . but why . . . ?"

"Why a cheese shop?"

Janice nods. Jebediah Jury (undertaker) has moved out and the new sign reads, "Fiona Jury:" There is then a blank space where "Undertaker" had once been written in gold paint.

"I've always fancied running a cheese shop, ever since I saw the most wonderful shop in Bath when John and I went there for a weekend away."

In the downstairs premises, where there once were coffins, there are now dressers and tables loaded with tiny wheels and wedges of cheese. On a small table, there is a minuscule cash register and a pair of gold-colored scales.

"I haven't decided yet whether to branch out into cold meats and possibly cakes. That's why I've left the sign blank. I was thinking maybe 'Fiona Jury: Delicatessen.' What do you think?"

"You could put tables and chairs outside and serve coffee

and cake," Janice suggests, picturing red-and-white tables lined up outside the shop window.

"Good idea," Fiona agrees, peering further into the interior of the shop.

"And the name?" Janice queries. "I guess Jebediah isn't a man I can imagine rustling up a couple of lattes with brownies on the side."

"Well, that's just it," Fiona says, sitting back and looking at Janice. "This is my business. It will be run by a woman. A woman who will find a way to manage it on her own."

Before Janice can smile or cry, she isn't sure which, they are interrupted by Adam and Decius, who bundle into the room.

"Well, are you coming out or not?" Decius spins on the spot by Adam's side. He really could be a circus dog. Janice imagines him balancing on his two paws on a ball. Then Decius glances at her and his expression (as always) says it all. *"Don't even go there."*

Fair enough.

Instead, Janice asks Adam, "Do you like your mum's changes to the doll's house?"

Adam looks at her as if she is mad. "Suppose," he offers, but she can see they have ventured into *Midsomer Murders* territory. The "how can you possibly like that" stuff.

She smiles to herself and joins them as they head for the stairs. Just before they leave the attic, Fiona says, "I've had an idea about Adam too. I'll tell you later if I get a chance, when he's not around."

Janice knows there is something she wants to say to Fiona too. She wants to mention that her friend Euan (the traveling bus driver) might be joining them on some of their walks. She wants to introduce Euan to Decius. She wonders how that meeting is going to go.

Later, as Janice lets herself into Mrs. B's home, she remembers that neither she nor Fiona got round to saying what they had planned to.

Mrs. B is in her normal armchair and seems in high spirits.

"Anything from Mycroft?" Janice asks, unloading a bottle of Hendricks gin and three bottles of tonic water from her bucket. She had avoided wine as, without Mycroft there to make a suggestion, she was unsure what to buy. However, she did recall once seeing a bottle of Hendricks on a tray along with some glasses, on one of the bookshelves.

"As I believe I once said, you are an *exceptional* cleaner," Mrs. B declares, spotting the gin. "You must tell me what I owe you."

"I think it might have been an exceptional *woman*?" Janice queries, arranging the bottles on the tray. As Mrs. B does not rise to this, she repeats, "Mycroft?"

Mrs. B rubs her hands together. "Yes, a little bit of news there. Shall we have a G&T as we discuss it?"

"Hot chocolate to start?" Janice suggests, as a compromise. She is not sure her cleaning rules allow for drinking this early.

"If you insist."

As Janice heads to the kitchen, she wonders what would be wrong with having a G&T with Mrs. B at two in the afternoon. Nothing at all, really. Since Euan challenged her rules of story collecting (one person, one story), she is finding herself questioning more of the things she has previously set in stone.

"So, Mycroft?" Janice says again, handing Mrs. B her hot chocolate and picking up her duster.

"Are you not joining me?" Mrs. B asks, glancing at her husband's old chair.

"Maybe in a bit." How can she say she must keep some of

this professional? She needs to feel she is earning her money. Geordie's return is looming, her bank balance is low, and she still hasn't been able to speak to anyone at the building society about the mortgage.

Mrs. B sniffs but after a while continues. "Mycroft is going for a two-pronged attack. He has been in touch with the committee that oversees the residential side of the college's assets, and he assures me that he has provided them with a list of legal queries that will keep them busy until Christmas. He said he even quoted a line from a statute from the time of Henry VIII." Mrs. B's feet start to swing to and fro. "I wouldn't be at all surprised if he made that statute up. He really does have a wicked sense of humor."

Janice cannot resist asking innocently, "Like the time the two of you were in Madagascar?"

Mrs. B snorts into her hot chocolate. "Oh, you'll have to do better than that. As I was saying, Mycroft is also trying another approach. It seems he is a member of the same club as the current Master. They've been discussing their shared interest in ornithology over a few bottles of Château Margaux." Mrs. B stares up to study the rafters. "Augustus always said one of Mycroft's greatest strengths was that you never saw him coming." She looks back at Janice and chuckles.

Once Janice has finished the cleaning she takes up Mrs. B's offer of a G&T and settles into the chair opposite her. "Come on then, Becky and the letters. What did she do next?"

"She wrote a letter to the prince. Now, we have to remember this is a woman with a spectacular temper . . ." Mrs. B gets side-tracked. "Do you know, she once struck one of her lovers in public with a riding whip? Apparently, he was a mild-mannered man, but that was too much, even for him. He left her in the restaurant and got into his car and refused to let her in. Becky simply opened the driver's door, threw the poor chauffeur out onto the gravel, then got in, started the car, and drove her lover home. What a woman!"

Mrs. B takes a taste of her G&T. "So you can imagine the sort of letter she wrote the Prince of Wales. Not only had he dumped her without a word, he had failed to act like a gentleman in providing her with some recompense. I imagine when he opened that letter, he feared the paper he held in his hands might very well burst into flames. She reminded him of their previous correspondence and of some of the choice phrases he had used, and of his comments about the king, among others."

"I bet she wished she could have seen his face when he read it."

"Oh, indeed. The Prince of Wales now had no option but to call in his advisors. There was even talk of Sir Basil from Special Branch being consulted. 'The Paris Woman' was talked of in hushed tones behind closed doors in Paris, London, and Windsor. When asked about the letters, Edward admitted that 'she has not burnt one of them,' and that he believed her to be a '£100,000 or nothing type.' All his previous cloying baby names were forgotten and he started calling Becky 'It.'"

"Much she would have cared," Janice suggests.

"I agree with you." Mrs. B nods. "On the next point, I have to say I disagree with some historians. Some argue that Becky was indeed considering blackmailing the prince. However, I do not believe she ever seriously contemplated this. She was a wealthy woman, and she earned her money by the patronage of rich men. I hardly think she would have risked her future income by an act that, should it become known, would scare off other men. She was not going to kill the goose—or rather, the gander—who laid the golden egg, if that is not too tortuous a metaphor."

"You think she was just after revenge?"

"Yes, I believe she wanted to make him suffer for not playing the game according to the rules. I certainly do not believe she did it because she was upset about the breakup. I suspect she was never greatly attached to Edward; he was just a means to an end."

"So what happened next?"

"Oh, you will like this . . . or maybe you won't . . ."

Janice raises an eyebrow at Mrs. B, who continues. "Our Becky got married. She chose for herself a wealthy man . . ."

"Of course."

". . . An air force officer whose father was a director of the Hotel Crillon and also of an exclusive department store."

"Let's hope she got a family discount," Janice interjects.

"It was an unsuitable match, one which Becky herself knew would not last. Her husband's tastes ran to literature, the occasional opera, and quiet nights in. And Becky's . . ."

"Didn't."

"Will you stop interrupting and pour us another drink," Mrs. B barks.

Grinning, Janice does as she is told.

"The marriage gave Becky three things she wanted: a respectable married name, money, and it enabled her to bring her daughter to Paris."

Janice looks up, midpour. "So she brought her home!"

"Well, for a while."

Janice sees that Mrs. B is studying her with a look of concern.

"Oh, don't tell me. She lets her get run over too?"

Mrs. B smiles a little sadly. "No. After a while, she discovered that neither motherhood nor marriage were really for her. She divorced her husband, who headed off to Japan, leaving Becky with a considerable financial settlement. And she sent her daughter away to school in England."

"Oh." Janice is not sure what she thinks of this. Isn't it what she and Mike did to Simon?

"Did you send Tiberius away to school?" she asks.

"Of course. He went to the same school his father had gone to."

"How old was he?"

"Eight."

Janice can feel the old woman stiffening beside her.

"You disapprove, Janice? We did what was best for our son. It was a school with an excellent academic record and was the right choice for him."

Janice wonders who Mrs. B is trying to convince.

"He may not have attended the local comprehensive, as no doubt your children did, but we believed in doing the best for him."

Mrs. B's anger is palpable. But then, so is hers. "Do you think because I am poor, and I am a cleaner I wouldn't want the best for my son? As it happens, our son, Simon, went away at twelve to a similar type of school. Why the hell do you think I started cleaning in the first place? Even with a scholarship, it took every penny I could earn." She slams her glass down on the table. "But at least I can admit I'm not sure it *was* the right choice. I'm not hanging on to some idea that because his father went there before him it must be the right thing." And because she is now so angry, she can't help it. She blurts, "And at least I didn't call my son Tiberius. Do you have any idea how cruel kids can be?"

There is complete silence.

It stretches on and on, and Janice dares not move, in case her leather armchair squeaks.

Mrs. B coughs. "His best friends were called Algernon and Euripides."

And Janice can't help it, she is laughing. "I'm sorry, Mrs. B."

"What, sorry we call our children such ridiculous names?" She doesn't wait for an answer. "No, I am the one who should apologize. I suspect you have guessed that Tiberius's upbringing is a sensitive subject for me. I do not always feel that Augustus and I made enough time for him. I think I have tried to convince myself that it was a result of our nomadic lifestyle, moving from country to country. But the truth is that Augustus and I were complete in each other's company and I realize now that must have been hard for our son."

"Have you ever talked about it with him?" Janice asks.

"No. Have you talked to . . . I believe you said your son's name was . . . Simon?"

Janice shakes her head.

"Oh, we are a right pair, aren't we?" Mrs. B reaches out and pats Janice's arm.

That evening, Janice decides to walk home to Geordie's house. It is not too far, and she would like the time to think. Did they do the right thing for Simon? She realizes she hasn't even told him yet that she has left his father. They had a very brief "Hello, how are you" conversation at the weekend, but the call had been cut short as friends had arrived at Simon's flat.

She calls his number.

"Hi, Mum, how're things?"

"Okay. Do you have five minutes?"

"Yes, what's up?"

She can hear the concern in his voice. How does she start? His might not be the perfect family, but at least she used to be able to reassure herself that they were still together. A base he could return to, if he ever needed to—which of course he didn't.

"Mum?"

"I've left your dad."

Silence.

"Simon? Did you hear me?"

"You guys'll make it up. You always do."

Is he trying to encourage her to go back? She feels she needs to be honest with her son—for once.

"No, we won't. Or rather, I won't. I have left him, and I will never go back."

There is another long silence, and she thinks Simon may have been cut off. Then she hears him give a long sigh. "Well, all I can say is, it's about bloody time!"

"What?" She can't quite believe what she is hearing.

"You heard me, Mum." He pauses. "Do you have any idea what it's been like watching how he treats you all these years? Don't think I don't know who always pulls it together and sorts things out. And I'm sorry, Mum, I know I should have been supportive and stayed in touch more, but I was so bloody angry with you for taking it."

"You were?" She knows she sounds incredulous—but also hopeful.

"Yes! I just thought there was nothing I could say. He treated you like shit and I wanted you to stand up to him. And in the end, I just couldn't watch it anymore."

"Oh, God, Simon, I'm sorry."

"Jesus, Mum, you have nothing to be sorry about. You have been amazing. I just wished you could see it. I couldn't bear watching him convince you that the way he saw things was right. It's why I rarely see him. I don't want to get sucked into his mad fucking world."

"Can I ask you something?"

"Anything, Mum. Anything you like."

"Did you hate being sent away to school? Did you blame me for letting that happen?"

"God, no. I really liked school. Okay, it was tough to start, being a scholarship boy and all that. But it gave me space to figure out who I was. I'm still great mates with the guys I met there and when I was at school, I could play sports twenty-four-seven which was all I ever wanted at that age."

She can't believe what she's hearing. Why did she never ask before? She feels lighter—ten years younger.

"Do you think we could have lunch sometime—if I came down to London?" Despite the feeling of relief, she is still tentative, feeling her way.

"Of course, Mum, I'd love that. Are you okay though? Where are you living? Are you still in the house?"

"I'm house-sitting at the moment for a friend."

Simon is suspicious; it seems he knows his dad. "He can't clear out the bank accounts, can he? Or run up debts?"

She doesn't say that he has already done that. But she reassures him that she made sure her name was taken off any joint credit cards years ago.

"And the mortgage?"

She can't help admiring her son's attention to detail.

"I'm trying to get in touch with the building society about that so he can't get money out on the mortgage, but I don't seem to be able to get ahold of anybody."

She can hear Simon laughing down the end of the phone.

"What? What is it?" She can feel herself smiling, but she has no idea why.

"Do you know what I do, Mum?"

"Not really"—she hates to admit this—"something in the city?"

"I work for the Financial Conduct Authority. Look, I won't be able to discuss your actual case, although I probably had a hand in assessing the contract that your mortgage is based on. But if you give me the name of the building society, I can find you the phone number of someone to speak to. And you can mention my name. Would that help?"

"Yes, it would." She suddenly feels like she's not alone.

"And Mum?"

"Yes?"

"Come and see me soon, all right?"

As she ends the call, she wonders if Mrs. B will ever feel like she does right now, after a conversation with Tiberius. Somehow, she doubts it.

TWENTY-NINE

The Quiet Voices

The car is not in the drive when she gets to the house, and she hopes that means Mike is out. She has heard very little from him since he took the car, just a few text messages. One (*i told u i needed car)* and then another, late at night, (*I stopped believing in love, but after seeing your smile I became a believer again. I love you, I think of you, I miss you)*. She can imagine him drunk, cutting and pasting this from the internet. The punctuation is a dead giveaway. The following morning, Mike is back to his old form: *cnt find iron*. She did think she may have seen him drive past the end of Geordie's drive the previous evening, but then feels she must have been imagining it—after all, a lot of people drive old estate cars, and she has never told him where she is staying.

The house is completely silent, and she knows immediately it is empty. She quickly collects the extra clothes and books she has come here to get, loading them into the hold-all she brought with her on the bus. Euan had been driving and she had sat up the front near him. He had been very strict about her not sitting too far forward and she could imagine him as the coxswain on a lifeboat, keeping his crew in line. He had offered to drop her wherever she wanted, even volunteering to drive her to the door. When she had smiled and queried what the other passengers might say, he had just laughed and said, "My bus, my rules." They are meeting up later this afternoon to walk Decius and Janice is excited in a good and a bad way. She has told Euan about her love for a fox terrier but not that his language leaves a lot to be desired.

She takes the things she needs from the wardrobe and bookshelves and then looks in the spare bedroom. The boxes are still there, but some are now open. She wonders what Mike is going to do with all the stock he—or rather, she—has bought. She contemplates taking some brushes but cannot for the life of her think what she would do with them. She quickly checks on the rest of the house. It is not as untidy as she expected, but it is pretty dirty. Still, she tries to convince herself, that is no longer her problem. She does take the iron out from the cupboard by the cooker and leaves it on the kitchen table with a note for Mike. She doesn't want him to think she has been sneaking around—after all, she has every right to be here. Finally, she looks through the post—nothing but a few bills. They will have to talk about these sometime and also what they are going to do with the house. Simon had texted her a number to call at the building society and the woman she spoke to had been very helpful, even offering to provide guidelines outlining procedures and legal requirements relating to their situation. Again, it made her feel that she was not alone. This had happened to many other couples, and they would get through it.

She is nervous as she approaches Mrs. YeahYeahYeah's door and asks Euan to wait at the end of the drive for her. She does not want these people invading her newfound happiness with even a look. And it *is* happiness, she has accepted that. She cannot get her head around whether she now has a "perfect moment" to look back on, but it doesn't matter. What she can acknowledge is that the bus driver who was never a geography teacher makes her happy. She tries not to look beyond that, for when she does, Nat King Cole starts singing in her ear. "There may be trouble ahead . . ." She preferred Sister Bernadette's whispering.

Mrs. YeahYeahYeah opens the door and turns away without even a glance at Janice. She is on the phone.

"Yeahyeahyeah . . . I know, yeah." She then disappears into the kitchen, just as Decius comes skidding through the archway. Janice guesses he can't wait to get away from Mrs. YeahYeahYeah either. As she collects his lead from the hook, she catches a glimpse of Tiberius in the "snug"—a barren, bare cube of a room off the kitchen. The sliding door into the snug is partly shut but she can see him appear and disappear in the gap as he paces back and forward. He is also on the phone, and he is not best pleased.

"Well, tell him to get it sorted. Do you want the bloody building or not?"

There is a pause.

"The Master said *what*?"

She can hear the sound of the wastepaper basket being kicked across the room.

"What the fuck's he got to do with it?"

Another pause.

"Her legal counsel? You're shitting me."

Janice definitely knows where Decius gets his language from. She also thinks Augustus was right: no one ever sees Mycroft coming.

Tiberius suddenly looks up and sees Janice watching him. There is nowhere for her to hide and there can be no doubt about it: she was listening. He looks at her, then at Decius, and then back at her, before slamming the sliding door shut.

She is shaking and she knows Decius's look mirrors her own.

Oh fuck.

"Are you okay?" Euan is clearly concerned when she comes striding down the drive with Decius running beside her.

"Let's just get out of here."

They walk in silence for some minutes and then it dawns on her that she doesn't have to deal with this all on her own. She is so used to Mike's disinterest and disdain that it only now occurs to her she could actually share this with someone, and that this someone is walking beside her. So she tells Euan about why she works for Mrs. YeahYeahYeah, their nicknames, and how she came to meet Mrs. B. Mrs. B takes a lot longer to explain, as does Becky's story. He is fascinated by Becky but is confused. "Right? Is she called Becky or not?"

Janice tells him of her love for *Vanity Fair* and how Mrs. B chose a true story for her that had a heroine (if you can call her this) who was like Thackeray's Becky Sharp.

"You could look her up. I bet we could find out her real name. Or would Mrs. B tell you?"

Janice tries to explain that she wants her left as Becky—somehow it feels important because of where the storytelling started. However, she does confess she would like to see a photograph of her.

Some things she leaves out of her recital: her outburst, Mrs. B needling her to find out her story, Scheherazade, and Mrs. B killing a man. But she covers almost everything else, and she finds Euan an appreciative and sympathetic audience. He laughs when she hopes he will and holds her hand as she explains the tough bits. He doesn't try and offer her advice but nor does he dismiss her concerns. As they reach Fiona and Adam's front door, he looks at Decius and then at her. "I think you're right to tread carefully." And she can't help noticing he sounds worried for her.

She rings the bell and as they wait, Euan crouches down and scratches Decius's head. She watches him carefully, suddenly anxious.

"I hope this is okay," Euan says, pulling a bag from his pocket.

There is no need for her to answer, Decius answers for them both and now he is climbing up onto Euan's knees.

"You said he liked bits of chicken. They're only small."

"You tart!" she says to Decius, laughing.

He gives his tail a perfunctory wag and looks briefly over his shoulder. It is as if he is raising an eyebrow at her. *"Takes one to know one."*

Fiona invites them in and chats with them in the hall as they wait for Adam, who is changing out of his school uniform. She is not coming with them today as she has an appointment with a bereaved family. Fiona keeps glancing from Euan to Janice as they talk and when Adam appears and they head for the door, she gives a thumbs-up sign to Janice behind his back.

"What's with the thumb signal, Mum?" Adam starts making a series of rapper hand signs to his mother. He then raises his eyes to the heavens and walks away, shaking his head.

Janice has told Euan a bit about Fiona and Adam, but not about the doll's house and her thoughts on it being an allegory for recovery. As they reach the fields, Euan and Adam start to look for a stick for Decius to chase. Part of their conversation floats back to her. It seems Euan is taking it slowly. He starts with a few comments about football. A bit of a response from Adam but not a lot. Adam mentions a sci-fi comic, but Euan doesn't go there (probably very wise). Euan mentions a Netflix series—this creates a bit of a flurry of chat, followed by silence. Then Euan hits the jackpot. Adam tells him about a new wildlife series about big cats he has seen, and they're off. Euan hasn't seen all of the series yet, but he has just read a book about the reintroduction of lions into Eastern Rwanda.

As they talk, pausing sometimes to throw a stick for Decius, she watches them and asks herself, if a heart can be broken, can it be put back together . . . perhaps not the same as before but so it is no longer the shattered wreck it was? She thinks of John and wishes he could see his son at this precise moment. She also wonders, as she stands ankle-deep in the wet grass, if she will ever go back to Tanzania. It has never been possible before because of circumstance and money, and Mike had never shown any interest—in fact, the complete opposite. But then she had been a mouse. Maybe if she were more of a lioness, she would find a way. Now, standing in a Cambridge meadow, with mist rising from the river, she thinks she would like to see the lionesses of Tanzania.

However interesting his chat with Euan is, it's clear that Adam only has so much time for conversation and soon he runs ahead with Decius. Euan drops back to walk with Janice, and they continue along the path in silence. Their silences are getting more companionable but sometimes they hit an awkward patch. As they watch Adam, she thinks this would be an ideal time to talk children, but she knows Euan doesn't have kids and she is still feeling her way with Simon and isn't ready to share this with him. And so they walk in silence—both aware that the inner teenagers are back. She has seen much less of them lately, but they still pop up. Now, they are scuffing at the ground with their school shoes. *What d'you wanna talk about . . . I dunno . . . What d'you wanna talk about . . . I dunno.*

Euan turns and kicks the teenagers into the long grass. "Would you like to hear about the conversations I collect?"

"Yes." She would, she really, really would.

"You overhear all sorts on the bus. They're not stories like yours, but they make me think or laugh. Sometimes both. Like the vicar who said to her friend, 'The trouble about being a vicar is, if you ask someone how they are, they actually tell you.' It made me think what that woman's life must be like and I wonder if anyone ever asks how she is and means it."

Janice smiles encouragingly. She can tell Euan is nervous. She finds his occasional dip into shyness endearing, but it strikes her that when he is driving the bus, he is different—completely at ease and confident. She thinks of the young man who was in charge of a lifeboat, battling against the waves. Perhaps he finds people more of a trial. "Go on," she says.

"I had a mother on the bus the other day who was taking her son for an injection—some inoculation or other—and she was trying to explain to the lad how it worked. You know, how you are given a bit of the disease and then your body learns how to fight it. And her son said, 'That's why I don't get colds.' So she asked, how come? And he told her it was because he picked his nose and ate his bogies."

Janice laughs and Euan walks a little faster, his muscles loosening as he talks. As he strides out, she can imagine him firm-footed on a pitching deck.

"There were two old boys on board one evening who had known each other for years. I'd say acquaintances rather than friends—maybe they went to school together, something like that. I recognized one of them straight away—artist bloke. Comes from Cambridge but nowadays you're more likely to see him on TV. You know the one, always wears a battered blue trilby. Anyway, the other guy was asking about his latest exhibition and then started joking that he should have bought a painting when he'd first started out. The artist said, 'Well buy one now; it would still be a good investment.' The other bloke laughed and said something like, fat chance he'd ever be able to afford it. Then he said, 'Tell you what, can I buy your hat?' and joked that maybe he could afford that. As the artist got off the bus he turned and called down the bus, 'Oy, Jimmy!' and he threw him his hat and then jumped off. I see Jimmy on the bus most weeks and he's still wearing the artist's hat."

Euan is on a roll and as he starts another story, Janice thinks that he has been too modest: these are definitely stories, not just conversations.

"There was a couple on the bus; I think they were both teachers—well, she certainly was because I heard one of the kids getting off calling her 'Miss' and another, 'Mrs. Rogers.' She was telling her husband that her last class had been Year Ten and that she had just taught the perfect lesson. She wasn't boasting; she was just saying it as it was. She explained she had a student teacher in with her and the girl had said at the end that she couldn't really tell what it was like, as she didn't see Mrs. Rogers sort out any bad behavior. Mr. Rogers then said that the girl had no idea what she had seen because it was clear his wife had the class working as one, and she had made it look easy—so I guess he must have been a teacher too. His wife said that no one would ever know what she'd done today—it would make no difference in the bigger scheme of things—but *she* would know, and she would be pretty certain that if that section came up in their GCSEs, her class would nail it."

So, Mrs. Rogers has her own "perfect moment," Janice reflects, and she takes Euan's hand as they walk.

"Do you ever collect stories when you're on the bus?" he asks.

"Yes, though usually I only get half a story as I'm there for such a short time, so I might make the rest up. But, yes, sometimes you hear something that makes your heart stop and you realize for that person it *is* their story. Like the lady I overheard whose mother was in a concentration camp in Germany during the war. She was due to go to the gas chamber, but they broke down and they had just called in the engineers—and that was astounding in itself, to think that these monstrosities were serviced."

"Yes, I read that some companies put the gas chambers they had designed in their corporate brochures," Euan remarks.

"It's unbelievable." Janice shakes her head. "Anyway, this woman's mother thinks she will die when the engineers come, but the following morning it's the Americans who enter the camp. And this young girl ends up marrying one of the men who liberated them. She wore a wedding dress made from his parachute silk."

"Now that is an amazing story," Euan comments.

"Do you ever have any trouble on the bus?" Janice suddenly wants to know. "I mean, people shouting or being rude and abusive to you."

Euan grins. "Of course. I'm a bus driver. We're considered fair game for some, especially the drunks."

Janice knows what this feels like. "What do you do?"

"I listen to the quiet voices."

Janice stops and looks at him. "What do you mean?"

"I figured out long ago that if I listen to the few people who shout at me, I am making them more important than they are. What they say will stay with me, upset me, and those loud voices will go on and on, even when the shouting has stopped. So instead, I listen very carefully for the quiet voices—which is most people. The people who teach a perfect lesson with nobody knowing. The children who eat their bogies. The artist who gives a man his hat. Or a vicar who just sometimes would like people to ask her how she is. Those people, the quiet people, seem to have more important things to say."

Janice could not agree with him more.

Later, they decide to go to the café where they first had lunch together, and to have afternoon tea. Janice thinks the inner teenagers have finally been kicked into touch and imagines them grumbling as they wander off across the field where they walked with Adam. *What shall we do . . . I dunno, what d'you wanna do . . . I dunno, what d'you wanna do . . .* She's glad to see the back of them.

Over tea and cakes, Janice and Euan cover a wide range of topics.

Favorite food: Janice, Mexican; Euan, Thai

Winning the lottery: Janice, house by the river, give up cleaning, holidays to Canada and Tanzania; Euan, doesn't want a big win, £550,000 would be perfect, sit on it for a while and think about it.

Janice thinks this is rather boring and persuades him to buy a new bike with his imaginary win.

Music and dancing (Janice threw these in together, in the hope that Euan likes dancing): Janice, basically anything you can dance to; Euan, eclectic taste in music, dare he say he likes folk music? Janice tells him most geography teachers do. And then he plays his ace. She mustn't laugh but he's always fancied learning to ballroom dance, especially the tango.

Once again, Janice imagines leaning across and kissing this man. And this time it seems like one day this might happen. Whether she thinks they could ever dance the tango together, however, is a thought for another day.

As these things skim across her mind, she looks out of the

window and sees her husband. He is dressed in a smart navy jacket with a badge on the pocket. She spots he is wearing his second-best pair of trousers and that they are badly pressed. He is holding a rolled-up umbrella in his right hand and suddenly he thrusts this upward toward the sky. This brings the group that is following him to an abrupt halt. He turns to face them and starts addressing them. She can't tell what he is saying but the group of middle-aged and elderly followers are obviously enjoying it and there are smiles all around. It seems Mike, the man of a thousand jobs, is now a tour guide. She actually thinks he will be good at this; he is a pleasant man on first meeting, and he knows his way around the city. No one need be with him for more than an hour. Then she thinks about the people he will be working for. How long before he tells them that the routes they have chosen are wrong? And a more worrying thought still, how long before he starts trying to sell the tourists he meets a set of versatile electronic brushes in an attractive weather-proof carry bag?

Euan interrupts her thought process. "What are you thinking? You are miles away."

"That it's not my problem."

"What isn't?"

Knowing there will never be a good time for this, she points toward the window. "That's my husband. But I'm glad to say he is no longer my problem."

"The guy in the blazer?"

"Yep."

"Ah, he's a tour guide then?"

"For the moment." And that is all she wants to say, so changes tack. "You said you would tell me another of your stories."

Euan is frowning and glances a few times toward the figure of Mike, who is now striding purposefully through the gates of King's College, umbrella held aloft. "Right," he says uncertainly.

"Your story?" Janice says encouragingly.

He turns back to her and gives a tiny shake of his head. "My story."

He takes a drink from his mug of tea and begins again. "Story number two is the reason I'm not married. I have been out with women"—he looks up, as if to reassure her—"in fact, quite a few, but the thing is, once a woman has been out with me, nine times out of ten, they either marry the next man they meet, or go back to an old love and marry him. And it seems to work for them; they seem really happy." He glances toward the gate that Mike has just disappeared through.

Janice wants to reassure him that he has nothing to worry about, but she does not want to enter into a long explanation. And anyway, she is much more interested in Euan's story. "So what happens?"

"Well, to start with, I didn't think anything was happening. It was only over the years that my ex-girlfriends—many of whom are still my friends . . ."

Ah, the women he has tea with. And she can't help thinking, good, he said they were all happily married.

". . . It's those women who said that when I was with them—and I'm not trying to blow my own trumpet here—that I really listened to them. And I suppose I must have done, because I was interested. Many of them talked about old relationships, often one in particular, and described what had gone wrong. Others would tell me about the sort of men they went out with, and I would ask why they chose these men, and they would tell me."

Janice is nodding; she is with him so far. She just doesn't think he has any idea of how unusual he is.

"Anyway, after a while, it could be weeks or months, they would have said all they wanted to say, and they would ask me what I thought. And because they said they wanted me to tell them, I did." He laughs. "Think I might have got that bit slightly wrong. Anyway, I hope I was never unkind, but I did answer the question—after all, they had asked for my opinion. I think you can imagine what happened quite quickly after that."

"Oh, yes."

"But I don't know if it's what I said, or that, frankly, after me, anything was better . . . but most of the women I have been out with have married the next man they met. As I said, sometimes that might have been an old love they found a way back to. Or a new romance—and not the type they had always gone for before."

Janice is now laughing. "I think you've provided a valuable service for the female community. But it's a bit sad for you though. Isn't there anyone you've ever wanted to marry?"

Now Euan is laughing. "I did once meet a girl in Ireland who I really liked. She was pretty and chatty—well, actually, more than chatty. She, well, let's say she was very talkative."

"You mean she never shut up."

Euan smiles but says nothing

"So what happened?"

"I took her to a beautiful spot overlooking the sea. I had the ring in my pocket. Anyway, I drew the box out and had it tight in my hand and there, looking out at the view, I asked her to marry me. The thing was, she was so busy talking, she didn't hear me. And I sat there and thought, do I say it again? And something made me just put the box back in my pocket."

Janice's laughter is suddenly cut short.

"I know what you're up to, you know!" Mike is towering over the table, umbrella in hand. He is glaring down at her.

"Mike, what are you doing here?"

Mike ignores Euan, who has swung round to look at who is speaking.

"I said, I *know* what you're up to. I followed you."

"What are you on about?"

"You know exactly what I'm talking about."

As he says this, she sees a strange look on her husband's face: he looks aggrieved and yet triumphant.

"The boys agreed, I never stood a chance." With this he turns on his heel and marches from the room, leaving a stunned silence behind him. Eventually, the murmur of conversation returns and the only two silent people in the room are Janice and Euan.

He leans across. "Are you okay?"

She nods and then realizes she is trying not to laugh.

"What is it?"

"I think my husband thinks I have run off with Geordie Bowman and, you know what, in some strange way, I think he's quite proud of the fact."

"You know Geordie Bowman?!"

Janice sighs but she is still smiling. Although how she is going to untangle this with Geordie, God only knows. "Yes, I know Geordie Bowman. Do you want to meet him?"

"Well, not particularly. I'm sure he's a nice bloke and all that, but I'm not really into opera."

And with that Janice decides that Geordie will be one of the first of her friends she will introduce Euan to. She has a feeling they will get on just fine.

THIRTY

The End of a Story

"You look different."

Janice stops waxing the table. She is waiting.

Mrs. B looks up from reading *The Times*.

"Well?" Janice asks. Better get it over with.

"No, that was it, just you look different." She chuckles. "I learned my lesson last time."

Janice gives some ground. "I am different. I'm happy."

"Well, that's good then. Anything you want to tell me?"

"No," Janice says, smiling, but then adds, "not yet, anyway."

Mrs. B sniffs and starts folding the paper. "So, shall we continue with Becky's story? I think this will be the last chapter, and it's a corker."

Janice applies some more wax to her cloth and settles down to polish and listen.

"Now, last time we were with Becky she was divorced and had sent her daughter off to school in England."

Janice interrupts. "I did talk to Simon in the end, and he said he really enjoyed his school. I'm going to see him next week for lunch." And then she wishes she hadn't said it, as she is sure things are going from bad to worse for Mrs. B and her son. "Anyway, back to Becky," she says hurriedly.

"Becky was soon back to her old tricks and before long was living in Cairo under the protection of a rich Italian banker. It was here that she caught the eye of our second prince . . ."

"Who wasn't a prince," Janice remembers.

"Exactly. He was a titled young gentleman, but his rank did not equate to the equivalent of a royal prince. However, I believe he never let that bother him overmuch and was happy to be referred to by this title when he traveled abroad—which was often, as he was a rich playboy. His name was Ali—"

"Prince Ali." Janice laughs. "Sorry, I was thinking of *Aladdin*."

"Ah, Scheherazade, the story of the boy with the lamp, as told in the eighteenth-century version of *Arabian Nights*?"

"Umm," Janice vaguely agrees, thinking instead of Disney's *Aladdin*.

"Well, I think for our story we will call him Prince Ali. Now, Prince Ali had spied the glorious Becky and being rich and young and rather foolish, thought he could win her over with brash displays. He had his boats—of which there were many—in fact, he once won a race in one of his speedboats in the Monte Carlo Regatta, but I digress. He decorated one boat with huge floral displays showing Becky's initials and he shone the same initials onto the hull of another. He was only in his early twenties so we should not judge him too harshly. His money was derived from a prosperous cotton business that he had inherited from his father at a young age. He was the only son and much spoiled by his mother and sisters. I believe the only check that was placed upon him was from his secretary, an older man who had worked in the Ministry for the Interior in Cairo, before taking up his post as part-secretary, part-mentor to the young man."

"Did Becky fall for it?"

"Not Becky. She would not come at the clicking of his fingers. As you know, there are rules, and a proper introduction was necessary."

"So did he find someone to introduce them?"

"Yes, he managed to find a female acquaintance to make the introduction. He did this when he was in Paris on a subsequent visit. I believe they lunched at the Hotel Majestic and shortly after, Becky moved into his suite there, where Prince Ali showered her with jewels and costly gifts."

"She sure falls on her feet."

"Or rather back," Mrs. B mutters. "There then followed a game of cat and mouse. Sometimes Becky would follow him on his travels—Deauville, Biarritz; sometimes she would delay her visit or not come at all. When he returned to Cairo, he desperately wanted Becky to join him there and eventually he feigned illness to get her to agree to come."

"But surely she wanted to be his . . . what did you call it? 'Keep?'"

"Yes, of course, but on her terms. Eventually, she boarded the Orient Express and headed for Egypt. When she got there, she found Prince Ali in rude good health and after a passionate reunion he proposed to her."

"How did the family take it?"

"Not at all well. They were horrified. Not only was Becky a woman with an eye-watering reputation, she was also not a Muslim."

"Was that a problem for Prince Ali?"

"Becky agreed to convert, and they decided on two ceremonies to mark their marriage."

"So were they happy?"

"I suspect for a while, but it was a very short while. They

had a lavish lifestyle in Egypt, of course. This was the time of the discovery of Tutankhamun, 1922. They dined with Lord Carnarvon and visited the site, Becky posing in one of the sarcophagi, her hands and riding whip laid across her breast—a sight I have to admit I would dearly have liked to have seen."

"Me, too." Janice has given up the polishing and is sitting with her elbows on the table, her head in her hands.

"However, theirs was to be a tempestuous relationship. Prince Ali made the mistake that many men do of falling in love with an exotic temptress but, once married, believing that woman should then behave like his mother."

"I can't imagine that went down well with Becky."

"Not at all, and we must not forget her temper. There are many examples of very public quarrels, but I will tell you of a few to give you a flavor. In one instance, in the foyer of a hotel, Prince Ali ripped a diamond bracelet from Becky's wrist and threw it at her. On another occasion, he threatened to throw her in the river, and she threatened to break a bottle of wine over his head. He roared at her that she was a tart and she screamed back that he was a pimp. Both carried bruises and scars from their bouts of physical fighting—confrontations that Prince Ali's long-suffering secretary often had to break up. On one occasion, Prince Ali left his wife at the theater, returning home without her. And on another, Becky threatened her husband with a pistol—she had taken to sleeping with a semi-automatic Browning under her pillow, on account of her staggeringly expensive jewelry."

"Were they still living in Cairo?"

"No, they traveled extensively, moving with the fashionable and the rich around the world. The fighting was worst when they were in Paris, because Becky thought nothing of taking up with some old friends, shall we say."

"She's something else," Janice has to admit.

"Almost a reincarnation of Becky Sharp, I feel. Well, our Becky, as I said, was soon back to her old tricks, and of course the fighting got worse and worse. Things came to a head on a thunderously hot night in July in 1923, when the couple were staying in London at the Savoy. They were in town for the Season and had booked a suite and additional rooms for their entourage, for a month. Becky always traveled with her maid and chauffeur; Prince Ali had a larger staff including, of course, his faithful secretary and his personal servant, an illiterate Sudanese boy who would wait for hours, crouched outside the door to the suite until called."

"Poor boy."

"Ah, but as Prince Ali said, he was 'a nothing.'"

"To him, maybe, but he'd have meant something to someone."

"Quite," Mrs. B agrees.

"Sorry, I interrupted. They were at the Savoy and it was a dark and stormy night . . ."

"Will you be serious." Mrs. B is back to barking. "The young couple went to the theater, Becky dressed in a white satin gown designed for her by Coco Chanel, after which they returned to the Savoy for dinner. This ended with the usual argument and Becky flounced up to their room and Prince Ali took a taxi out into the night. Becky did not go to sleep though, as she was making arrangements for her early return to Paris. This had been the reason for this particular evening's quarrel—he wanted her to stay in London, she didn't. I can only presume that this argument continued when Prince Ali eventually returned to their room, because at two a.m. on July tenth, 1923, Becky fired three shots into the back of her husband's head and killed him."

"She did *what*?"

"You heard," Mrs. B says, looking decidedly pleased with herself.

"What? How? Whoa! Did anyone see?"

"A night porter carrying some luggage was passing by as the couple came out into the corridor—fighting as usual—Becky in her white gown, Prince Ali now in a florid dressing gown. Prince Ali showed the porter some marks on his face, furiously claiming his wife had hit him and demanding to speak to the manager. As this is going on, Becky is trying to pull him back into the room and her small dog is running around in circles in the corridor, yapping. The poor porter sent a message down with the lift attendant and then hurried around the corner to the next suite to try and finish delivering the luggage. That's when he heard three shots. He raced back and found Prince Ali lying in the corridor in a pool of blood and Becky standing in the doorway with a gun in her hand, which she then threw aside."

"What about the boy, the one who sat outside the door?"

"I wondered if you would remember him. It seems nobody else did and I believe he was never asked to give evidence."

"Good God. What happened to Becky? Ah, the letters . . . did she still have the letters?"

"You are jumping ahead, Janice, but you are certainly traveling in the right direction. After much huffing and puffing, Becky was arrested and sent to Holloway, although not to a sordid cell; she was accommodated in the hospital wing. And eventually, she was sent for trial. During this time, I think it is interesting to see the transformation of Becky. At first, I believe she was truly terrified. She quite clearly said, 'I have shot him' and kept repeating 'What have I done?' For her first appearance in front of the police, she managed to change out of her blood-stained white gown into a smart green suit. By the time she was seen in court, she was dressed in black but still arrayed in a fabulous selection of her jewelry. Come the main trial, she was in somber black with no jewels and had perfected the art of weeping and swooning."

"You think this all became an act?"

"I think after the initial shock of what she'd done had passed, she became the Becky we know once more—a woman totally committed to looking after her own self-interest."

"What happened at the trial, and what about the letters?"

"One thing at a time. As soon as it was known who the woman in the Savoy shooting was, the news spread like wildfire among the Prince of Wales's faction, and now Special Branch was also involved. They acted swiftly, and despite the fact he had appointments scheduled in the UK, Edward was whisked away on an 'official' trip to Canada. The association with Becky would be bad enough but if she were to publish the letters, well . . . Time had only made them a more dangerous weapon. The endearments and indiscretions were bad enough, but more than that, they painted the prince as a man who was fornicating and partying while millions died. The full horror of the First World War was by now better understood and his conduct during it would have been viewed in the most critical light."

"Do we know what he thought?"

"Not in detail but the letters to his then mistress—still not Wallis Simpson—showed he was a very worried man indeed."

"Did Becky use the letters?"

"At this point, I would like you to remember Mycroft and one of his maxims."

"Never write anything down?"

"Indeed. So, if you imagine men like Mycroft scurrying around in the background, I think it would be safe to assume that a deal was done whilst Becky was in Holloway. There is talk of certain important personages arriving on trains to London possibly carrying certain packages. What we do know is that the judge ruled that Becky's past life was inadmissible in evidence."

"Really?"

"Yes, really, and quite frankly, astounding. However, Prince Ali's life could be inspected in detail and that was what Becky's eminent barrister did. He painted Prince Ali in the worst possible light: a wife beater, a bully, and a man with unnatural sexual tastes that no decent woman should ever have to hear about, let alone submit to. The inference was that Prince Ali's relationship with his secretary was of the worst possible kind and that he also forced his sodomite practices on his wife. All during this evidence, Becky wept and swooned, often needing to be half-carried from the court. A great performance, I feel, from a woman who offered sodomy as an à la carte speciality."

"But Becky actually admitted shooting him."

"You have forgotten the worst sin that Prince Ali committed: he was a foreigner."

"But so was Becky. And she can hardly have held these views—at least two of her lovers were Egyptian, and didn't she save one from an assassin?"

Mrs. B nods. "But as we know, Becky was primarily concerned with looking after number one, so for now she was a gently spoken French woman, bravely giving her evidence through an interpreter. And of course, you have to remember that while they were both foreign, she was white."

Janice is silent. She knows what's coming but she has only just realized the implications.

"The jury heard the evidence and within a relatively short period returned with a verdict of Not Guilty."

Mrs. B glances at Janice and pauses before continuing. "The crowd, as I believe they say, went wild. And Becky was free to return to Paris, which she did, picking up the threads of her old life. I think it's interesting to note that the play the couple went to see on the night that Becky shot her husband dead was *The Merry Widow*." Once again, Mrs. B looks at Janice, but Janice cannot look at her. "She lived there, in an apartment opposite the Ritz, until she died at eighty. I believe she was still supported by several pensions from old lovers at the time of her death. I imagine during those years she must have bumped into Edward and Mrs. Simpson, as they lived in the Ritz for quite some time when they moved to Paris . . ." Mrs. B breaks off her recital. "What is it, Janice? What's wrong?"

Janice does not move a muscle, in case a movement or a glance exposes her thoughts. She certainly cannot look at Mrs. B.

Mrs. B half leans toward Janice, watching her closely, but continues with the end of her tale. "When Becky died, it is said that the last of her lovers, a banker, I believe, came to her apartment and destroyed her studbook—the record she kept of her customers' preferences, and also some letters written by a man who had once been the Prince of Wales." She pauses again, frowning at Janice, then continues. "It seems Becky kept a few of Edward's letters to the very end." Mrs. B now leans forward until she is nearly touching the table. "Janice, what is wrong?"

Janice looks quickly at her and in a voice she hardly recognizes, forces herself to say brightly, "Great story, Mrs. B. Thank you for telling me. So the letters, and the deal, yes I can see, that's how *she* got away with it."

Immediately, she knows her mistake. She cannot clean this up, cannot tidy it away into a cupboard. The inflection reverberates and she trembles with it: not she, but *she*. The *she* that tells of something shared. Janice wants to take that word and bundle it into a dark place where no one will ever find it. She sits completely still, listening to her own breathing, which she makes as quiet as she can, despite the pounding of her heart.

Mrs. B sits back and does not say a word. Janice understands that there is no need for her to say anything. No need to tell Mrs. B her secret. The old woman already knows there are two women in this room who have killed someone. And Janice, like Becky, got away with it.

THIRTY-ONE

The Untold Story

She has no idea how long she has been staring at the electric fire. It must have been some time as there are now two mugs of tea on the table to the side of her. It feels odd that it is tea, not hot chocolate or brandy. Perhaps Mrs. B has loaded it with sugar—for shock. But Mrs. B does not look shocked; she looks like she has been sitting in that chair for a very long time waiting for this moment. Janice notices her face is the white of fine linen and feels a stab of anguish for what two cups of tea has cost her friend. Janice takes one of the cups, nursing it in her hands but not drinking it.

"When my father died, I was ten and my sister, Joy, was five."

It is the place to start. When everything changed is the beginning of her story.

"He had known he was dying and, being an academic, I think he organized his death like he had his work. He created piles of books and papers in his study, and I remember wondering, if I pushed at one, would they all come tumbling down? When I first came here and saw your books, I thought of him." She looks up and scans the now-tidy bookshelves. "For weeks, before he eventually went into the hospital, people came and went, sometimes taking a bundle of books away with them. My sister and I would sit on the stairs and watch. We had been told by our parents that he was dying but we didn't really know what it meant. This felt like we might be moving house." She pauses. "I don't believe my father would have been frightened of dying; his work made him think of man in terms of millennia, not three score years and ten, but I think he wanted to prepare the ground for what would come next. So, he organized his work, and I know he put what money he could into a trust for our education." Janice cups her hands more firmly around her untasted tea, holding it closer to her body, craving the warmth against her heart. "I think the only thing he forgot to do was say goodbye."

Mrs. B leans forward. "Drink some tea, Janice; it will help."

"Will it?" She looks at the old lady beside her.

Mrs. B looks back. "No. I don't suppose it will."

Janice takes a sip anyway and feels the warmth ease her throat. "I find it hard to describe my parents. My father, I can only capture as fragments of memories, like a mirror that has been broken. Each piece that is left gives me a bright glimpse of him." She shakes her head. "I know I am probably idolizing a father I never really knew but I do believe he was a good man, and I did love him so." She doesn't want the tears, but they come anyway.

"And your mother?"

"I think when my dad died, she just got up and left. I don't mean she physically left us; I think she saw her life as being over and . . . I was going to say she was distant, but it was much more than that . . . Even at ten, I knew my mother had gone too. She went through the motions—or some of them—but that was it."

"What happened after he died?"

Janice ignores this. "I wish you could have known my sister,

Joy, as a little girl." Suddenly it is vital that Mrs. B understands this, that she sees Janice's younger sister. "I thought of her when you described Becky's brother. She was a child like that." She is struggling to find the words. "When you give a child a name, how do you ever know they will suit that name?" She knows parents can make a terrible mistake with a name. She does not wait for Mrs. B to answer, rushing on. "With Joy, my parents got it completely and utterly right. She was like that little boy you talked of; she chatted away to herself and everyone else. It was like she had found out a secret that really made her laugh and she wanted you to share this amazing joke. If she was cross, she was very cross, but it never lasted long and then she would suddenly fall asleep. And she could sleep anywhere: in a chair, while she was eating, or halfway up the stairs. And that's when I would watch her. Her hands would clench and unclench as she slept; her cheeks looked so round and soft—and they were soft. Sometimes I would reach out and touch the tip of her nose and trace a path with my finger across her cheek."

Janice takes another sip of tea. "I don't know if she missed Dad when he died; I suppose she must have done, but it was Mum she missed the most. There were times she still appeared to be happy, but now it came in fits and starts, and she became so eager to please everyone, especially Mum." Janice stops and looks at Mrs. B for several seconds. "It was so hard to watch her change and to see all the things she did to try and make Mum happy when none of it worked."

"It must have been very hard for you too, Janice. Was there anyone else around to help you?"

"We had to move when Dad died, as we were in a house owned by the university. That's when we went to Northampton. Mum's sister, Yvonne, lived there. We had a small house around the corner from her and I thought maybe it would change things—her sister would make her happy or my aunt would see Joy was so unhappy and she would do something to help."

"And did she help?"

"If taking my mum out and getting her pissed was helping, she certainly did that. But, no, not a lot else. She was all talk." As she says this, it occurs to Janice that she married a man like her aunt. She can't believe that she has only just thought of it, or that she allowed herself to do something so breathtakingly stupid.

Mrs. B gently takes Janice's empty mug from her and places it on the table.

"What was your mum like before your dad died?"

"Most of the time I can't remember and then I'll get a sudden picture of something: her baking, her tying my sister's hair, her checking my book from school to make sure I was doing my reading. But now I don't even know if these are real memories or what I wished for."

"So, who did those things for you and your sister once your dad died?"

"I did most of it. Sometimes Mum and my aunt would go out at night and not come back until a couple of days later. They would bring loads of sweets and cheap sparkly crap and act like they had just been to the shops and that we should be pleased. But Joy got so scared when Mum was away, even though I lied about where Mum was and tried to cook us stuff and get things ready that she needed for school; she knew I was just trying to cover up. By then I was twelve and Joy was seven. She was very bright, my sister." Janice can't help saying this with pride. "I tried everything from pleading with Mum to shouting at her, but it didn't make any difference. She just acted like I wasn't there—and me making a fuss made things so much worse for Joy as she wanted it to be real, a nice treat that Mum was giving us."

"Did anyone see what was going on, try to help you? A neighbor or a teacher?"

Janice, once again, ignores Mrs. B's question. She knows she has something she wants to tell her. "My sister was christened Joy, but I wasn't baptized Janice. Well, I suppose I was. It's my middle name, after my grandmother—who I never knew."

"What were you christened?"

"Hope." Janice closes her eyes on the memory and the painful irony. "We were from a traditional family and names like Mercy, Grace, and Happy were quite common. Hope and Joy. Can you imagine what that felt like? When we moved to our new school in Northampton, I started calling myself by my middle name."

"What did your mother call you?"

"As little as possible. I can hardly remember her speaking my name."

"And what about your sister? What did she call you?"

"She usually called me 'sis' or sometimes Hope. At school, she was very good and remembered to call me Janice. She's smart like that. Picks things up quickly."

The room goes quiet, both women lost in their thoughts.

Eventually, Mrs. B sighs and asks gently, "Would you like me to call you Hope?"

"Not unless you would like me to call you Rosie." Both women try to smile, but it seems to be an art that is lost to them.

Mrs. B pulls herself up straighter in her chair. "I want to know why no one saw what was going on with you and your sister," she says, returning to her earlier question.

"We didn't really know our neighbors and I made my sister promise not to say anything at school. I was sure that what I was doing was wrong and that if anyone found out I was looking after her on my own I would get into terrible trouble." Janice shakes her head. "It seems unbelievable now."

"But did no one at school ever ask you about your home life?"

"The money Dad put aside meant my sister and I went to a private school—a convent." Janice thinks that in another life she would have joked about this with Mrs. B, laughed because she had been right; she was educated by nuns. "School was very formal. The teachers were not friendly, approachable women. Only one teacher, who taught English—Sister Bernadette—took a real interest in me. She was kind and sometimes at break or at lunchtime—never after school, because I had to make sure I was home—she would let me sort through books with her and give me biscuits for helping."

"She should have done more," Mrs. B states, as a fact.

Janice wonders how this can matter now. What made a difference was what happened back then, and she will always be grateful to Sister Bernadette. She needs to hold on to her small acts of kindness as a good thing, otherwise what else does she have?

She looks at the woman beside her and sees the tears that she thought were hers belong to the old lady. She thinks of the night that they laughed and cried—when she could not tell the difference between the two. Now she can no longer tell who is crying. She feels like she is looking down from a great height. Can she let herself fall? It certainly won't be a leap, but maybe she could just let go? If she can do it anywhere, it is here among the books, with this woman.

"My mum met someone—a man who worked where she did. Mum was an office manager; I don't really know what he did. One day he just started turning up."

"What was he like?"

"Oh, there was nothing Ray couldn't do. And the difference in my mum was astonishing. Now she was laughing, singing around the house, making an effort with how she looked. Joy was so happy, and she would sit and watch her get dressed and she kept telling Mum how pretty she looked."

"And you?"

"I was so angry. Why didn't Joy, who was so sweet and lovely, make my mum feel that way? Part of me wanted my sister to be angry like me. But part of me wanted to be happy like her—to just give in to it all. I guess somehow I wanted to believe it would be okay and that Mum would start behaving like a mother should."

"And did she?" Mrs. B asks, like someone who already knows the answer.

"What do you think?" Janice replies, like a woman who, also, knows the answer.

"After . . . I don't know how long, Ray moved in with us. He didn't bring much with him except some weights and a punching bag that sat in the lounge opposite the TV. Looking back, I wonder why he bothered. After all, he would soon discover Mum made a great punch bag. He was a small man, thin, and wiry, with quick movements. You wouldn't think that he would have filled up the house much, but he did. You could feel him everywhere. And even if he wasn't in the room, he was there inside you because you were scared he would come in."

"Was he abusive toward you and your sister?" Mrs. B asks directly.

"Not to start with, and never in the way you mean. Now, I can see he was one of those people who are naturally violent—any change in his emotions would trigger a physical response, usually an aggressive one. But that wasn't obvious to start with. All we knew, my sister and I, was that he was watching us. We would be on the sofa with the TV on, me and Joy curled up together, and I would look up and see him just looking at us with his eyes half-closed. After a while, I think I realized it wasn't me that interested him, but Joy. He watched her most when she was in one of her happy moods, when she was a bit like she had been as a toddler. He studied her like she was something he had never seen before."

"And your mother, what was she doing whilst all this was going on?"

"She was busy. Busy cooking, busy talking, busy tidying up after him, and busy fixing her hair and nails. But most of all she was busy laughing at everything Ray said. And he would laugh back and then my sister would try and join in, though most of the time she had no idea what the two of them were laughing about."

"And you?"

"I wanted them all to shut up. It became one of those unbearable sounds, like a car alarm that goes on and on and on. All this tinny laughter ricocheting around the house. I just couldn't join in and so I sat silent a lot of the time, watching my sister and watching him. That's when he started making jokes about me being a moody teenager and everyone joined in on those, even my sister. And the laughter would start up again."

"Oh, Janice." The words are barely a whisper.

"I can't do this, Mrs. B," Janice suddenly declares, defeated.

"You can, Janice. You are an exceptional woman and I think a very brave one."

Janice knows she is not. She asks, "How many stories do you think there are in the world? Seven? Eight? I can't remember how many. I read in a magazine somewhere that there are only a certain number of stories ever told."

Mrs. B sits quietly, watching her.

Janice sighs. "You and I both know what's coming, don't we? It is a predictable story. It has been played out in hovels and palaces around the world since the beginning of time. There are no new stories, Mrs. B."

"But this is *your* story, Janice, and I believe you need to tell it."

"Do I? Will it make any difference? I can't change the ending."

"That's where I think you're wrong," Mrs. B says simply. She pauses, before adding, "One of Augustus's favorite quotes from the philosopher Cicero was, 'While there's life, there's hope.' He needed that as he battled cancer—and I know it helped him—even though the cancer took him in the end." She reaches out and takes her friend's hand. Her friend called Hope. "Sometimes we all need a bit of hope."

Janice looks down at their two hands clasped together—chalk white and polished cedar. She turns her head and stares out of the beautiful window. The sky is now clear of the rain clouds that gathered earlier in the day and the light is sharp—washed fresh. She wants the pure, clean light to fill her with hope, but she can't capture that feeling, can't capture her name. It slips through her fingers like the diffracted sunshine that's making patterns on the oak table. She looks around at the shelves of books, every one of which she has handled, and she begins to think there may be a way. A way of finding that hope. She is, after all, a collector of stories and a storyteller. Maybe she could tell her story as she has told other stories?

So, she starts. "This is the story of a girl who lived with her small sister in a town where they made shoes. Their house was not a big one but it had enough room for the two girls and their mother and a man who was not their father. The mother loved this man very much. She even loved him when he scored her with a lino cutter, making her bleed. The blood that fell like water drops onto the floor was the same color red as the roses he bought her to say he was sorry."

Janice looks at Mrs. B, who nods very slightly.

"The man said he loved the mother, but he never said he loved her daughters. Why should he? They were not of his blood and the girl understood this. She also knew he would not love her because when she looked at him, her look said, 'I know who you really are.' The small, thin man rarely looked at her, and the girl thought that he had seen her look and he knew what it meant. Instead, the man watched her sister. This sister wanted the world to think she was happy, so she laughed and played as if she were. And she tried to make other people happy because she believed if she could make these people happy, the happiness would be catching, and she would be able to collect some of it for herself. Sometimes the man would pretend she made him happy and throw the small sister high in the air, laughing, and other times he would drop her and pretend it was an accident. Then he would turn his back and smile. He did not think anyone saw the smile, not the mother or the sister who was crying. But the girl saw him because she had promised herself that if she was awake, she would not take her eyes off him."

Janice feels the cool pressure of Mrs. B's hand in hers and she holds onto the frail but firm hand as if this will stop her falling. She is not sure such a tiny hand can do this, but she knows Mrs. B will not let go and will fall with her if she needs to.

"One day the man came home, and he said he had a present for the mother. It was a dog. The mother laughed nervously because she did not like dogs, then she laughed some more to make sure that the man did not know this. The dog was small like the man and strong like him, but whereas the man was thin, the dog was broad, like a small boulder. The sister laughed like her mother when she saw the dog and even though she was afraid, she patted him. The older girl looked at the dog in the same way she looked at the man, but unlike the man, the dog looked back at her. The girl thought about a book she had read at school that said all God's creatures had started life as fish swimming in the sea. She knew the dog had started life as a shark because he still had the same eyes.

"The sister tried to make friends with the dog because she knew the man loved the dog. He spoke to the dog with a different voice and rolled around the floor playing with him. The sister tried to do the same but the small, thin man made the dog nip at her fingers and toes. And the blood that the girl wiped off her sister's skin when she kissed her better was the same color as the mother's blood that dropped onto the floor like water. The man did not buy the little sister flowers the color of her blood, but he did laugh when she wasn't looking. The girl knew he did this because she never stopped watching him.

"One sunny day, when the mother was out shopping, the girl was in her room reading a book. She could do this because the man was out with his friends. So, for once, she did not have to watch him, but through the window, she did watch her sister, who was having a tea party in the garden with her dolls. As the girl was very tired from all this watching, she soon fell asleep.

"When she woke, she could hear the little sister crying and the man shouting. There was also another sound, which was sickening and horrible, but she did not know what this was. The girl ran faster than she had ever run before in her life and she saw the man was holding her little sister as if she was one of her sister's dolls and he was shaking her. He had his face very close to the little sister's face and as he shouted, he was spitting. The girl saw that the dog was spitting too. The dog was lying down as he spat, and his spit looked like the foam from the dirty part of the river by the brewery. The man was angry because the dog had joined the dolls for the tea party. As the dolls were not very hungry, the dog had eaten all the chocolate the sister had laid out on plates for them, as well as his own. The man said the sister had done this on purpose to make his dog sick.

"The girl was very afraid, but she was also very angry with herself because she had fallen asleep and had not been watching. So, she ran at the man who was not their father and did not stop hitting him until he dropped her sister on the floor. He then turned and looked at her as if he would like to shake her like a doll too, or worse. So, the girl grabbed her sister's hand and ran up the stairs to their bedroom. The man was quick, but for once they were quicker. When they reached their bedroom, the girl pushed her sister through the door and pulled it shut. She did not go in the bedroom with her as she had seen what the man could do to doors when he was angry, and she thought this time he would have to kick his way through her as well as the door.

"The man ran up the stairs very fast toward her and the girl was more frightened than she had ever been in her life. But she did not want this man to get to her sister who she loved so much, so she ran at him too. And that's when it happened. The small, thin man had small feet. If he had had bigger feet, if he had been slower, it might not have happened. But his small foot slipped on the top step and the girl pushed him with all her might down the stairs."

Mrs. B goes to speak, but Janice has to finish this; she has to tell her everything.

"The man now lay like a broken man. His arm was crooked, and his leg was crooked, but his voice was still working, and he used this to throw things at the girl. She didn't know what all his words meant, except they meant trouble for her sister. So, she did not go to help him, and she did not phone for an ambulance as the nuns had taught her. Instead, she sat at the top of the stairs and looked down on him through the banisters. She did not know what to do. All she could hear was the sound of her sister sobbing behind the bedroom door and the crooked man screaming at her, telling her what he would do to her sister to punish the girl.

"That's when the girl saw the weights that the man used to keep him strong; they were behind her on the landing. When she could not bear the words anymore, she pulled the weights toward the edge of the top step and, with both her feet, she pushed them off. And then the shouting stopped. The girl went down the stairs and stepped over the broken man and went to the kitchen and got a cloth. She took the cloth and wiped the heavy weights of her fingerprints before dropping them back at the bottom of the stairs, the same way the crooked man had dropped her sister. She did not look at the dog as she did this, but she knew she did not have to. She knew she did not have to be frightened of him anymore. Then she went to the back door where she kept her old skipping rope and she put that half-way up the stairs. The girl then waited with her sister in their bedroom. She sat with her on the bottom bunk and held her hand and whispered very, very softly in her ear."

THIRTY-TWO

Grief Is Not as Heavy as Guilt

"You shouldn't feel guilty about what you did, you do know that, Janice? You were protecting your sister." Mrs. B is in earnest.

Where does she even start? How can she explain the things she does and does not feel guilty about? Both long lists, but one a lot longer than the other. Then it strikes her that maybe she should just tell Mrs. B. After all, they've come this far.

"Do you think if we asked him, Stan would get us a bottle of brandy? I'd like to tell you about this, but I don't think I can do it without a drink, and I don't think my legs are working."

"Join the club," Mrs. B barks, and this short response strengthens Janice like a shot of brandy might. It reminds her of other times when they have bickered and tried to score points off each other. Mrs. B reaches for her phone and in a very short time, Stan is at the door. It just so happens he does have a small bottle in his locker and he would be very happy to lend it to them to save them (or him) popping out.

Once Janice has taken her first sip of brandy she begins. "First, Mrs. B, I have never felt guilty for killing Ray. I know I should and in the middle of the night I can summon up guilt for *not* feeling guilty. I know that most people would never understand that. How can you take someone's life and not feel bad about it? But the truth is, I don't."

"I'm glad to hear it," Mrs. B says, and her tone makes Janice feel that if Mrs. B had been there that day, she would not have had to push Ray down the stairs because Mrs. B would gladly have done it for her.

"I don't feel guilty for lying to the police, either. I said I was sorry that there was so much stuff on the stairs when Ray ran up to find the vet's number. He was in a hurry, and I think he tripped and then slipped. No, my sister and I had not seen it; we had been reading in our bedroom. I'm not sure, looking back, what the police actually thought. There was one man, a young detective, who I think suspected something more had happened, but he kept asking if there had been someone else in the house. I know they confirmed where Mum was, but they knew Ray of old and, I can see now, they thought there might have been a fight. But Joy and I kept telling the truth—no one else had been in the house. And I don't think anyone realized the implications of this. I do think they knew what sort of man Ray was though; it turns out he had a record of violence against women, and you only had to look at Mum, look at our house, to know. Even the walls were bruised."

Mrs. B nods, swilling her brandy around in her glass. She had insisted on Augustus's best glasses.

"And I don't feel guilty that, over the years, I have told my sister, again and again, this version of events and that it was an accident—"

"It *was* an accident," Mrs. B interrupts.

They both know this is a lie, but Janice thinks how good it is to have this woman as her champion. Oh, if only she had known her when she was younger. Or maybe it wouldn't have worked? Perhaps some relationships blossom because they are formed at a specific time and space in your life?

She returns to her sister. "I honestly thought Joy believed this version and that as she was so young, this is what she remembered."

"But?" Mrs. B can tell there is more.

"When I last saw my sister—it was the time I went to stay with her in Canada—she did something right at the end of the visit and, well, I don't know what to think."

Mrs. B waits.

"We'd had such a good time. I got to know my nephew, nieces, and brother-in-law so much better, but as they were at school and work, Joy and I had all day to ourselves. It was wonderful. She was changing jobs at the time so could take three whole weeks off—she's a specialist pediatric nurse. She's very bright, my sister." Janice feels this is worth repeating. "We did talk about what it had been like growing up, of course we did, but it was good. Even if the memories weren't great, and some were very painful, saying it and sharing it with the one person who knew what it was like helped both of us. But she never directly mentioned that day and everything she said that was sort of related reassured me that the version I had told her was what she remembered. Then, on the last night, it was just the two of us and she went to her desk, drew out some paper and an old fountain pen and wrote down, 'I remember what you did.' Nothing else, just that."

"Did she say anything?"

"No, she just started making supper."

"Did she appear upset?"

"Not at all. If anything, she smiled a little."

"Maybe she does remember and was telling you it was okay?" Mrs. B suggests.

"No, it was all wrong. If she had wanted to talk about Ray, there were plenty of chances to do that during the visit. And the smile just wouldn't fit with telling your older sister, 'Look, I know you killed him . . . '"

"But?"

"Now I'm worried that maybe I'm wrong, and all this time she has known and had to live with it. And yet I don't know how to ask her about it. And the trouble is, I know I don't ring her as much or Skype like we used to and . . . well, I miss her."

"I think you should ring her when you get home this evening and talk to her. I believe after everything you've been through together there is nothing you could not ask your sister. Is she happy now?"

Janice is touched that Mrs. B wants to know this. "Yes, yes she is. I don't think she will ever be like the child, the sister, I knew at the beginning, but maybe she would have grown up differently anyway. Meeting her husband made a massive difference to her. I think that was like you and Augustus: they met and that was it. And having children just added to that. Yes, I think they helped so much because she could be such a different mother to them."

Mrs. B nods, as if satisfied. "You should ask her, Janice. You must not let that relationship go. I don't have any siblings and would have very much liked to have had a sister. And these days, the distance doesn't have to be such a great barrier."

Janice agrees but thinks the barrier feels so much bigger when your husband has spent all your savings and you're facing the prospect of paying a mortgage and trying to find somewhere else to live.

"Now, tell me the other side of it. You've talked about what you don't feel guilty about. What is it that troubles you so much?" Mrs. B reaches out and pours them a second brandy.

"How do you know I'm troubled?"

"Oh, Janice, I knew it from the first time we met." She smiles. "Anyway, I'm a spy; I'm trained to notice these things."

Janice takes a deep breath. She hopes Mrs. B is comfortable, as this could take a while. "I feel guilty most of the time and have done so for pretty much all of my life, it seems. I feel guilty I didn't really protect my sister. As an adult, I can see there was very little I could do, but I still feel guilty she didn't have the childhood she deserved. I feel guilty that what happened after Ray died made life harder for her, and that did feel like my responsibility."

"What did happen?"

"I told you that when Dad died, Mum had all but left with him. What I realize now was that that was her way of coping—something of her was still left. Because when Ray died, she suddenly became such a presence, a force—if that's the way to describe it. But it wasn't us she concentrated on; everything was focused on her sorrow. It didn't seem to matter that he had beaten her; she was inconsolable. Even as time went on and the initial shock wore off, she was in so much pain that it was like it was physical. I used to wonder if cancer was like this. Had my dad been in so much pain when he died? And she could see nothing but her own suffering so Joy, who was eight by then—I mean she was just a little girl, wanting and needing love and—"

"There was you too, Janice. You were only a teenager."

"I knew I didn't deserve better, but Joy did; she hadn't done anything."

"I thought you said you didn't feel guilty?" Mrs. B challenges.

"Perhaps guilt is like a disease; you can have it without knowing you do." Janice realizes this is something she has never considered before. Perhaps guilt is forever in her blood?

"Anyway, I tried my best with Mum, but I was the last person she wanted. I think she knew. She never said anything but she knew those weights weren't on the stairs. She never told the police that. Occasionally, she would spend time with Joy and would cuddle up with her on the sofa. I would try and make time for that, find the right movies, bring them sweets they liked. I didn't have to be there with them. I could just sit on the other chair and watch them as they watched the film." She wonders how much of her childhood was spent watching others.

"Oh, Janice," Mrs. B says, and it is an echo of her earlier sadness.

"Then Mum started going out again and not coming back—sometimes for days. I would try and keep things together; there was usually some cash and coupons around, and in the early days she did leave us some money. But when she started drinking in earnest, I think she just forgot. So, I feel guilty about this too; maybe she wouldn't have drunk as much if things had been different."

"And maybe Ray would have killed your mother or you or your sister. Have you thought of that?" Mrs. B says tartly.

She shrugs; she has thought of every possible "what if" scenario. She turns toward Mrs. B; there is something she wants to say. "I never for a moment thought you were a drinker, Mrs. B. I know alcoholics all too well."

Mrs. B shakes her head as if this is irrelevant. "I still feel angry that you can feel guilty about all this, Janice."

"I don't think guilt asks permission to come in. I don't think it knocks and waits politely on the mat."

"Like Japanese knotweed," Mrs. B says. Janice knows she is trying to make her smile and it almost works.

"What else do you feel guilty about?" the old lady asks.

"I feel bad that I never saw my mother as a victim in all of this:

she had moved to a foreign country, her husband had died, and she had to take up work she didn't enjoy; she was served badly by her drunken sister, she was abused, and then had to deal with another death. I feel guilty I didn't understand or feel sorrier for her."

"And?"

Janice thinks Mrs. B would have been a good interrogator; she always seems to know when there is something more.

"I feel guilty that when Social Services eventually got involved—a neighbor, I think—I was relieved. And even though our foster care wasn't perfect, it didn't all rest on me anymore. And yet I still can't help feeling that I let Joy down."

"Nonsense!" Mrs. B barks this like it's made her very angry.

Before Mrs. B can say anything else, Janice continues. "And the thing I feel most guilty about is that when my mother died fifteen years ago, an alcoholic, in a Salvation Army hostel, not only had I not been able to save her, I wasn't even sorry that she died."

"My dear, you had done all you possibly could. You cannot take this on your shoulders, believe me. Was there no one there for you, looking after you during all this time?"

What can she say? She met Mike at the office where she was working when she was eighteen. She had thought he might look after her, or that they would look after each other. How wrong could she possibly have been? She doesn't want to revisit the years with her husband so she explains it to Mrs. B in the only way she can think of.

"The girl in the story did meet a man who she hoped might help her. The man was not a prince or a king, but the girl was happy with that; more than anything, she wanted a man who was kind. However, it turned out the man believed himself to be an emperor. And he wore a very fine set of new clothes."

The bark of laughter works better than the brandy and Janice smiles as she reaches out and clasps Mrs. B's hand.

THIRTY-THREE

Two Sides to Every Story

"I didn't know you knew Geordie Bowman!"

She is sitting in Geordie's chair by the Aga, and for a moment the voice throws her—she had just been thinking of her sister, and hearing her in Geordie's house feels like she has wandered into a strange dream.

"Sis, are you there?"

"Oh, yes. I'm actually sitting in his chair now."

"But he's in Canada. Don't tell me you're with him!"

Her heart lurches at her younger sister's eagerness. "No, no, I'm house-sitting for him in England."

"But how do you know him?"

"I'm just his cleaner."

"Oh, I don't think so; you should read the email he sent me. He's got us VIP tickets for Saturday and wants us to join him for drinks afterward. I always knew you were a dark horse, Sis."

"It's so lovely to hear you, Joy." Janice pulls her feet up onto Geordie's chair and hugs her knees. She feels like she is going to cry—again.

"You okay, Sis? You sound odd."

"I've left Mike."

"What, for good?"

"Yes." Why is it both Joy and Simon need to check this?

"Well, about bloody time!"

Was she the only one who didn't see that she should have left her husband years ago?

"You okay, Sis?" Joy repeats, but she sounds happier now. Happy, Janice thinks, that her sister has finally left her fuckwit of a husband.

"I'm fine. I was going to ring you tonight. I wanted to ask you something."

"Fire away . . . Hang on, first let me pour a glass of wine. Have you got one?"

"No, but I'll get one." Janice doesn't really want more drink, but it has been a tradition that they share a glass of wine while they speak on the phone. She realizes they haven't done this for some time.

"Okay, what d'you want to know?" Her sister is back.

"The last night, when I was with you in Canada. You wrote something on a piece of paper and I wasn't sure what it meant."

Her sister is gently laughing. It's not the sound of someone who has reminded her sister she killed someone. "I wasn't sure you remembered. But then, you did so much."

"Remembered what?"

"It was one of the times Mum went off. I think she was gone for about two weeks that time. I know it was a long time. I think I must have been about ten? So what would that have made you?"

"Fifteen."

"You must remember this?" her sister insists.

Janice doesn't know what her sister is on about, but now she knows it can't be about Ray and she is trembling with relief. She takes a sip of the red wine she has beside her on the Aga.

"As I said, Mum had gone, I think that time she had left some money but not a lot. And it was over Christmas. Hope, you *must* remember that?" her sister insists again.

And, with her old name, the memory returns to her. She had thought her mum must come back in time for Christmas, but she hadn't. They had broken up a day or two before Christmas Eve and she had worked late into the night decorating the house. Her sister had helped her and then, when she was asleep, Janice had added extra bits to surprise her. She tried to make Joy some presents and refurbish things of hers her sister would like. She only had so much money and she used most of it on food, but she had bought her one present, something new. She had chosen a gift she thought her father might have picked.

"Yes, I remember now," she tells the sister who she loves more than anyone else in the world.

"You bought me a fountain pen. I still have it. That's why I wrote that note with the same pen; I thought you would see and understand."

"I understand now," is all she can manage to say. "Joy?"

"Yes."

She has to ask her, she has to know, once and for all. "Do you remember what happened to Ray?"

"Of course, you don't forget something like that."

"But do you really know?"

"What?" Her sister sounds suspicious.

Silence. She cannot find the words.

Her sister helps her. "What, that you killed him?"

Her breath comes out in a rush. She always says it: her sister is very bright.

"You there, Sis?" Joy sounds concerned.

"How long have you known?"

"Always. I knew the weights and skipping rope weren't on the stairs. I just didn't think you wanted to talk about it."

Janice doesn't know where to start. "And you're . . . you're okay with it?"

"Of course. He was going to kill us, Hope. Don't kid yourself it would have stopped there. You do know you are the best sister in the world, don't you? You do know how much I love you? You have *never* let me down."

Janice can't stop the tears now. "I'm just so sorry it wasn't better for you."

"I had you; it was okay."

Janice thinks of Fiona and how she had told her the same thing: Adam has you.

"Can I ask you something I've always wondered?" her sister asks.

"Anything."

"Did you kill the dog, too?"

Janice is laughing now, and even though she loves dogs, and an animal's death shouldn't be funny, she can't help saying, "No. You did."

Her sister is also laughing. "Fuck, he was an evil bastard. Well, they say dogs get like their owners."

Janice knows this can't always be true—you only have to look at how some fox terriers turn out.

"Will you come and see me soon?" Joy asks.

"I really want to, but I have to sort out where I'm living and . . ." Janice finds it hard to admit to her younger sister that she has money troubles.

"Sod that. We'll work out some dates and I'll send you a ticket."

"But you can't do that."

"Of course I can. I'm your sister."

And Janice finds she has no answer to that.

THIRTY-FOUR

The Boy and the Dog

Janice has managed to clean pretty much all of the house without bumping into Mrs. YeahYeahYeah. If she hears her coming into one section, she scoots into another. She thinks it is a good thing that the wooden floors make footsteps so loud as it's easy to hear her employer approaching. As she glides as quietly as she can from room to room (she left her shoes by the front door), Decius follows her. He's been giving her his, *"What the fuck is wrong with you, woman?"* look, but she doesn't care. She's been thinking of her sister (and how bright she is) and about Mrs. B. She knows that just telling Mrs. B her story has made a difference to her—that and talking to her sister. Nothing has changed but everything has shifted—in a good way.

She has received a text from Euan, and they are meeting later to walk Decius with Adam. She can't decide if she could ever tell Euan her story. She would like to think she could, but there is no scenario she can think of—and she has conjured up many—in which she would find the words. So instead, she is thinking about two other things. Possibly learning the tango with him, and picturing a time when they might go to Canada together. For this, she allows her imagination the luxury of no money troubles and a new wardrobe of clothes.

"Ah, there you are."

She spins round at Tiberius's words. She hadn't heard him coming. She sees he is wearing sheepskin moccasins and she also notices, for the first time, he has very bandy legs.

"Can you tell me what is the meaning of this?" he demands, holding up a bottle of brandy that is three-quarters empty. She's no expert on brandy but she's pretty certain this is the bottle that she and Mrs. B shared some of yesterday.

She remains silent, even though thoughts are rattling through her head like a Gatling gun.

Have you been bothering Mrs. B again?

Is Mrs. B okay?

What a shit son you really are.

Has Mycroft been up to something?

You have incredibly bandy legs.

That's Stan's brandy.

Mustn't say anything to get him into trouble.

Why do you think you can talk to me like this?

Her final thought is the one that sticks: *What makes this supercilious man think he can talk to people like they are some sort of sub-species?*

"I *said*, what is the meaning of this?"

Decius nudges her leg, just in time. She looks down at him and remembers what's at stake. His expression is particularly eloquent this morning; *"Just don't go there."*

"I'm sorry, I have no idea what you're talking about," Janice says, sweeping past him with the specially designed, long-handled floor duster (with cashmere filaments).

Tiberius reaches out and grabs her arm. It is not a strong grip, but nevertheless, he is touching her, and she feels the degradation deep inside. She stops stock-still and looks at his hand and then up at his face. He hastily removes his hand.

"Do not ever, *ever* presume to touch me again," she says in a voice that barely contains her rage.

From the ground just to the left of her comes a low guttural growl. Decius has lost all his bounce, and she can tell that if she were to put her hand on him now his flank would be rigid muscle. The dog does not take his eyes off Tiberius for a second. She knows she is in trouble but part of her celebrates that, as she found her inner lioness, the dog she loves is a wolf by her side.

The spell is broken by Tiberius leaving the room.

"I don't think this is working, do you?" It's not a question. "Finish at the end of this week. My wife will pay what is due."

Her fury gets her to the boot room to find her coat and fetch Decius's lead. It gets her down the drive and across the lane and into the field. By the time she is halfway to Fiona and Adam's house, she is weakening and beginning to feel sick. She does not want to look at Decius who is bouncing proudly along beside her. She cannot see his face, but she knows what it would say.

"Oh Decius, what have we done?" she says out loud.

He turns to look at her and she was right, his expression was just as she expected: *"That fucking showed him, the twat."*

How do you tell a fox terrier that everything is ruined, and you won't be seeing each other again?

And Adam? Oh God, what is she going to say to Adam? This upsets her more than her own pain, as she feels she has betrayed a child. And Adam is still such a child. She has to find a way around this. She knows Tiberius will never reconsider her position. Decius chose his side and there is no way back from that. But perhaps she could get Adam to approach Mrs. Yeah-YeahYeah about dog walking? She doesn't have to know that Adam knows her, and she will need someone to take her place.

"What's wrong?" Euan is striding toward her before she gets to the start of the path to Fiona and Adam's front door.

Is it that obvious? Or maybe the lifeboatman is an old hand at spotting trouble? She tries to form the sentences she needs but they come out as single words that make no sense. Euan steps toward her and folds her into him, wrapping his arms and coat (that would keep you warm climbing Snowdon) around her. As she sobs, she can feel the fleece of his coat against her face, and his chin and cheek against her hair. But most of all, she feels the comfort of being held by someone she is falling in love with.

Eventually, they untangle, having to spin on the spot to unwind Decius's lead that has become wrapped around their legs. "We will find a way out of this," he tells her. She would like to believe him, but he has never met Tiberius.

She takes a deep breath. "We'll see," is all she can manage.

By now, Adam is in the drive and he and Decius are taking part in their bouncing, circling greeting ritual. This only makes her feel worse. She will just have to find a way for Adam to see Decius at the very least. She sees Fiona standing in the doorway and heads over to her. She explains as quickly as she can what has just happened.

"But that's terrible." Fiona puts her hand on her arm, and she is struck by the contrast of how she feels compared to when Tiberius touched her. "Look, I've been meaning to say something to you for ages, and now might be a good time to tell you and Adam." Fiona calls across to her son.

"Adam, Janice has been telling me that she might not be able to walk Decius anymore. She is hoping she can work something out so you can still see him, but I've had this idea. I've even spoken to some breeders. How would you like a dog like Decius?"

Janice can see the car crash coming before Fiona does. But

then, she loves this fox terrier, and she knows there could never be another dog like Decius.

Adam stands still for almost thirty seconds. Then he bellows, "What, and you think one day you could just get me a new dad too? Just buy me a new one. New dad, new fucking dog." He's shifting his weight from foot to foot. "What is wrong with you all?" Now he is screaming at them. Janice glances to her right and sees Fiona's face is completely white and her mouth is open. "What is wrong with you people?" he repeats. "You never talk about Dad or if you do, he has to be some perfect fucking hero who never did anything wrong. Well, sometimes he was crap. Why won't anyone just say it? Sometimes he let us all down. He couldn't get up in the morning or couldn't do anything 'cos he was so doped up. But no, it's Dad, the perfect dad."

He stamps his foot hard on the ground and it is part small boy, part furious adult. "Do you think I love him less because he was shit sometimes, or wouldn't miss him if you said these things?" He spins around to Janice. "And no one ever talks about him. You . . . you," he hurls at her, "I thought you might be different. I thought you might ask me about him." Adam is crying now, and she can see Euan plant his feet more squarely on the ground, and through her shock, it makes her think of a man steadying himself before a wave hits. "How could you think I would want another dog? And you think I don't know why we never go into the woods? It's always the fields or the meadow. What do you think I'm going to do? Find a tree like Dad and fucking hang myself? What is wrong with you all?" And with that, he turns and he runs. He dodges past Euan and, with Decius fast by his side, he sprints as if his life depends on it. Janice watches as he puts as much distance as he possibly can between himself and the people who have let him down. In the stunned silence that follows, all she can think is that she is glad Decius is with him.

Fiona crashes down so she is sitting on the low garden wall. It is as if her legs have given out on her without warning. She starts to rock back and forward. The sound she makes is like nothing Janice has ever heard before; it is like listening to an animal in pain. She takes one step toward Fiona and then, uncertainly, one in the direction Adam has gone. Euan is suddenly at her side. "Let's get Fiona inside." He turns to the figure on the wall and crouches down beside her. "Fiona, come with me and Janice. We're going to find Adam and help him, but first, you need to help us."

Her cry catches on her intake of breath and she looks up at him. He repeats, "I can help you, Fiona, but we need your help."

She stops rocking and looks uncertainly at Janice. Janice takes her hands and helps her to her feet. "Come on inside."

Fiona half stumbles with them into the house, and Janice leads them all into the kitchen as she doesn't know where else to go. She sits beside Fiona at the kitchen table. Euan pulls another chair around so he can look directly at Fiona. "Now, Fiona, where do you think Adam would go?"

She shakes her head. It's as if she has lost the power of speech.

"Would he go to a friend's or is he more likely to want to be on his own?"

"He doesn't have many friends," Fiona manages and she starts to cry. Janice takes her hand.

"So he's more likely to be on his own. Where would he go? He mentioned a field, a meadow, and a wood." Fiona flinches at the mention of the woods, but Euan keeps going. "Anywhere else you can think of?" Fiona shakes her head. "Does he have a mobile?"

At this Fiona perks up. "Yes. Can we track him through that?"

Euan starts to say something, but Janice interrupts him.

She knows what Adam's mobile looks like and she can see it sitting on the kitchen dresser. "Not to worry," Euan says to Fiona and grabs a notebook and pen from beside the phone. Then he checks his watch. He quickly scribbles a list. "Fiona, this is what I want you to do."

She looks up at him, and Janice is torn by the look of hope and anxiety in her eyes.

Euan smiles at her. "It will be all right, Fiona. Adam is a sensible lad; he's just upset and needs some time on his own. What we're going to do now is just a precaution, okay." He repeats, "He's going to be fine." Euan then shows her the list he has made. "Janice and I are going to do a quick sweep of the three places he mentioned. You need to stay here in case he comes back. We will all take each other's mobile numbers so we can stay in touch. He checks his watch again. "Sunset is in an hour, so we'll give it forty minutes maximum to look, then we'll come back here. While we're away, I want you to complete that list for me and collect some things. We need a recent photo . . ."

Fiona looks up at him in alarm.

"This is just a precaution. At work they call me Checkpoint Charlie; I just can't help being over-prepared." He smiles down at her. "I used to work for the RNLI. This is just standard stuff, but best to be on the safe side. We probably won't need any of it."

Fiona lets out a breath and nods.

"So, you're going to get me a photo, write down a description of what he is wearing—"

Fiona interrupts. "He didn't have a coat; he only had a school shirt on."

"All the more reason why he'll come back quickly," Euan says reassuringly. "I also want you to list his friends—names and numbers. And any social media he's on. Do you know his passwords?"

Fiona nods.

"Good. Then I want you to think of other places he might go, especially somewhere that might be important for him and his dad. Just list them down here." He points to the notebook. "Right, we're going to head off, but we'll be back in forty minutes, if not sooner. He won't have gone far. And he has Decius with him. He won't let anything happen to that dog, you can depend upon it. He won't put him in any danger."

Fiona looks up at him. "What was I thinking of? I can't believe I was so stupid. I just thought . . ." She can't finish.

Janice gives her a quick hug around the shoulders. "You were just thinking about what would make him happy. There's nothing wrong with that. It'll work out; he just needs some time, that's all."

Janice follows Euan into the hallway. "So what do we do now?"

"Do you know where the woods are? I know the meadow and fields, as I've been there with you. Would you be okay to go to the woods?"

"Yes, it's not far," she says.

"You're sure you're okay with that?'" Euan asks, suddenly anxious.

"Really, I'll be okay."

"Right, no more than forty minutes, then we meet back here."

"What then? What if we don't find him?"

"We call the police."

"What, so soon? Don't we have to wait a few hours or something?"

"No, absolutely not. We call them straight away. Adam is a child, he is distressed, and not dressed for a cold night. They have the manpower we may need." He leans forward and kisses her swiftly on the cheek. "I said *may* need. I'm just being

Checkpoint Charlie. And remember, I wasn't kidding when I said he won't let anything happen to Decius."

They split up at the end of the drive and Janice walks and then half runs to the woods. Now she is on her own she thinks about all that Adam said. Why hadn't she asked him about his dad? She had certainly sensed he knew more about his troubles than Fiona was prepared to admit. Why not ask him then? Had she not wanted to upset him? Or did she think it wasn't her place as she was "just the cleaner"? She has been angry with Mike for seeing only the limitations and stigma associated with her job. Has she hidden behind it too? *Don't get involved Janice, you're only the cleaner.*

She reaches the edge of the wood and heads down the main path, last autumn's leaves crackling underfoot. As the trail leads down, she can see mist gathering in the hollow and this frightens her far more than the dark shapes of trees rising up on each side of her. What if Adam goes down to the river? Could he lose his way, miss his footing as the mist rises? She calls as she walks, and occasionally roars "Decius," into the gloom. She is past caring what anyone might think. She knows her dog would answer her. And as she thinks this, she feels part of her breaking. He stood by her side and defended her and now she has no way to even spend an occasional few hours with him. She stops this thought in its tracks. She needs to find Adam. This is not the time to feel sorry for herself. "Adam!" she shouts as loudly as she can, again and again, until her throat aches.

She heads off the main path, taking a spur to the edge of the woods that looks out over the broad Cambridge countryside. She knows exactly where she's going. It's one of the tallest trees on the small ridge. It's the oak tree that Adam's father, John, climbed before hanging himself. He chose one of the highest branches, so Janice presumes he must have stood on the branch for some time looking at the view. What had that poor man been thinking? Or maybe he'd been beyond rational thought? She finds the tree she's looking for and circles it, hoping to see a crouching figure, arms wrapped around a small dog. Nothing.

By the time she gets back to the house, Euan is already there and is on the phone to the local police. Fiona is more composed and offers her a cup of tea and thanks. "You okay?" Janice asks her.

"Yes, Euan is being amazing."

Janice has to agree with her. She's too distressed to consider it now but she is aware that he is a man quietly in control. He is an ordinary man who is extraordinary. But isn't that what her favorite stories are about? She is distracted by more people arriving in the kitchen. Fiona makes some hasty introductions. Euan has asked Fiona to gather any neighbors she can think of who would help in a search. They need to be ready when the police arrive. Without knowing what else to do, Janice starts to organize more cups of tea and to dig out thermos flasks and water bottles.

The next few hours stutter past. Sometimes there is a flurry of activity, sometimes things stall as calls are made or groups are reorganized. Janice has to hand it to the police, they are amazing—calm, kind, and professional, and—what she hadn't expected—sometimes humorous, keeping Fiona's spirits up. Nothing seems too much trouble, and she gets no sense they are expecting anything but a good outcome. She draws Euan aside on one of his trips back to the house. "Do you think they're worried?" It is now eleven p.m., the temperature has dropped, and the police cars and lights remind Janice of a crime scene. "They're being very thorough," he says, before heading out again. But she can tell by the tone of his voice he is anxious.

She hears the cry from the kitchen. It cuts through the night, and she pushes past a neighbor to get outside. In the drive, Fiona is on her knees in the gravel, her arms wrapped around her son. Adam is bent over her, and it is impossible to see where mother starts and son begins. They sway gently together. She can hear Adam's voice repeating, "I'm sorry, Mum." Standing back slightly from the two figures is Tiberius. There is no sign of Decius, and Janice is suddenly afraid. The tableau abruptly breaks apart. The police surround the figures, helping them inside; neighbor turns to neighbor and the murmur of relieved conversation rises above the sound of police cars starting their engines. Figures wander across her field of vision. She cannot see a dog anywhere and she cannot see Euan.

Across the driveway, she sees that Tiberius is looking at her. She weaves between the stragglers to get to him. As she approaches, she can see he is rigid with anger. He doesn't even wait for her to get within ten feet of him.

"You have been using a twelve-year-old boy to walk our pedigree dog whilst taking the money. Not only is that dishonest and fraudulent but it has put a valuable animal at risk—"

She stops him. "Where's Decius?"

"He is back home where he belongs, but that is no thanks to you. He has been missing for over seven hours, and you did not have the courtesy or decency to call us—"

Again, she interrupts, her relief making her brave. "Were you in?"

"That is beside the point."

"I called the house every hour to let you know what was happening, but no one answered."

"As it so happens, we were at a wine tasting—"

"Who brought Decius home?"

"The boy did."

Ah, Adam must have read the tag on his collar. Euan had been right—he wouldn't let anything happen to Decius.

"Was he waiting for you when you got home then?"

"Yes . . ."

"How long had he been waiting?"

"I neither know nor care. That is not the issue here."

But it is an issue for her. She is distressed by the thought of Adam waiting on the back step in the cold, whilst Fiona was going out of her mind with worry. Of course Adam wouldn't have known there was a key safe to use when no one was home that would have let him into the back porch and boot room. Her only comfort is the thought that Decius was with him. Suddenly she feels utterly exhausted. "Okay, the main thing is that Adam is home now, and Decius is fine. So all's well."

"All is very far from well—"

"Look, all *is* well. You have no idea what Adam has been through." Despite her overwhelming tiredness, she wants to make some push to help Adam. "He really does love your dog; he would never let anything happen to Decius. I can understand you no longer wish to employ me. But please, *please* would you consider letting him be your dog walker? He really is very sensible. I mean, he found your address and got your dog home safely."

Tiberius blows out a sharp breath and shakes his head as if he can't believe what he is hearing. "Is there something wrong with you? Are you a complete simpleton? You think I would entrust a valuable animal to that boy, just because you think it would—"

Janice suddenly holds her hand up in the air, all tiredness

miraculously gone. She thrusts her palm toward Tiberius as if she was one of the police officers on the drive and has decided to start directing traffic. Tiberius stops midsentence and looks from side to side in confusion. "Would you do me and the rest of the world a favor and shut up, you pompous arse!" Janice roars. Everyone around stops as if playing musical statues. "I have to tell you, I have never met such a rude, arrogant, self-opinionated snob in my life. You are without doubt the most ignorant man I have ever met. And I was married to a complete imbecile, so trust me, I know what I'm talking about. As for calling me fraudulent, why, you are nothing but a common thief. You know it and I know it." She spins around on her heel to look at the people on the drive, who suddenly burst into life. "And now they know it too."

Tiberius has turned a deep shade of crimson. "That is certainly slanderous, and I have a good mind to—"

Janice steps toward him, and Tiberius takes a hasty step back into the flowerbed. "You just try me. You wouldn't dare, you pathetic excuse for a human being. It is only out of respect for your mother, who is worth a hundred of you, that I do not tell you to BUGGER OFF!"

She spins once more on her heel and marches away, walking straight into Euan.

"Illogical ending but otherwise magnificent." He is laughing. "And Janice?"

"Yes!" she shouts.

"Remind me never to piss you off."

THIRTY-FIVE

Words Written on Paper

This time the ceiling is the palest of greens. Janice is getting used to waking up in different beds. This one is neither too soft nor too hard, and she thinks of the story of Goldilocks and the three bears. She is in bed on her own and she can't quite decide if this is a good or a bad thing. By the time the house had been cleared of people and Janice had prepared bacon and egg sandwiches for Fiona, Euan, Adam, and herself it was two thirty a.m., and Fiona had insisted they stay over. She had taken Janice tactfully aside and inquired as to the sleeping arrangements. For a brief second, Janice had been tempted, but now she is glad she opted for separate rooms—she thinks.

Adam had wanted to come to the kitchen to see Euan and Janice. He had thanked Euan and apologized to her, before taking his food and drink up to his room. He had looked so small and white and shaken—but Janice thought she could glimpse the man he would become. There had been a certain dignity in the way he spoke, and she felt he meant what he had said. And she had meant it too when she told him how sorry she was that she hadn't asked about John and said she would like to know more about his dad and hoped he would take her through some photos one day soon. Neither of them mentioned Decius.

Lying in this new bed, staring at the ceiling, she tries to think about what lies ahead, but she gets nowhere—so much is uncertain. Instead, she thinks of how she feels about what has happened to her over the past few weeks. It's difficult to untangle this, but she is left with a sense of extremes. It is as if her emotions have been shot all around a pinball machine and there are only two places for them to fall. Either in the prize slot (lots of stars lighting up) or they are catapulted into the bowels of the machine. She wonders why she ever complained that her life was boring—wouldn't that be better? She dismisses the thought immediately. At least now she knows she's alive.

On the good side of her emotional pinball are: very definitely, Euan—she likes to start with him, and it strikes her that she would like to end with him too. So Sister Bernadette had been right when she whispered into her ear in the café overlooking King's College.

Also, very firmly on the positive side are her feelings about her sister and Mrs. B. She includes her other friends in this too and decides there and then to stop telling herself she is just a cleaner. There is nothing wrong with being a cleaner, but she can be a friend too. After all, she is a multitasking woman who can use a blowtorch, sander, and chainsaw.

Then there is the way she feels about her past, her story. She knows this is not all good, but she does appreciate that she has unburdened some of her guilt. She is now at ease with how she looked after her sister. And if not exactly at peace with what she did to Ray, she knows she can live with it. She wonders if part of storytelling is not only about sharing the good things in life but also enabling the storyteller to send the bad things out, to let them disperse like dust in the wind.

She thinks about Simon, too. He had to postpone their lunch but is coming up to Cambridge in a few days' time to take her out and is going to stay over. He very definitely falls on the good side. She can't wait to see him, and now she has left Mike, and Simon has been able to say what has been keeping him away, she can look forward to him being part of her life. She is also able to look back at his childhood with a less jaundiced eye. She *was* a good mother to him and she thinks, like Joy, she made certain that her son had a completely different upbringing to her.

It is much harder to think about the things that fall into the pit of her emotional pinball machine. But she feels she needs to take these out and examine them too. She deals with the easiest first. What is she going to do when Geordie gets back in less than a week? She has little money and currently nowhere to go. She thinks back to sitting in her car outside the old barns—there is the same sense of panic, but she realizes there is no longer a feeling of despair. She will find a way. Now she has people she could ask for help. She has friends and . . . she gets stuck here, what would she call Euan? Boyfriend does not describe a fifty-five-year-old man, and they are not "lovers." At least, not yet. The thought makes her heart race faster and the pulse of it reminds her of the staccato steps of the tango. She tries to concentrate. Not "lover" so . . . what? She once read a story about a Scottish couple—very appropriate for a man from Aberdeen—and whilst the tale was not remarkable enough to make it into her mental library, she came across a phrase she liked. The unmarried couple living together referred to each other as their "bidey-in." She thinks one day she would like Euan to be her bidey-in.

The last two things she knows she has to take out and examine are much harder to deal with. One very much in the present, one from the past. There is a fox terrier that she loves who she now knows she cannot see. And, included in this, is the fact that a young boy who has lost his dad cannot see him either. There is nowhere to go with this thought. All that is left is grief and loss. She knows saying "he is only a dog," is no way to describe Decius. And anyway, she now appreciates he is a wolf.

The final thing she thinks about is her mother. She knows this is at the heart of the guilt that for years has eaten away at her like a cancer. She can reconcile her feelings about her sister, but at the core of her she believes she let her mother down. Particularly as her mother slipped into alcoholism. Logic and reason have no place here. They cannot help her. She believes that her actions led to her mother's drinking and, ultimately, her death. The fact that she could not mourn her death only pushes the guilt, like a knife, in deeper.

There is a knock, and Fiona pops her head around the door. "I've brought you some tea." The jolt back to the present makes her feel hopeful for Fiona. She does have a chance to put things right with Adam. Over their late-night snack, she told them she and Adam had had a long talk in his bedroom when he got back. She said there had been lots of tears but also, she felt what had happened had forced them to be more honest with each other. She said she was sure they would look back on this awful night as a good thing.

Fiona sits on the edge of the bed. "So, tell me more about Euan. He is *lovely*." As Janice explains a bit about how they met and her current circumstances, she remembers she has only heard two of his four (or possibly five) stories. "So, do you guys think this is a serious thing?" Fiona asks. Janice is not ready to share her thoughts on a bidey-in, so just laughs and thanks her for the tea.

Adam appears briefly at breakfast. It is a Saturday, so he has no school to rush off to. He is quiet and withdrawn, and

Janice thinks of all that the young boy is dealing with in terms of loss: his father, John; and now Decius. As she pours herself a second coffee, she sees Euan go over to Fiona. He says something quietly to her and Fiona looks up at him in surprise, and there is something else in her look that Janice can't quite read. She nods at Euan and pats his arm, and Euan leaves the room. Janice looks at her enquiringly.

"Euan asked if he could have a few words with Adam."

The two of them sit for some time, sharing coffee and chatting about how good the police and neighbors were. Fiona is thinking of ways to thank everyone, and Janice reassures her that knowing Adam is back safely will be enough. The minutes pass by, and Janice is increasingly intrigued about what Euan can be talking to Adam about.

Eventually, after about an hour, the door opens, and they both come in. Neither say anything or act like anything is different, but Janice can see the change in Adam and she knows his mother will certainly notice it too. Adam has not been transformed into a happy twelve-year-old but he looks less pinched about the face and more relaxed. Both women realize that he has also been crying. He makes himself some toast and sits in one of the comfy chairs by the French windows. Janice and Fiona continue to chat self-consciously.

"Mum, can we go into town today?"

"Yes, of course," Fiona replies quickly. Then she waits; is there going to be more? Any explanation of why he wants to go?

Adam munches through his toast unperturbed, and Fiona eventually looks at Janice and shrugs. It seems that normal twelve-year-old communication has resumed.

As Janice and Euan leave the house she asks him, "What did you say to Adam?" He looks over his shoulder as if he's worried the boy might hear.

"I'll tell you about it later."

They head to a bar by the river in Cambridge for a late lunch. The sun is shining but there are rain clouds gathering; it looks like it's going to be a typical, showery spring day.

The bar is busy with students and shoppers, but they find a table along one of the side walls and order a mix of tapas and some red wine.

"You were going to tell me about Adam," Janice says, before remembering she has said nothing to him about what he did last night. She interrupts herself to add this in, but he cuts her short. He is clearly embarrassed by her thanks, and she is reminded how people can be such a mix—shy one moment, supremely confident the next.

"So?" she prompts again.

He is frowning into his wine and Janice thinks of when Euan told her of the boy drowning when he worked for the RNLI in Ireland.

"I just asked him about his dad." He looks up. "I know he said he could love him with all his faults but I could see how hard it is for him. He is just a boy after all, and so he does want to think the best of his father. On the other hand, there must be times when he is so bloody angry with him for leaving them."

Janice nods; she can see this.

"I got him to write down on a piece of paper good things about his dad—just on one side, great memories and why he loved him. Then, and this was much harder, on the other side of the paper he needed to put down the things that upset him and made him angry. I think it's important knowing those things are part of his dad too."

Euan is back to studying the wine in his glass. "What you end up with is a better picture of the man. Both sides are true, but you can't separate them. You can't have one without the other. You can tear a piece of paper across, but you can't split it apart."

He looks up. "I don't know if it helped. It seemed to a little. And the thing is, I know Fiona got it wrong with the dog, but she will be there for him one hundred percent. One good parent can make a lot of difference."

As Euan drinks his wine and looks out at the river, Janice wonders what happened to Euan's mum. He has talked about his dad, but never his mum. She also thinks that maybe, just maybe, a man who can be this sensitive might understand her story. She knows that she could not bear to be with another man who she had to hide her story from.

He looks back at her. "I think maybe I should tell you the third of my stories. I didn't come up with that idea about the paper; someone showed it to me."

"What happened? Your mother?"

"Yes." He draws a deep breath. "When I was seven my mother killed herself. That's why my dad wanted a complete change. He went from being a fisherman who liked books to a bookshop owner who liked fishing. He made a right mess of it to start with, but he got there in the end, and I think, in some ways, that's what saved him."

"I am sure having you helped too." As she says this, she wishes her mum could have seen her sister like that.

Euan nods. "Yes, I think we kind of muddled through together. I grew to love books, and you can find all sorts of stuff in them. I think that thing about the paper came from a book my dad read. I didn't always cope very well and got into fights and stuff. Nicked a *lot* of sweets," he says, half-smiling. "I was just so angry. So, when I heard Adam shouting, I did understand a bit of how he felt."

Janice realizes this is what he must have told Fiona in the kitchen. The look on her face, she now realizes, was sympathy.

"I keep my mum's death as one of my stories because what happened is part of who I am; it made my dad and me different together, and . . ." He pauses. "I keep it because I loved my mum."

"Do you know why she killed herself?'

"She lost a baby. It would have been a daughter. My dad told me more about this when I grew up—as a child I didn't really know what was going on. I knew I had lost a sister and then the next thing I knew were the arguments about drink."

"Your mum drank?"

"Yes. I think she couldn't cope with Dad recovering, even a little, from the loss and she had nowhere to go. Her grief left her stranded. Her family were supportive, but it was in the days of, 'Just get on with it.' We were from a fishing community, and life could be pretty brutal. There wasn't the support she needed, and she slowly drank herself to death. Although it turns out it wasn't so slow; Mum was a small woman and she was pretty determined. I sometimes think if she could have got hold of pills or a gun, she would have ended it sooner."

Janice can feel the blood drain from her face as the hope seeps from her heart. She knows, in the same way she knows there is a glass in her hand, a river flowing by the window, and a sun in the sky, she will never be able to tell this man that she did something that led to her own mother drinking herself to death. And to tell him that she was not sorry that her mum died would be completely and utterly impossible. She looks out of the window and she thinks there is some regret that is beyond tears.

She stands up. She notices she is remarkably controlled. It comes from a calm hopelessness. "I can't do this, Euan. I thought I could, but it's impossible."

He looks up, confused, and then she can see the hurt.

She busies herself getting her bag and coat off the chair.

"Janice, no, please. Can't we talk?"

She thinks if he asks her to talk about books and stories she might break down and cry . . . she might stay . . . but he says nothing more; he just watches her. She cannot look at him.

She finds herself standing at the end of a road, at a crossroads. She had got up from the café chair and she had walked and walked. She watches the cars stream past—black, gray, then a splash of color, bright against a road darkened by a March downpour. Bicycles hug the curb, then wriggle to avoid a puddle. They come so close she could reach out a hand and push them over.

Her phone rings. She thinks it will be Euan, but realizes from the screen it is Stan. As soon as she hears his voice she knows, and she starts to run. As she turns the corner into the lane leading to the college, she sees the ambulance pulling up.

THIRTY-SIX

End of an Era

The chapel is full, and Janice feels like she is watching an old film in black and white. Black for the mourners. White for the flowers—lilies, narcissi, roses, and she thinks she can detect the smell of hyacinths. She doesn't think this combination suits the woman she knew. Each flower on their own might, but all together she finds the fragrance cloying—suffocating. But, she admits, she would not find much joy in anything today.

At the front of the chapel, she sees a woman in a dress coat—charcoal black. She is weeping and it strikes her as surprising. Most of the time she didn't think she liked her. The sobs are shaking her body and she sees her pull a handkerchief from her pocket. Then the woman turns and beckons to her. This surprises her more than the weeping. The woman reaches a hand out as she approaches, and whispers, "I've saved you a place." Then she turns to the thick-set man beside her. "This is my husband, George. I don't know if you've met him before." Janice sits down beside Mavis and thanks her. "Well, I know Carrie-Louise was very fond of you. She often said so. She said you were a woman who hid your light under a bushel." Janice finds her eyes filling up; she can hear Carrie-Louise saying it, but she knows she would have added, "darling," at the end.

Carrie-Louise died of a stroke. It had been very sudden, and for once Janice thinks the phrase, "It was very quick," can be seen as a blessing. She didn't have the trauma of a long deterioration or have to cope with losing her voice. Janice knows she would have faced all of this with grace and good humor, but she thinks Carrie-Louise would have preferred it this way. She is just sad that she cannot see that Mavis, her oldest friend, did really love her. She can hear her say, "Well . . . darling . . . bless her . . . so she really was . . . lovely . . . after all." She also wishes that they had just chosen white roses for the coffin. She was such an elegant woman. Janice can't help feeling she would have found the fussiness a bit vulgar. "Oh, darling . . . always keep it . . . very simple . . . that's the way."

As she makes her way back up the aisle after the service, she sees a familiar figure sitting on the last pew: Mrs. B. Tiberius is standing to the side of her. She is dressed in black apart from the white plaster cast she wears on her arm. The spiral stairs had for once defeated her and she had tumbled headlong off them. She is also sporting a spectacular black eye. Janice wants to go and talk to her but remembers all too clearly her last encounter with Tiberius. Mrs. B leans over and says something to her son, and he looks toward her. He does the tiniest of nods in her direction and then turns and leaves the chapel. Janice can't help wondering if he has brought his dog with him. Mrs. B gestures for her to come over.

"Come and sit with me, Janice, whilst Tiberius gets the car."

"I didn't know you knew Carrie-Louise."

"Cambridge is a small city and her husband, Ernest, and Augustus were friends. I thought Augustus would want me to come."

"She was a lovely woman. I think you would have liked her."

Mrs. B nods. "Interesting name," she comments.

"It suited her; she was an interesting woman. Brave, too." Her thoughts drift to names—she has never felt less like her birth name. "Do you have a middle name?" she asks, distracting herself from her own thoughts.

"Mary."

Janice smiles.

"What's that smile for? Are you thinking of the virtuous Virgin Mary, or maybe the flawed Mary Magdalene?"

"Oh no. Mary, Mary, quite contrary." Despite the day, and the sense of sorrow she feels on so many fronts, Janice keeps smiling, and she experiences a small easing of her heart. "Anyway, how are you, Mrs. B?"

"Well, as you can see, out and about again. Thank you for the flowers and for coming to visit."

"You weren't a very good patient, were you, Mrs. B?" Janice comments.

"I told you when I first met you, I will not be surrounded by fools. And the hospital I was admitted to seems to have been blessed with more than its fair share of idiots. I do believe one of the consultants may well have been dropped on his head at birth."

Janice would have given much to see Mrs. B's run-in with this particular senior consultant.

"The volunteers were a little better. One particularly patronizing woman insisted on wearing T-shirts emblazoned with sayings such as, 'Please be kind to animals.' I thanked her for reminding me and told her I would think twice before I put my next kitten into a wheelie-bin."

"Oh, Mrs. B." Janice is shaking her head but can't help laughing.

"Oh, I wouldn't feel too sorry for her. I'm pretty certain she spat in my soup."

"Not a vegan, then?"

Mrs. B snorts.

"So, what now?" she asks the old lady.

"I was just going to inquire the same about you."

"Oh, things are moving along slowly. My son, Simon, came to stay, which was wonderful, and also good because he spoke to Mike and got him to let me have the car back and also persuaded him to agree to sell the house." She doesn't tell Mrs. B that Mike kept complaining because he felt that Geordie Bowman could well afford to buy him out. Or that she has since seen Mike driving the BMW belonging to the landlady of his local pub. It seems Mike did not struggle to find a replacement for her, and it appears he is finding comfort in the arms of a buxom widow in her late fifties. All she can think is that she's surprised she didn't see it coming. She could almost feel sorry for the widow. Almost, but not quite. She had always looked at Janice like she was "just a cleaner" when she visited the pub with Mike.

She realizes she's been staring off into the distance and looks back at Mrs. B. "I've found somewhere small to live until the sale goes through." She doesn't tell Mrs. B that this is a hostel and that she hates it. She doesn't tell anyone that. Maybe misplaced pride but she hopes it won't be for too long. Instead, she adds, "My friend, Fiona, is great, and I stay over with her sometimes. Her son is Adam, the boy I told you about."

"Ah, yes. How is he getting on?"

"He's okay. I think he's coming around to the idea of them getting a dog." She realizes she doesn't have to explain any more to Mrs. B. She knows all about the time Adam ran away and has even spoken to Tiberius to try and persuade him to take Adam on as a dog walker—but to no avail.

"How about you, Mrs. B? How are things? And how's Mycroft?"

"I think you could say I have stood Mycroft down. I am moving."

"Oh, Mrs. B, no! Your books . . . Augustus . . . please, there must be a way." She doesn't say she can't bear the thought of not being able to spend time among Mrs. B's books—but she cannot help thinking it.

"No, there comes a time when you have to accept that change is inevitable. I cannot manage the stairs . . . and Tiberius . . ."

"Yes?"

"I do know that my son is the villain of the piece, but he is my son and so I would prefer to come to an arrangement with him. It wasn't that difficult."

I bet it wasn't, Janice thinks, remembering the £2 million. "Where will you go?"

"We've found a ground-floor apartment by the river. It's a reasonable size, so I will be able to bring many of my books with me, and Tiberius has agreed to return some of my wine. I shall sit there drinking my claret watching the river." Mrs. B raises an eyebrow. "I believe they run bridge nights on a Wednesday."

"I bet they do craft afternoons as well; you'll enjoy that," Janice suggests.

"I won't because I certainly will not be going," Mrs. B says with feeling.

"Quiz nights?"

"Sod off, Janice."

The old lady takes Janice's hand in hers.

"You will come and clean for me, won't you? And even if you won't, will you come and drink gin with me?"

"I will do both, Mrs. B," Janice agrees.

"You look different."

Janice knows this is not going to be good. "And?"

"Last time I said that, you said you were happy," Mrs. B comments.

"And?" Janice prompts when Mrs. B keeps silent.

"Well, now you don't look at all happy. Would you like to tell me about it?"

"I don't think I could, Mrs. B." How can she say she came so close to getting it right, but in the end, her guilt, or what was left of it, cut her off from her happy ending? And she doesn't think she has much to complain of. After all, family is the thing she missed most as a child and she now has the chance of building a future with her son and her sister. Joy has already been busy looking up dates for her visit.

"Are you sure?"

Janice nods. She knows she cannot tell Mrs. B about Euan. He still texts her regularly. She cannot bring herself to delete his number but some days she only reads his messages four or five times. Decius, she tries not to think of. She just carries his loss like a wound that won't heal.

"I have been thinking about *Vanity Fair*," Mrs. B says, squeezing her hand. Janice is relieved she has changed the subject.

"You are not an Amelia. But I think the tragedy is that your mother was, and she did not get a happy ending. You were her child and were not responsible for her, Janice. The fact there was no faithful William Dobbin to save her proves that life is much crueler than fiction. But it certainly wasn't your fault."

"So, am I Becky Sharp?"

"No, she was ultimately a selfish woman and you are the most selfless woman it has been my pleasure to meet. But I do sometimes wish you would find a bit more 'Becky' in you and claim some happiness for yourself." As Mrs. B says this, Janice wonders how she could ever have thought of herself as a lioness. "Anyway, enough of this, here comes my pompous arse of a son."

Janice looks up in surprise. "He told you what I said?"

"Yes, he was livid," Mrs. B is laughing now.

"What did you say?"

"Nothing. I couldn't speak. But I nearly wet myself laughing," Mrs. B remembers fondly. "Best make yourself scarce, but will you come to me on Monday? The removers should have me in and straight by then."

"I can help you get things sorted, Mrs. B."

"Nonsense. Let Tiberius pay for that. After all, he can afford it."

THIRTY-SEVEN

We Are All Storytellers

Mrs. B's new apartment is set in a large mock-Georgian house arranged around a courtyard. There is a fountain in the middle of the courtyard and numerous statues are placed tastefully around the extensive gardens. Janice is sure Mrs. B will have hated it on sight. A large reception area connects with communal rooms and corridors leading to individual apartments. Janice is pleased to find there is no smell of urine or cabbage but there is the powerful fragrance of plug-in air fresheners. She hopes Mrs. B doesn't have to spend too much time in the lounges or dining room.

Mrs. B's front door opens into a large hallway, with room enough for a table and two chairs. As Mrs. B ushers her in, Janice thinks this bodes well for the rest of her new home, which Mrs. B has told her is made up of a kitchen, a bathroom, two bedrooms, and a large living-dining room. She says most rooms have views over the gardens to the river. Mrs. B appears in an excellent mood and chats away happily to Janice. As this is definitely not normal for Mrs. B, she wonders if she has been drinking—but knows better than to ask. As she follows her into the hallway, Janice thinks of the first time she met this woman (dressed in purple and red) and followed her past stuffed squirrels, a didgeridoo, suitcases, and a bag of old golf clubs.

"Mrs. B, what did you do with all the things you had in storage?"

"I donated them to the college," Mrs. B says gleefully.

"Oh, I bet they were delighted," Janice says appreciatively. Then she stops, and Mrs. B stops too. On the chair by the door to the main room is a cycle helmet. She swings around to face Mrs. B.

"What have you done? Who's in there?" She points a thumb toward the door.

"Well, as you are an intelligent woman, I presume you already know the answer to that." Mrs. B does not look precisely guilty, more defiant.

"What have you done, Mrs. B?" Janice says more slowly. She can feel her heart racing and her palms growing damp.

"The young man in there contacted me because he was worried about you. He also has a gift for you. I have to say, I found him to be extremely pleasant and surprisingly well-read for a bus driver. But these days education has moved on so much."

Janice knows Mrs. B is trying to buy herself time, but she is finding it hard to concentrate knowing who is behind the door. She imagines Euan looking anxious and this only makes things worse. She says, irrelevantly, "He's fifty-five, so he's hardly what you'd call young; his father ran a bookshop, and he used to be a coxswain on a lifeboat."

"Now that is most interesting. He told me about the shop but not the lifeboat. I can't help but feel one would be in safe hands with him."

Now Janice is really worried. She can tell by the way Mrs. B is talking that she is nervous, and this is so unlike her.

"Janice, I have a confession to make." She pauses. "I want you to know I thought long and hard about this. I felt, in this instance, I needed to be a storyteller too. And I have told Euan your story."

"You've done *what*?" Janice shouts, then, glancing at the door, she repeats in an angry whisper, "You've done what? How dare you!"

Mrs. B sinks down on the chair and puts Euan's cycle helmet on her lap. Janice resists the urge to ask if she is all right.

"I appreciate in doing this I have betrayed your trust and risked your friendship. Not something I would do lightly, I can promise you. I thought long and hard about it, ever since Euan came to visit me the first time. I took this drastic step for two reasons . . ."

Janice notices she is holding on to the cycle helmet as one might a lifebuoy.

". . . Firstly, because I think unfounded guilt is getting in the way of you telling this man what he clearly needs to know and I believe that, should you ever overcome this, which I strongly doubt, you still would not tell the story as it needs to be told."

Janice tries to interrupt, but Mrs. B holds up her hand to stop her. "I know you, Janice, you will tell the story with your sister at the heart of it. But this is *your* story, Janice, and I wish for once you would see that. You were a child and very badly served. You were not responsible for your mother's death or her drinking." Mrs. B is shaking her head as she says this, and Janice can see her distress. "It makes me very, very angry to think that no one helped you. You were a child, Janice; you should *never* have been carrying such a heavy burden." She passes a shaking hand over her eyes and takes a deep breath. Janice is no longer trying to interrupt her and sits down heavily on the second chair in the hallway.

"The second reason I told your story was because I could

see from the time we have spent together that meeting this man made a difference to you. He made you happy. And if there is ever a woman who deserves to be happy, it is you. I would do anything, *anything,* to have another hour with Augustus. Do not pass this opportunity by because of a foolish, misplaced feeling of guilt. Now, please do my nerves, and Euan, a favor and go and talk to the poor man."

Janice does not know what to say, so says nothing. But she does stand up and opens the door. She steps into the room and closes the door behind her. Euan is standing with his back to her, looking out across the garden to the river. He turns around to face her.

"If you don't want to see me, I'll go." He nods to the hallway. "I could hear most of what Rosie said."

All she can think is, "Rosie!" And that it is so good to see him again. He looks tired.

"She is right, you know. It wasn't your fault, Janice. But does us saying that make any difference to you? It doesn't really matter what we think."

"And you don't think it was my fault?" she asks.

He turns back to look at the river. "Of course not, Janice. I just feel desperately sorry for you . . . and sad." He turns and looks quickly over his shoulder. "How's Adam doing?"

She is thrown by the change of subject, but partly relieved. And of course, he would want to know about Adam. "He's getting there I think; I hope he'll be okay," she says.

"He may or may not be," he says.

"I know it will take time," she reasons.

He shrugs, still with his back to her.

"I really do hope he'll be all right—in the end," she says, thrown by Euan's unusual pessimism.

He still doesn't turn around.

"Maybe, but perhaps he could have spent a bit more time with his dad. He must think about that," he says.

"I'm sure he did all he could do. I know they used to go camping together." She is bemused by the change in him.

"I know he told me he noticed more than Fiona thought he did. Perhaps it would have been better if he'd talked to someone who could have helped his dad."

"Where's this coming from, Euan?" She is starting to get not just confused, but irritated.

"Well, maybe he could have done more, that's all I'm saying."

"What are you on about?"

"Well, something must have made John the way he was. And you know, fathers and sons . . ."

Something in Janice snaps. "He is twelve years old, for God's sake! Adam is only a child!" And this she shouts at him. The lioness is back.

He spins round to face her. "Exactly, Janice. He is a child. He is the same age you were. You will fight for Adam, please will you fight for the Janice who was twelve?"

She stares at him.

He says, more softly, holding out his hand to her. "Please fight for her, Janice. Someone has to."

She puts her hand toward his and he pulls her toward him. As he wraps his arms around her, he murmurs into her hair. "I'd fight them all for you, Janice, but I think the only person who can really do this for her, is you."

As she stands there, she can feel the beat of his heart and she suddenly remembers one of the few photos she has of her and her sister as children. She thinks she needs to get this picture out and look at that little girl, to look at herself. That girl called Hope. She was so young, as Euan says—as young as Adam, and he is still such a boy.

After a while, as if reading her thoughts, he says, "I have a picture for you."

She pulls away. "What, of me?" She's confused.

"No, but I would like to see that." He puts his hand into his jacket pocket and pulls out a sepia photo of a young woman. "This is Becky."

"Really?" The young woman staring back at her has large, dark eyes and a firm, determined-looking chin. Her expression is impossible to read. Could this be a woman who shot a husband she had got tired of? It's hard to tell from the photo. Could it be a Becky Sharp? Yes, she thinks she could certainly be that. Janice looks across the room and realizes she has left Mrs. B in her hallway. She pulls open the door and Mrs. B is still sitting on the chair. Janice can't help feeling that she is looking very pleased with herself.

"Forgiven?" she asks, in a jaunty voice.

"Possibly," Janice says and leans down and kisses her. She adds, "Tricky. Too tricky by half." She then helps the old lady to her feet and steers her to her battered old armchair beside a new flame-effect fire with a marble surround. Mrs. B looks at this scornfully as she sits down.

"Have you seen this, Mrs. B?" She hands her the photo of Becky. Mrs. B looks at it and hands it back. "Yes, indeed. Very interesting. Do you want to know her real name?"

Janice shakes her head and studies the picture of the youthful face in front of her. "Not a beauty but I'd say she had great presence."

Mrs. B snorts. "So, you are sure you don't want me to introduce you properly?"

"No, I think I want her to simply be 'Becky.' I don't know why that matters but I think I'd rather keep it that way."

Janice looks up as Mrs. B reaches across and takes another

look at the photograph. "Of course, this doesn't really do her justice, you know," Mrs. B says, and casts Janice a sly glance.

"What?" Janice and Euan exclaim in unison. Tricky doesn't begin to describe this woman. "You've met her?" Janice demands.

Mrs. B puts her head on one side. "I think it would be more accurate to say I have seen her. She was drinking in the Paris Ritz one day, with a very unpleasant little lapdog and an enormous and vociferous American. Augustus recognized her. Of course, she was quite an old lady by then, but he had been aware of her during his time running the Paris Station."

"Oh my God! What was she like?"

"She was one of those women you can tell has a depth beyond their purely superficial look. She had a certain something."

"Is that why you told me her story? Because you had seen her? I've wondered why you chose her."

"I cannot really explain that," Mrs. B muses. "Possibly fate—if I could believe in that. Maybe it was simply because I had been thinking of Augustus and when we talked of stories—"

"*You* talked of stories," Janice interrupts.

"Ah, yes, when *I* started talking about stories, for some reason I recalled Augustus telling me about her as we sat in the Ritz having supper that evening. Normally he was very discreet, but we had shared some Champagne, and I think he knew I would find her tale fascinating."

"Do you think he knew about the letters and what happened?"

"I wouldn't be at all surprised, but there he did keep a professional silence." Mrs. B looks at her from under her shaggy eyebrows and Janice wonders if she is being told the complete truth.

The doorbell goes, and Janice comments, "Saved by the bell?"

Mrs. B keeps her expression blank and starts to struggle to her feet.

"Shall I get it?" Janice offers, realizing she is not going to get any more out of the ex-spy.

"No, best not. That will be Tiberius with the wine. I can only stand a small amount of excitement in one day and you calling my son a thief might send me over the edge." Mrs. B is back to grinning.

Janice opens the door into the hallway for Mrs. B and pushes it closed behind her. She and Euan are left alone once more.

"Rosie is something else," he comments, nodding toward the door.

"Rosie!" Janice can't help saying.

"Well, I'm not calling her Mrs. B, and she said 'Lady' was too formal." He puts an arm around her. "You and me? We okay?"

"Oh, I'd say more than okay."

"We don't have to rush things, Janice, just take it one day at a time. Could we do that?"

She nods. "One step at a time." And not for the first time, she wonders if this man would like to dance with her.

They can hear voices in the hall and they sit down quietly on the sofa. Janice feels like a naughty schoolgirl, hiding from the headmaster. She hears the front door close and then, in a sudden rush, the living room door bursts open. Through it bundles a bouncing fox terrier, toes pointed, head held high. He leaps toward Janice like he has been pulled toward her on a taut string. As he lands bodily on top of her, his face says it all: *Fuck it, you took your time.*

For some minutes Janice cannot speak to anyone else; she is far too busy telling Decius how much she has missed him. Eventually, she raises her head. "Oh, *thank you* Mrs. B; you brought him to see me."

"Not brought. Bought."

"I'm not with you."

"Oh, the nuns really wasted their time with you."

"What do you mean?"

"I said bought not brought. Part of my negotiations with my son—who would probably sell his grandmother, if he had one—was that as I would be living on my own somewhere new, I would need a dog for company and security. As it just so happened, I had a particular dog in mind."

"But you don't want a dog," Janice exclaims. "I didn't even think you liked dogs."

"Don't be ridiculous. Of course I don't want a dog," Mrs. B barks as she sits down in her armchair, but Janice can see the tell-tale twitch in the side of her face. "He is yours. And I hope you appreciate him because I believe that fox terrier cost the bones of £2 million."

Janice cannot move; she just keeps staring straight ahead of her. Then she launches herself at the old woman, trying not to crush her as she hugs her. "I bloody love you, Mrs. B!"

As she hugs her, Mrs. B starts to make small gurgling noises. Her gurgling turns to a coughing splutter and Janice is reminded of the time she told her that her son had called his dog Decius. Janice steps back and watches as Mrs. B slaps both arms of the chair and tears of laughter start to run down her wrinkled face.

"What is it, Mrs. B?" Janice asks, but this only seems to make her laugh even more and all the old lady can manage to say in a strangled voice is, "Mycroft."

"Has Mycroft done something?" Janice says, sitting beside her on the carpet, one hand on Mrs. B's knee and one arm around Decius.

All Mrs. B can do is nod and rock back and forward.

Janice looks at Euan and shakes her head uncomprehendingly.

Mrs. B gives a last chortle and pats Decius on the head. "I may have exaggerated this good dog's worth somewhat, now I come to think of it." She grins. "I'm not sure it was a full £2 million."

Janice sits back on her heels. "What do you mean?"

"Jarndyce versus Jarndyce," Mrs. B declares and makes a sound remarkably like a giggle.

Janice shakes her head.

"I think I'd better explain," Mrs. B says.

"I think you better had," Janice says, getting up and sitting back on the sofa beside Euan. Decius parks his bottom contentedly on her foot.

Mrs. B begins to make happy humming sounds. "I think what my son may have overlooked is that any legal costs pertaining to his father's trust . . ."

"The £2 million?" Euan clarifies.

Mrs. B nods and continues. "Yes, any costs that occur come out of the capital sum before the legacy is passed on. And it does seem that Mycroft is an extraordinarily expensive attorney. Worth every penny, of course."

Janice is confused. "But I thought he wasn't going to charge you anything?"

"Ah, the dear man wasn't, until he realized the full sum would go to my villainous son"—here she looks a little sadly at Janice—"then he felt that it might be a good idea to harvest a largish slice of the pie for himself."

"And you don't mind?" Euan looks as confused as Janice.

Mrs. B glances from one to the other. "You should never, ever underestimate Mycroft." She then turns specifically to Janice. "And you should never give up hope, for Hope changes everything." She makes a tiny bowing movement to Janice. Janice returns the bow. "As it was," Mrs. B continues, "Mycroft donated his fee to the college on the understanding that he and I have some say in the conversion of my old home into a library. There will be ample funds to achieve this, and Mycroft has been talking to the Master about naming the new library after Augustus." Mrs. B smiles mistily.

"Oh, Mrs. B, that's wonderful." Janice then mutters, "No one ever sees Mycroft coming, do they?"

"Indeed, they do not, my dear. And no," Mrs. B adds, as if reading her thoughts, "I am not going to tell you about our time in Madagascar."

Janice's laugh is cut short. "Will Tiberius be angry? He won't be able to take Decius back?"

"Oh no, my dear, Mycroft was particularly stringent about including him fully in the terms of the agreement that we both signed. I believe drawing it up took a considerable amount of time and may have cost Tiberius quite a few thousand pounds."

Mrs. B gazes vaguely up at the ceiling and Janice is strongly reminded of her friend, Fred Spink. "It is quite amazing how costs can accumulate," Mrs. B says dreamily. "Now, I do think we might open a special bottle of wine to celebrate," she adds, looking back at the two of them.

After drinking a very good bottle of Augustus's pinot noir, Euan and Janice say their goodbyes and, along with Decius, make their way back down the path into town, Euan wheeling his bike and Janice holding tight to Decius's lead as if he might suddenly disappear into thin air if she let go. "We must go and see Adam."

"I've been thinking about that," Euan says, negotiating a bollard. "Decius is a pedigree hound, isn't he?"

"Of course," Janice says, looking down fondly at Decius's curly head.

"Well, how about a 'Son of Decius' for Adam?"

"Oh, I think that is a great idea. But maybe let's not mention it straight away. You know what happened last time."

They walk on in silence, then Janice remembers something. "You never told me your fourth story."

"Oh, I don't know, maybe I don't need more. How about you? You still going to be collecting other people's stories?"

She nods. "I don't think I could stop. And I wouldn't want to. I think it's in people's stories that you discover the best of what we can be."

"And what do you want to be?" Euan asks, glancing at her profile.

Janice is not at all sure, but she is certain that, with this man walking by her side, she will figure it out along the way. So, she just smiles at him and shakes her head.

"A new story?" he suggests hopefully.

"Oh, I think so. And maybe you're right, perhaps I'll have three or four stories. I think I've got some catching up to do." She reaches out and takes his hand. "Anyway, come on, I thought you said you were going for five stories?"

"Well, I think maybe some were a bit of wishful thinking." He glances down at her. "Okay, well do you want bus driver learns to dance? Or we could go for bus driver wins the lottery?"

"Oh, I think the dancing, don't you?"

"Whatever you say," Euan agrees.

They walk on in silence.

"Well, do you fancy going dancing?" he asks her.

"Yes, I do. Where were you thinking? Is there a tango class somewhere we could try?"

"I was thinking maybe Argentina," he suggests tentatively.

"Argentina? Be serious."

"Oh, I was, and I thought maybe we could come back via Canada. I'm sure Adam would look after Decius."

Janice gives him a double look.

It is only then that she notices that Euan is wheeling along beside him a rather smart, new carbon-fiber bike.

Author's Note

I came across the story of "Becky"—in reality, a woman called Marguerite Alibert—while reading Adrian Phillip's excellent book about Edward VIII, *The King Who Had to Go*. Marguerite gets the briefest of mentions, but it was clear that there was a woman who became involved with the future king and who then went on to get away with murder. I was fascinated to find out more and I turned to Andrew Rose's book about the scandal, *The Prince, the Princess and the Perfect Murder*, as well as investigating news reports and documentaries about the subject.

There is debate about whether Marguerite did intend to blackmail the Prince of Wales and what role the letters played in her trial and acquittal. However, there is no doubt she was an important woman in the prince's early sexual life and that he sent her many indiscreet letters.

I have to say I agree with Mrs. B's reading of Marguerite's character—a Becky Sharp, for sure. And I am certain Mrs. B knows more about those letters than she is saying . . .

Sally Page